IRON ANGEL

SORDID AFFAIRS

Book II

A Novel

By

P.F. BUSCH

NOVELS BY P.F. BUSCH

THE LYRICIST

IRON ANGEL THE FRENCH YEARS BOOK 1

IRON ANGEL SORDID AFFAIRS BOOK II

COMING SOON

IRON ANGEL THE TRIAL BOOK III

Acknowledgments

My infinite love to Carl, my love, ever so brilliant, wise and loving and to Monique, Matt, Bradley and Nicole for your wise suggestions and all around support. My heart belongs to you.

A great many thanks to Marc Siegel, physician, writer, novelist, and host of Fox's News Sunday House Call. Thank you Marc, for your encouragement.

Gratefulness to Laura Taylor, editor and romance novelist and to my dear friend Elizabeth Juncosa, thanks for your insight and support.

To Dominique,
with great affection

Historical Timeline

1848-1852 Charles-Louis Napoléon Bonaparte first elected President of the French Second Republic

1852-1870 Napoléon III Emperor of the Second French Empire

1849-1861 Victor Emmanuel II King of Piedmont and Sardinia

1861-1878 Victor Emmanuel II King of a unified Italy

1846-1878 Pope Pius IX

1861-1888 King William I of Prussia

July 1870 France declares war on Prussia

September 1870 France is defeated End of Second Empire

By 1867, Victor Emmanuel II, King of Piedmont—Sardinia and appointed Monarch of the United Kingdom of Italy in March 1861, had taken over with the help of Giuseppe Garibaldi and his Red Shirts forces most of the Principalities attached to the domain of Pope Pius 9th. Irate, the Pontiff referred to his 'appalling' condition as an insult to God. "I am but a prisoner in my own kingdom," he'd written to all heads of States. The French Emperor had maintained a French garrison in Civitavecchia for quite some time to protect the Pope and Rome.

The defeat of the French by the Prussians in the Franco-Prussian war of 1870 helped the excommunicated Victor Emmanuel II to capture Rome after the French withdrew their forces. He entered Rome in September 1870 and made the Eternal City his capital in July 1871.

IRON ANGEL   SORDID AFFAIRS

A NOVEL

Chapter 1

"The Count must be a lion, but he must also remember how to play the fox."

- Niccolo Machiavelli 1469-1527

In a stealth location away from curious onlookers in the waters of Toulon—the French naval town—the Tempête sat moored as it awaited its influential passengers.

The trip south, from Paris to Toulon, had been long. The French diplomats and the influential ecclesiastical negotiators were anxious to climb aboard the recently modernized *Tempête*. The vessel was the property of the Duke de Bourbonne, Jean-Louis-Pierre de Pleyssis, the brilliant aristocratic adventurer summoned to France three years earlier from America by Charles Louis Napoléon III, Emperor of France. The Duke was to serve as the appeaser to the Pope in the forthcoming Italian political negotiations, which involved the reunification of Rome to the kingdom of Italy.

Chapter 2

Somewhere in the Méditerranée

Jean-Louis-Pierre de Pleyssis and his American wife, Gabriella de Conte Thornsen, sailed across the deep blue waters of the Méditerranée. Accompanied by a large French delegation of diplomats and high-placed, influential ecclesiastics, their destination was the port of Pisa on the Italian coast. From there they would sail northeast on the Arno River to Florence where the Duchess' maternal ancestors owned large estates. Cardinal Philippe Thornsen, Gabriella's cherished cousin, awaited their arrival. They would tour the lovely villages in and around their lands and then continue on to Rome. The Cardinal had pre-arranged for a Papal audience with Pius IX.

In the lavish dining room of the vessel, Jean-Louis-Pierre de Pleyssis, Duke de Bourbonne, sat in a large leather and mahogany framed chair, his arm wrapped around his wife's shoulders. Both listened intently to the trusted advisors who spoke about the complicated task ahead.

"As we're all aware in this cabin, the annexation of most of the Papal States took place in the late 1860's. Now, nine years later, WE, the French, who protected the Pope's assets, re-established the Holy See's temporal power, and returned him to Rome in 1850 after his flight to Gaeta; WE, now dear friends, are sent there to mollify both sides!" Gérard de Guarnier, a former naval officer who had been a close friend to the Emperor during his exile in England, proclaimed sarcastically. He raised both of his hands toward the heavens, exasperated. "Let it be known that France is not opposed to Victor Emmanuel's actions. In fact, it is greatly in favor of the reunification process. All of us present know quite well, how difficult it was for Louis Napoléon to let the Italian liberals down in '49. *Sacré-bleu*, sixteen years earlier the Emperor had been a member of the Carbonari!" de Guarnier clarified grandiosely to Gabriella and the men assembled in the cabin as if revealing a cherished secret. "Yet, it would have been a catastrophe in France if the support from the Catholic electorate in the provinces waned. We had to rebuke the Italian militant troops. Eighty per cent of our population is Catholic. It was not a good time to entice the provinces against the Emperor. Regardless, we want our troops to return home and that is the last order from Paris," he continued, exasperated by the turn of events. He stared at the Duchess as if the last statement was directed at her.

"The Pope no longer trusts the defending French troops, we were told that His reasons for the long awaited return to Rome in 1850 were our overtly modern view of the world. The Papacy had always sided with the Monarchy, and Charles Louis's demand of a less theocratic State disturbed the Pontiff immensely. Yet, he owes us much," Mathieu Garnelle, another former retired officer intoned. "Consequently, we need to pacify both sides. Victor Emmanuel's fervent supporters want the King to be situated in central Italy and they are quite weary of the power Rome still possesses over the Italian nation."

"Envoys from Emmanuel II will attend the delicate negotiations," Colonel Jean-Marie Bouverin remarked in a professorial tone. "Essentially, the King's final quest is Rome as the capital of Italy."

The Duke sat silently taking in the statements. He straightened his large body in the armchair as he assessed the expertise of the men assigned to work with him.

"The French army collaborated with the Holy See," he interrupted, "and French troops have protected their forces from Garibaldi, who was intent, let's not forget, on taking over the Papal States. This time, the French will not stand in the way. Instead, we'll serve as pacifier. We will facilitate the task on both sides and France will gain in the negotiation," Jean-Louis-Pierre de Pleyssis stated. "I am determined to close the deal. Defeat is not an option. Our task is to prepare the Pope for the eventuality of the loss of His lands and of Rome itself. Another area of contention we should expect from the reunification forces," he paused and finished the brandy in his glass, "will be to excise for the Pope small pockets of land in and around the city. Furthermore, the opposition should accept His absolute control over Vatican City and of all the Cathedrals in the surrounding hills. Financial reparations will be expected, but how much, no one knows." The statuesque French man lifted his shoulder to his ear and pressed his lips together as his chin jutted forward. "This as well, gentlemen, will be an area of contention with the King's forces," the Duke stated flatly.

"We need a show of force," Arnier continued, "perhaps by the French garrison in Civitavecchia. But it is inevitable, Italy will seize the remaining lands."

"Again," the Duke opined, "France is not adverse to the idea. In fact, the Emperor's turn against the Prime Minister of Piedmont, Count Camillo Benso di Cavour after France and Piedmont's victory over Austria was, in my view, a major mistake. The Piedmontese had agreed to give up Nice and Savoy—and they did. Had Austria been forced to give up Venetia, as called upon by the informal treaty between the Emperor and di Cavour, I doubt that Italy would have supported Prussia in '66 in its war against Austria. Now, we have to be concerned about a very powerful force on our North Eastern border. I would have advised otherwise had I been in France when this major miscalculation was undertaken," the Duke snapped pretentiously. "The Catholics in our country would have aligned themselves with the policy of the Emperor, and the Papal States would have been under Italian control earlier and with fewer lives lost," he asserted.

"The Papacy will no longer accept democratic forces working for the advancement of modernity after the revolutions of 1848 and 1850." The Count de Bregnanne, a corpulent man continued, "for God's sake, the Pope had to escape his lands under the cover of a simple priest chasuble and seek solace in the fortress of Gaeta!"

"Trust or not, the Pontiff should not forget that the French army re-established the Holy See's temporal power!" Jean-Marie Bouverin retorted angrily.

Gabriella de-Conte-Thornsen-de Pleyssis stood. She ambled away from the group, seating behind the Duke's desk. Intently, she listened to the discussion.

"Distrust of the French is not a novel reaction from the Italians," Gabriella responded in her informal American demeanor. It was a clear contrast to her husband's formality. "The Emperor's intent, Napoléon I that is, was to abase the church after his excommunication from the Catholic Church over his marriage to Joséphine. The arrest of the Pope and the announcement that the Pope had no formal temporal authority was not an endearing gesture to the Pontiff and his archbishops in the Holy See!"

"That's ancient history, Gaby," the Duke reminded her flippantly.

"Eh bien, Mon Cher, Italians have a long memory! But let me remind you of more recent events. In exchange for French protection in '49 and the expulsion of Garibaldi from Rome, Charles-Louis Napoléon," she caught her *faux pas* and smiled, "the Emperor asked for a general amnesty, more liberal laws and the continued institution of the Code Napoléon! Frankly, even Philippe, who possesses quite liberal values, was shocked by the obligations placed on the Pontiff." She held the stare of each of the men present—very much aware that her husband had imposed her presence upon them.

"Not for long," the Duke presaged. "The sole objective now is to reflect an image of solidarity with the Pontiff in order to assuage the eventual loss of his properties. I think we will be able to accomplish that reasonably well," he concluded, his glare fixated on one of the bishops whose gaze of sheer irony focused on the Duchess. "The nationalists want the King in close proximity to the heart of Italy—not solely on its Northern provinces. The anti-clerical ideas sweeping Europe are going to work in favor of Victor Emmanuel."

Although Jean-Louis possessed great distaste for the man, Cousin Philippe would be an astute diplomat. Rome would fall promptly when the French garrison left the peninsula.

"Gentlemen, the reunification of the Pope's former land-based properties to the Kingdom of Italy is of great importance to the Emperor's projects of modernization and trade. However, it has to be done diplomatically. Retaliation against the French would be counterproductive. The generals who counsel the Emperor are presently innerving more than one power with their ill-advised rhetoric. Let us not add to the conflicts."

Garnelle lifted his head, clearly miffed. "There are many reasons to keep the oratory. If the Prussian King Wilhelm I and his Chancellor, Otto von Bismarck, decide to place a Hohenzollern on the throne of Spain, we will be cornered on all sides, Jean-Louis-Pierre."

"We need to succeed, and succeed we will," the Duke insisted, obliterating the remark. "We will not overtly display the alliance with Victor Emmanuel II. I have chosen Venice for the talks. We have appeased the Carbonari. The burgeoning and potentially powerful class of wealthy bourgeois and intellectuals no longer want to pledge their allegiance to the titled landowners. This very reason essentially still wields political and economic influence in Rome and in the former Papal States," the Duke clarified curtly. He paused and looked around the table for a possible question. Silence reigned. "The masses in Rome regard us as the protector of the Pontiff and of his lands. And although we have been, the world situation now is such that we no longer want nor need that role," the Duke stated flatly. "Victor Emmanuel has his eyes on Rome. He will not regress, and he will conquer the city and its port by force if need be."

He may not try it initially, but Jean-Louis sensed that, in less than a year, Rome would be the capital of the Kingdom of Italy. It was his job along with the delegation, under a stealth agreement that France would help the Italian Monarch repossess Rome with a signed agreement from the Pontiff. The Church essentially had homes through its Cathedrals all over the world. There was no need, in his view, for the Pontiff to exert any secular power over any government. Gaby regarded the situation differently. Many altercations over this very issue had come to pass with his American wife.

France had to walk a delicate line. Some supporters of the Church in the former Kingdom of Naples might make the current negotiations go south. He was prepared—or as prepared as he could be.

The conference continued late into the night. The mission would change the course of history. Each one of them knew it, and they had dedicated their lives to its success. There would be no turning back.

Chapter 3

Two days later, the Duke, perched on the side corner of the Captain's chair, cast a skeptical glance at his wife. He sensed that her intent was to sway his orders by sweet-talking the Commanding Officer, Cunnan Adams Holmes. Having the last word was a way of life for Gaby. He would have to be doubly cautious and take extra safety measures to protect her.

Free at last from all the conventions she had had to suffer while in Paris, Gaby was now in seventh heaven. She enjoyed the independence being at sea afforded her. This time around she had his permission to roam around the ship freely. Recently, she had begun to train in the martial arts that had slowly filtered from the Asian continent. She never ceased to amaze him.

"Mon Dieu, living on a Southern plantation during the Civil War was no piece of cake. I have sharp shooting skills, you know that, Cunnan. Why this constant practice? Gustav taught me not to miss my targets," she argued vehemently. "Throughout the length of the Civil War, I used their well honed lessons of survival and vigilance," she countered repeatedly, lifting her shoulders, while she stared, annoyed, at the heavens. Gustav, her servant and former slave, was married to Tita, another former slave who had been given her freedom papers by Gaby's mother. The couple had practically raised Gaby.

Undaunted by her complaints, he and the first in command still made her practice daily on the ski shoot on the ship.

"Practice makes perfect, Gaby!" Cunnan would repeat when she pleaded with him to let her be. He loved Gaby like a daughter. Her charm and spontaneity were uncommon in this time and age.

Gaby knew that she could sway Cunnan's resolve sometimes. With Jean-Louis, it was useless to even try. She had respect for the position she was about to be initiated into. Despite her constant push to acquire more freedom, she listened and obeyed all of their orders to the best of her abilities.

"Rule number one," she would giggle as she mimicked the men in her life, "stay aloof, and do not become overly friendly with anyone." *Eh bien*, she had had to learn that one quite well in Paris! Her artist friends, the ones she had met in Paris were acceptable—others less so. She had learned to make herself less approachable in France—and that was a good thing.

Chapter 4

Venice appeared magnificent from afar. Ensconced in Jean-Louis' arms behind the steering wheel, Gaby admired the magnificence of the emerging coast.

"Life will be wonderful, Jean-Louis, I know. I will be supportive, and I will try to stay out of your way whenever possible." She glimpsed up, rotated from her torso and stretched to reach and kiss his lips. You made the right decision by letting me share this adventure with you. It would have been dreadful if I'd stayed in Paris."

He pressed her closer to his chest. "My life would have been miserable without you, Gaby," he replied solemnly.

"Look at the crowd! Is that for us?"

"Yes," he replied, none too happy.

"Are they expecting an aria from me?" she questioned, amused by his reaction. "I just can't wait to meet with the director of La Fenice. I will attend as many concerts as I can in the Teatro, Jean-Louis. You know, Verdi composed and played his opera *La Traviata* in this very theatre. I understand that it was a glorious rendition of Dumas fils's novel, _La Dame aux Camellias_. I love that opera, and I sing its arias magnificently!" She smiled coyly. "I also heard in one of the salons in Paris that the Russian composer Tchaikovsky comes to Venice during the winter. A very wealthy Russian Baronne is supposedly financially mentoring his musical career!" She stopped her monologue, entranced by the sight of the magnificence upon her.

Jean-Louis had told her to be as careful as possible, but to also enjoy the city.

"Remember *Chérie*, that you will be surrounded by security guards at all times, therefore do not be overly suspicious. Enjoy and appreciate. It is a culture like no other."

"My mother inculcated in my youthful spirit Italian traditions," she retorted, a bit miffed at his statement. After all, she was the one with the Italian lineage. "Naturally, Venetia was still under Austrian rule when she left Florence to marry my father. I had to learn how to speak and write the language, you know that, but I now wish I had been a great deal more assiduous. I should have listened more intently when she spoke to Ayden about the history and culture of Venice."

She noticed Jean-Louis' questioning glance.

"Ayden Bartley . . . her lover. I overheard them talking at times." Gabriella did not divulge more.

He never questioned Gaby about her past. She always appeared sad when she recalled events from her childhood. He couldn't fathom a mother who had been hanged for her beliefs! He did not know his mother—she had died in childbirth. But hearsay had it that the Duchess had been a lovely and surprisingly enough, for the culture of the times, an adoring wife. Let bygones be bygones. They did not need family. They had each other.

"These days, Gaby," the Duke continued, "the rich merchants' intent on copying the traditions of the most learned aristocrats has surpassed them many times over. They hire the very best painters, sculptors, musicians, dancers, and singers to work and play in their homes. Many of these families live like Counts and Kings because of the great wealth they've accumulated through trade with the East. Italy is clearly a respected center for your friends, *les artistes*!" he chuckled.

A stunned gaze flashed on her face, followed by a sideways inflamed glance directed at him. She lapsed into silence. A smile lit his icy blue eyes. He gathered her in his arms and pressed her body even closer to his. "I love you, Gaby, be patient with me, Chérie." She heaved a long sigh and continued to stare at the crowd on the Piazetta. The 18th century paintings she had studied as a child came alive. Flabbergasted, she gawped, a vision of the paintings from the *vedudisti,* the painters of views she'd studied with her Italian tutor as a child, flared before her eyes.

The influential merchants and aristocrats that she was about to meet were on the Piazetta, waiting.

He lowered the telescope so that she could focus on the large group as he reiterated much of the intelligence he had received. They were ready. He stayed close to her a while longer.

"Oh, by the way, my love, most of these people will use my title when addressing me . . . and you, obviously. Do not look the other way when you are called Duchess!"

As he doubled over, she cringed. It had been an embarrassing faux pas in England. She recalled all too clearly, one of Luke Edomberg's friends had called her Your Grace; she had looked behind her to glimpse at the person he was speaking to. She turned crimson at the thought.

"Well, as you can see, my wife truly embraces the spirit of the Revolution. She does not even respond to a title. A real *citoyenne,* don't you think?" Jean-Louis had quipped.

She could have murdered him! The only redeeming factor of this most difficult moment was that it stayed, inculcated in her mind—never to be repeated again!

"I will absolutely love the title," she retorted pretentiously, rolling her green eyes to the sky. "I am ready to storm Venice, Monsieur le Duc!"

Years ago, Jean-Louis had visited Venice. Actually, he had been an honored guest to the wealthy Austrian aristocrats who governed the *Bellissima*. The knowledge that he had experienced this beautiful city without her, most likely with another woman, was difficult to concede. However, Gaby reminded herself that she was the only woman in his life now. After all he had never lied about his less than saintly love life before their encounter.

She grasped the telescope and focused once more. Philippe stood on the embankment along with a large group of dignitaries. All obviously awaiting their arrival.

The Cardinal, the Beloved, Jean-Louis reflected caustically, must have arrived a couple of days earlier. He had stayed in Rome after they had departed for Venice. Now his presence on the Piazetta de Saint Marco indicated that he would represent the Catholic Church in the negotiations. Next to him stood another group of men in robes—the Vatican's delegation.

The King of Italy, Victor Emmanuel II stood tall and alone as he gazed at the *Tempête,* which sailed into the lagoon. Venice, the richest, largest and most influential city of the Kingdom had been under his control since 1866, a gift from the Prussian King, Wilhelm I. After the Austrians' defeat, Victor Emmanuel II had received Venetia from the soldier aristocrat himself. It must have been quite difficult for the proud Venetians to realign themselves behind one leader—a Sardinian king of all things. Like Giuseppe Garibaldi, the Venetians would have preferred a Republican government after a long bout under Austrian rule. Alas, for the sake of the nation, Garibaldi had opted for peace with Victor Emmanuel.

The opposition would be fierce. Jean-Louis trembled at the very thought that Gaby could come to harm. He'd heard about a shrewd noble, "a man not unlike myself—a dashing aristocrat," he'd mocked, as he'd recounted to Gaby the intelligence that had been forthcoming, "his name is Count

Jacopo de Castriodrianni. I have been told that women fall for him at the very sound of his name," he'd scoffed.

"Eh bien, Mon Cher, beware!" she'd intoned rapidly. "I was told when we visited Rome that the Count has a *maitresse attitrée,* whom he loves passionately. Regardless, it does not stop him from loving every pretty woman he chooses to have in his bed at night!"

"The Count is quite difficult to read, Jean-Louis," Philippe, Cardinal Thornsen, Gabriella's cherished cousin, had inserted in the few significant words they'd shared while the group was still in Rome. "Presumably now, he's aligned with the King . . . and the Pontiff."

"And the Pontiff? " Jean-Louis echoed.

"And the Pontiff," Philippe asserted. "De Castriodrianni's family has governed, for almost one hundred and fifty years, the two largest Papal States. Under the Risorgimento, he has been ousted from his lands . . . somewhat."

The Cardinal must have read his mind, Jean-Louis recalled, for immediately, Philippe had explained. "He likes his privileged standing. His financial power over the states is still astronomical. The man talks the talk and walks the walk. At the end of the day, he gives up nothing of his original requests—and there are many; he then makes you feel that you have gotten your way."

"A sly fox!" Another diplomat attached to the King had added. "When you review your treaty, he has given up nothing of substance and you are shut off. Talk to the Austrians, they will tell you about Jacopo de Castriodrianni. By the way, with this fellow watch the Duchess as well. He will pray on her, both physically and emotionally—that's a given!" Domenici de Burro had told Jean-Louis bluntly.

Jean-Louis had not deigned to elevate the impertinence with a specific question.

A grave mistake he would regret. Jealousy and pretension sometimes blind the very best!

By and by, the advisors strove to cover all pertinent information. Jean-Louis needed to sway many to his side of the fence. Rome as the capital of Italy, Victor Emmanuel would not compromise, and the modernization of the old continent, less religious powers and more trade, were the Monarch's goals. The peninsula was very well suited. The king had done it all before. He would not lose the final battle.

The Duke shared with Gaby the information that he received daily. It was in her interest and for her safety to be aware of the full situation. Besides, he wanted to discuss the prevailing situation away from the negotiating table. Her judgment was trustworthy. Brilliant, with a prodigious memory, Gaby listened intently and she spoke fluent Italian.

She had not been surprised when he had relented and asked her to accompany him. He remembered that day quite well in Normandy.

"Were you surprised when I decided to take you with me?" he'd asked her again a few days before their engagement.

"No, I would have been horrified, if you had not," was her fiery response. "Mon Dieu, what in the world would I have done in Paris without you and you without me? Jean-Louis, were you serious or was it some kind of *badinage*?" She'd expected an answer that he had not given.

Saying no to her would have been unachievable. He would have succumbed-again. Might as well let her assume that he had pondered the idea. He smiled as he looked down at her. Overall, he did not remember ever saying no to her about anything. Well, one time, her singing—it had been an immense sacrifice. He was well aware of that. But he had not forbidden the pursuit of her beloved musical skills. After all in Paris, in his privileged circle, it was unheard of to have a wife who wanted to pursue a profession, artistic or not? Instead, he'd built a splendid theater in their home. She still attended her courses at the *Conservatoire* every day and was directly involved in most rehearsals. The only restriction was the stage at the opéra. But here again, the theatre that he had built for her as a wedding present was the envy of every maestro in Europe. She had it all, he thought. A lucky woman, a very lucky woman, indeed! He gathered her closer. Perhaps, to reassure himself that he was absolutely correct.

"Gaby, our relationship may suffer at times. Under duress and pressure, I might become a less affable man, perhaps even more controlling than I have been in the past. Venice is not Paris," he candidly shared.

She shot him a questioning gaze.

"It goes with the territory, Gaby. As you know, I'm an amiable and adaptable person to live with," he countered. "I may be less agreeable at times. Nevertheless, the challenge and excitement of the endeavor will surely make up for my difficult moments."

Amused at the pretentious assertion, she giggled. A confused expression flashed on his manly face.

"Jean-Louis, I adore you, you are the most charming, stimulating, fascinating man that I have ever encountered. Consequently, on this note, I wish that I had been the only chosen one to experience or to acknowledge all of your graces. But *mi amor*, adaptable, that's decidedly pushing the bar to another level, maybe two or three! Darling, you are the most controlling person I ever had the pleasure to spend time with." She noticed his contrite expression. "And the only man I cannot fathom to live without!"

She slid her hands under his shirt, lifted it and pressed her lips to his taut abdomen. When he stood and towered over her, that part of his body she controlled. His response was predictable. Dazed with passion and longing, he would encircle her in his arms and usually took her to bed!

Human behavior? How oddly simplistic it was to expose, when the sweet sensation of passion flowed madly in the veins of a couple in love. In a fleeting instant, the mind would part ways from the most complicated, multifaceted mental intrigues, solely to be absorbed by an effortless animalistic response that dispersed all intellectual complexities. The body reacted to sensual impulses and the mind trailed it. Or . . . was it the other way around? She did not know. She did not care.

Chapter 5

Their arrival in Venice resulted in a splendid visual feast. Canals as far as the eyes could see. Black gondolas with sumptuous seating sailed through the choppy water under elegant bridges, small barges loosely attached to tall reeds emerged from the water while others were moored to the quays.

As she watched from afar, she noticed a crowd around the king.

"Oh, dear God, Jean-Louis, look!" She passed the binoculars over. "There is a demonstration. The King has been attacked? Oh, Dear God, Philippe! His bodyguards surround him. Has he been shot? Stabbed? I can't see him, Jean-Louis," she exclaimed dread in her voice. Almost as quickly as the attack happened, the military forced the crowd who had pounced on the attackers, away from the Monarch. Four men with blankets over their heads were led away by a military patrol. Victor Emmanuel, straight as a rod, straightened a sash that hung across his chest and regally, he marched stoically back to his original place of honor. The curia followed him. She saw Philippe. All happened so promptly that for an instant she thought she'd fallen asleep and had dreamed the horrific scenario.

"Eh bien," Jean-Louis stated, "I believe that an attempt on the Sovereign has just occurred." He left quickly for the stern to speak with his own security force.

"Are we at risk?" she asked Cunnan.

"No, my dearest, everything seems to have returned to normal. Watch, the King awaits our arrival." Cunnan turned and nodded to Gaby's security officers.

A short while later, they walked to the gangway and stepped down on a smaller boat to reach the mainland.

In less formal barges, passengers threw flowers at the delegation's passage.

As they disembarked, the Monarch strode to meet them. Quickly dozens of soldiers surrounded the French delegation and they were guided away from the populace.

They had crossed the Piazetta and had walked to the *Piazza San Marco* with its adjoining *Palazzo de Doges*. The magnificent *Basilica di San Marco*, with its golden murals, Byzantine icons, and rounded domes, emphasized the history of the former powerful City-State, more so than the great fervor toward the Church. The accompanying diplomats entered. Many lifted their gaze above to stare at the half-moon mosaic on the tympanum of the central portal, which represented Christ and the Last Judgment.

Before covering her head, with a black mantilla, Gaby stared up at the *Campanile* and blew a kiss at the Archangel Gabriel, which stood, solemn, at the very top of the tower. Piously, she trailed the others and strolled in the glorious church. The traditions of the Catholic Church were awe-inspiring. She loved it. After a long, but delicious Italian culinary feast, in one of the dining rooms in the *Palazzo de Doges*, they were escorted to their new residence.

The *Palazzo Gritti*, their home away from home was a veritable museum. Through its bronze portico, a pink and pearly white *parterre* extended the length and width of the brown ochre mansion. Tall wooden doors opened onto a vast courtyard bordered by large *Bellini* sculptures. They partly hid the elegant entrance to the main foyer. Liveried *domestiques* dressed in purple and yellow stood in two orderly rows, with their head slightly bowed. All awaited their future masters—

the Duke and Duchess de Bourbonne and the French delegation.

Early Renaissance works from Genovese and Tarrantino dominated the grand entrance of the palazzo. Heavy silk tapestries adorned the walls of the foyer with exquisite pastoral hunting scenes. Shaken and flushed at the incomparable beauty before her, Gaby sensed a fleeting moment of ancestral pride. Quickly, she jerked her head, shook her curls from side to side down her back and she lifted her chin. Why not? After all, her mother had a long aristocratic Florentine lineage. Nowadays all were Italians unified under one king.

Their private apartment boasted priceless paintings and Italian and French decorative arts similar to Jean-Louis's ancestral home in the Loire. Italian Renaissance paintings, Baroque sculptures, and intricately woven tapestries told stories of the great Papal Counts in their estates. Astonished, she stroked her hands on the fine silk bedspread and she stroked the long and thick matching *tentures* that hung down from the four bed posters. She came to rest on a satin, pink and white settee that stood across from a rosewood *coiffeuse*.

"Eh bien, Jean-Louis, I will just love it here!"

The mirror reflected a very happy, young woman whose lover strode to her and placed his mouth in the crook of her neck.

"I thought a smaller residence, closer to one of the canals, would be allotted. Instead our new home is a vast and very impressive palace!"

"What were you thinking, Gaby, that it would be similar to our love nest in the Faubourg?" A smile tugged at the corner of his mouth.

"No, of course, I understand that the delegation will share our quarters," she shot a furious glance in his direction, much too aware of her choice of words that he never failed to postulate. "They will share the Palazzo, but . . . I feel right at home in this magnificent residence," she remarked. "I will love it here. I am convinced that we will have a wonderful time." She squeezed his hand one more time as the butler reappeared, accompanied by a large number of security men. "It will be a challenging adventure," she murmured, almost to herself, as they continued their guided tour of the Palazzo in a more sedate manner.

Jean-Louis did not respond. When the doors closed in their private apartment, he gathered her in his arms and kissed her.

"Hopefully, Gaby . . ." He paused, skeptical of 'the wonderful time'. "As long as we have each other, we will make our own music." He kissed her again before she could babble on the never-ending charms of Venice.

The next few days would be social. He was prepared. He would make sure she would be prepared as well.

Chapter 6

The day after their arrival, a lavish ball was held in the couple's honor. The Venetian estate of the now defunct Count Camillo di Cavour was the location for the momentous event. Di Cavour, a Piedmontese, had been appointed as Sardinia's former chief minister in the late 1850's. He had seen in Charles Louis Napoléon III a very strong ally—one that would help him liberate his nation from Austrian rule. The reunification of the rich northern Italian provinces under the Sardinian ruler Victor Emmanuel II had been his most fervent goal. In fact, he had achieved his goals beyond his wildest imagination. Had he lived longer, he would have seen many of the City States allying themselves under Victor Emmanuel II. The conservative Monarch led Italy as a united country devoid of Austrian, Prussian and French tentacles. With all of its tumbles, Italian nationalism had emerged and strengthened.

Jean-Louis-Pierre de Pleyssis, along with the major players in the new world order, were upstairs above the grand ballroom, speaking about the wealth of Cavour and King Emmanuel II's design on Rome.

Meanwhile, on the first floor in the grand ballroom, the Roman society who had followed the international negotiators to Venice, reveled in the gossip that surrounded the Duke and Duchess de Bourbonne.

"Giuseppe, tell me," the Countessa di Rialto questioned her ardent devotee, Luigi di Berlozza, a principal negotiator in line with the Duke, "what is the Duchess' lineage? I recall that you spent a lot of time in New Orleans. Did you know her family?"

"Yes, the Duchess' mother, Caterina de-Conte, a distant cousin to the Sardinian statesman, Count Camillo di Cavour, had offered to her Irish husband, a seemingly splendid proposal—the purchase of a cotton brokerage firm in Louisiana. Her fervent hope had been that the old man would leave her behind to enjoy a bit more freedom on the old continent."

"She wanted to stay in Italy while he traveled or settled in the New World?" the Countessa questioned curiously.

"I believe so. Ian Thornsen was already a wealthy, part Irish, part English merchant whose family had bought or been given a title long ago. He still possessed large land holdings along the western Loire River. Staggering to many of his noble friends, the Count followed his learned wife's advice. He sold many of his lands and departed to the new world where many European aristocrats did not want to go—yet. Unfortunately for the lovely Caterina, Ian forced her to join him in his adventuresome venture. The Count then purchased huge parcels of land in the fertile area south of New Orleans, in Natchez and in Lafayette as well. With slavery very much in existence, his business flourished and his wealth tripled. His marriage, however, disintegrated. The reason—slavery."

"Slavery?" the elegant Countess asked disdainfully. "Caterina fell in love with one of her slaves?"

"No. The young, beautiful and passionate wife of the Count was taken from her very social life in Italy to the still closed social circles in New Orleans. Unwisely, Ian left her in the city to mix and mingle—on her own. It was not long before Caterina's passionate nature found a willing Northerner—of all things—to teach her the traditions of the South!" Luigi chuckled. "Aydan Bartley, the abolitionist taught her the customs of the South quite well. He convinced her to serve a cause bigger than herself. Often, Caterina would travel with him to Boston and New York. She began to empathize with the eloquent speeches given by Daniel Webster and Frederick Douglas in Faneuil Hall. She became an avid and committed abolitionist. To further complicate the issue, she fell passionately in love with the man who had introduced her to the momentous civil rights movement."

"She left her husband for an abolitionist? Had she lost her mind?" the incredulous Countessa scoffed.

"Yes and no. Caterina was intent on giving her slaves freedom papers. Ian wouldn't hear of it. After all, his plantations were lucrative, and he was a wealthy and respected man. He was not about to lose his fortune because of his wife's aversion to an accepted and legal way of life. The marriage went from bad to worse. Ian became very involved with a Creole woman in New Orleans. Caterina had her lover move in with her in the Justine—her rightful plantation. Ian firmly believed that the fault for the break-up lay with her Italian volatility. Regrettably, it was not long before she recognized that she was with child. Not from the man she loved, but from a man who failed to acknowledge the sanctity of life—her husband! Everyone thought at the time that the Duchess de Bourbonne was Bartley's child until one met her. She had her father's identical facial features, down to a minuscule *café au lait* birthmark on the right side of her neck. The situation became unbearable for both."

"Did he move back in?" Now, the Countessa was immersed in the story.

"Yes, he felt responsible for the child. Nonetheless, the following year, he returned to New Orleans."

"What about Caterina?"

"She pursued her passionate life with Aydan. They lived together and traveled a great deal of the time."

"I wish my husband had been sympathetic to my affairs," the Countessa laughed gaily. Gracefully, she detangled the dark brown curl on her cheek and passed a gloved hand over her intricately woven dark purple silk skirt. She glanced sideways at a nearby mirror and flashed a brief smile. Her elderly husband had recently passed. Since the loss, she'd drowned her sorrow in the company of wealthy and very young men in many of Europe's frivolous cities.

"Actually, they tried to be civil to one another at first. After the birth of the child however, the relationship deteriorated rapidly. Although, I confess that Ian was very proud of his daughter's musical accomplishments." Luigi came closer to Viola Maria. "Ian and I were quite close while I served in Louisiana, but his relationship with his daughter was always secretive. Every time he spoke of her, he appeared sheepish. There is a secret," he announced evasively. "However, I have been unable to read it."

"She does not seem to have suffered much." Viola Maria countered haughtily.

"Correct once again, my dear Countessa. She is quite accomplished. Ian was most proper when he separated from Caterina. He gave his wife the large, lucrative and very beautiful sugar plantation on the river, *La Justine*. The gift of two hundred fifty slaves was also part of the bargain. She gave them all their freedom papers as quickly as the ink dried on the transaction! Caterina had invested a lot of her own money in Ian's venture. Consequently, in her eyes it was a fair arrangement. Ian moved out of the plantation and settled permanently in New Orleans. There he was a revered social elite. He took up residence in the French quarter with the equally beautiful and very polished Adelaide Henriette Zelimat. But you asked about the Duchess?" He stepped closer to the Countessa and lovingly swept a loose curl away from her flawless profile. Ian stunned me late one evening when he revealed that Gabriella, the Duchess, had become a real burden to him."

"Why, Caterina turned the Duchess against her own legitimate father?" Once more the curiosity in the Countessa's low and delicious voice rose.

"No, I do not believe so. It appeared that Caterina had very little to do with the child as well. Gabriella-de-Conte Thornsen, the Duchess, spent most of her early years on her plantation with her servants, and at a convent in New Orleans. What I believe disturbed Ian most, was that 'the girl', the Duchess, as he referred to her, possessed an uncanny resemblance to her mother. Not physically, but in her demeanor and stubborn disposition. It drove Ian crazy. On these grounds, he professed more than once, in private to me, that he could not bear his daughter's presence in his happy home. By then he had fathered three sons with Adelaide."

Viola Maria was about to pursue her conversation, when the guests lowered their voices. The music brought to a standstill. The dancing ceased. All eyes riveted to the second floor and focused on the impressive couple. The Duke and the Duchess held hands, as they stood regal awaiting their formal introduction.

Chapter 7

Cunnan, seated at a table with colleagues from the French delegation, observed the couple stepping down the staircase.

In effect, Gabriella had been born against all odds. "My mother consulted midwives who'd studied medicinal plants all over Natchez and New Orleans to terminate the pregnancy. Her tenacity and diligence in the preparation and application of potions were obviously useless," she liked to tell her friends as she struggled against her mirth.

She'd grown into a very accomplished and breath-taking young woman. Cunnan considered.

"All the herbal tisanes my mother drank to expel the fetus must have worked in my favor," she would divulge. "More research should be undertaken; perhaps these unknown substances have properties that enhance intelligence and musical talents!"

Both parents had financed her education. She, in turn, had taken every opportunity to excel in the academic disciplines offered. She spoke French, Italian and German fluently. History and international relations she adored. With an adventurous spirit, she had been determined to live a full and exciting life—on her own terms, until her passionate encounter with Jean-Louis-Pierre.

Philippe, now Cardinal Thornsen, inhabited the plantation next to hers. At a tender age the two cousins, deprived of parental affection and a warmhearted family life, had developed an unusually close relationship. While riding on their vast plantations, they would often pretend to be Southern ambassadors involved in great negotiations across international boundaries. Their goal: to ease the tensions of a conflicted world with peaceful suggestions to the world's autocratic leaders. The imaginary games would solve delicate world crises. Naturally grand words of praise for the two diligent ambassadors of peace would always terminate their invented scenario.

"If we can't be loved by our parents," Gabriella would declare grandly to her cousin, "then at least we have our imaginary friends who are in awe of our genius." In their make-believe world, he would use religion and faith as his entrance to the grand political salons. And she would delight with her musical talents as she gained entrance to the world's most sophisticated aristocratic courts. Their dependence upon one another had often been questioned.

Keen intelligence coupled with a vivid intuition—qualities not sought often enough in a woman—she often wondered why would slave owners who had children with their slaves would provide a superior education to those daughter's from the improper union. Fathers rarely put too much faith or money in their legitimate daughter's education. In that sense, she had been fortunate. She had been given the chance and she had jumped at the opportunity.

With the Cardinal, the parental situation had prompted a sadistic revenge on the young man. Philippe's mother had been the long time mistress of a protestant Bishop. After years of hypocrisy and of a guilt-ridden life, the ecclesiastic had decided to return to the African colonies to preach the Gospel—in essence, to atone for his sins. Philippe's mother, the once splendid Virginia Cathers, had lost her mind. Shortly after the Bishop's departure, she had been placed in a *maison de fou*—a sanitarium down the river. While on an infrequent river outing on the Mississippi, she had committed suicide. Rejected, mal-treated, an embarrassment to his father who was uncertain of his son's genetic lineage, Philippe's arduous young life had taken a vicious turn. His father, a politically astute plantation owner, had sent his son to the Vatican in Rome to hone his musical talent—his angelic voice. Knowing all along the causal effect, the father had given his consent to castrate the child in order to preserve his great vocal gift. The Vatican's surgeon had castrated Philippe at the tender age of eleven.

Upon his return, the only salvation for the future Cardinal had been his cousin, his dear Gabriella.

Consequently, the two young rejected souls matured well, considering the horrendous hardships they had experienced and survived. The relationship had been sealed with an unbreakable tie. In effect, Gabriella's and Philippe Thornsen's destinies and roles in the world were not as bizarre as Jean-Louis-Pierre de Pleyssis assumed.

Philippe had resolved to return to Rome to fulfill his intellectual religious calling in the Jesuit order. The scholarly canon of the Jesuits appealed to him. At the seminary, he displayed an intellectual agility that secured an influential position within the curia. His letters depicted the beginning of a new world order. His ideas titillated Gabriella.

After the end of the Civil War, Gabriella had embarked on the adventure she devised years ago. The Académie De Musique in Paris extended an invitation, which she accepted. As she prepared to sail to France, the conviction that she was the captain of her life inculcated in her spirit a fearless determination.

Cunnan nodded to a group of delegates passing by.

Jean-Louis, in contrast, believed that he had a duty to hasten the modernization prospects of France. His political philosophy went a lot further than what he led others to believe. He was astute, conservative, and he possessed a total aversion for control of any kind.

"The Empire should serve the people well in areas of education and work creation. That is primordial. Then, we in the privileged class could proceed with a renewed authority toward the modern advancement of the not so distant 20th century." Otto von Bismarck, another aristocrat, served the world in his capacity as the right hand man of the Prussian king, William I. Both men sensed that aristocrats and members of the populace were no different from a physical and an emotional point of view. The difference lay in a lucky or unlucky birth! However, Jean-Louis-Pierre differentiated between the educated class and the masses that still struggled for an honest meal. Education was far removed from the uncultivated mind of the working class. To place grand ideas of intellectual freedom in the spirit, without first providing basic social reforms with a simple path to adhere to, was in actuality an exercise in futility for humanity.

The responsibility to settle the world's conflicts relied on members of the privileged class. The next generation would pick up the slack if Jean-Louis-Pierre attained his goal of social reforms. But for now, all the shouts about a democratic republic needed to be disregarded and countered with great authority. Otherwise, it would be the premier setting to create a nasty civil war.

Both Gabriella and Jean-Louis-Pierre were unlikely partners from two different continents. They had met and had fallen crazily in love. Now, both pursued a path to alter history.

Jean-Louis-Pierre had fought many wars in Asia. He had lent his services to the Northern American states to fight and to achieve victory over the Southern states—much to the chagrin of his adored Southern Belle wife. Gabriella still harbored the indelible scars inflicted by the Federalists in her native Louisiana.

He fought for modern ideas, and the eventual betterment of the common man. She, in essence, abandoned her dream of touring Europe's major opera houses.

Cunnan heaved a great sigh and stood. He ambled toward the couple.

Chapter 8

Silence reigned in the grand ballroom. The powerful Duke and Duchess de Bourbonne descended the rounded marble staircase and found themselves surrounded by a great number of guests who anxiously awaited a formal introduction.

Much later in the evening they became separated. Jean-Louis was led away by a group of military men who walked briskly toward a smoking room situated across from the ballroom. Cognac in hand, he strolled to the fireplace. From this vantage point, he rested his arm on the sculpted rosewood mantle and calmly observed Gaby, immersed in animated conversation and surrounded by elegantly dressed women.

Jean-Louis reminisced about his fateful crossing when he sailed back to France shortly before the attempted pirate's attack on Gaby's ship. His departure from the United States had been particularly gloomy. He admired the new nation across the Atlantic immensely. One of his last business ventures in Boston had been to commission the firm of the late famed architect Charles Bulfinch to re-design his recently purchased home in Louisburg Square. He had wanted to own a home to return to the United States. The three-story house was within walking distance of the famed Faneuil Hall, the very meeting place where many enlightened people had spoken their majestic words. He had even entertained the idea of settling down with a witty and interesting woman—an American woman who would be flexible and understanding about his volatile nature. Quite nice, indeed, had it panned out! Fate worked in mysterious ways, the Duke reflected. The beautiful brunette who stood across the room from him had changed his personal life forever. Change was an understatement. She controlled his every breath! Aversion to a monogamous relationship had been a sentiment that he had counted on pursuing for the rest of his earthly life. He loved his freedom and women too much. As he sailed toward Brest to meet with Charles-Louis-Napoléon, he longed to return to his adopted country. Then, the incident had occurred. He grinned. His transformation had been mind-boggling!

He loved the sea, the adventure that it provided, the fear that it instilled, the dangers and the challenges that it commanded. He had sailed for close to ten years now. Many of the conflicts had threatened his life and properties. He was an aristocrat with real conservative ties and beliefs—that was an asset, he thought. Governments often learned from the grave mistakes of the past. It was usually the negligible, repeated errors that provoked the vicious cycle of discontent and war. In his time, the aristocratic ruling class still possessed the upper hand. Bismarck and the crowned King of Sardinia, Victor Emmanuel II, shared a very good understanding of where they needed to take their countries. Absolutism through divine intervention was no longer needed nor wanted. Conversely, to prosper Europe needed conservative values with nationalistic ideals, which would embrace trade and modernity. Although the ideas of the Enlightenment, he thought, should not be disregarded. The Age of Reason in Europe had paid the heavy price of revolution for its challenge to the Old Order. The youthful United States comprehended the Enlightened ideas of the previous century and practiced most of its values. Finally, slavery had been outlawed. The moral deviance of history had not yet touched the nascent United States of America.

Gabriella spun on her heels. She glanced sensually in his direction and winked. Surrounded by diplomats who pressed for delicate information, he acknowledged their comments with a distant nod. A smile lit her emerald green eyes. He smiled back.

Chapter 9

A succession of grand balls continued throughout the month to formally introduce the Duke and Duchess de Bourbonne to Venice. As usual, Jean-Louis-Pierre and Gabriella de Pleyssis made their formal entrance hand in hand. Italy was in the midst of a golden age of Romanticism. The couple's sensual gesture caught the fancy of the young aristocrats. It was modern, gossips declared. Many yearned for a romantic and passionate life.

It was said that the couple had a most unusual connection.

Dukes and Duchesses, Counts and Countesses, Marquis and Marquises were in attendance. Italian women in their courtly and very sophisticated attires rivaled the elegance of their French counterparts. Rumors flowed in every hall. The couple's passionate but conflicted love affair in Paris was the talk of the *soirée*. In addition, Jean-Louis' less than perfect amorous past was splashed across the pages of the Venetian Gazette—the offspring of the 16th century *Notizzie Scritte*.

The powerful and enigmatic French Duke displayed very little emotion as the diplomatic corps of the forthcoming negotiations showed their respect. Women spoke of his masculine magnetism. Men delighted in Gabriella's appealing demeanor and very sensual assets.

Signora Fionna di Masaretti spoke candidly. Surrounded by a large group of acquaintances, the Venetian beauty recounted to all who wanted to hear the spicy episode she experienced first hand earlier that day. "The Count, my husband, sent me over to the *Palazzo Gritti* this afternoon. As you are surely aware, the use of the palace of our celebrated *Doge*, Andrea Gritti, has been gallantly placed at the disposal of the Duke and his Duchess. After all, the *Palazzo Gritti* was the residence of the Vatican's ambassadors when they visited *La Serenissima*. Marino asked me to visit our national guests. I'd hope to meet with him personally . . ." She smiled and winked at her friend. "To make him feel . . . should we say, welcome. To possibly remind him of our famous hospitality and culture, perhaps even . . . to soften the hard edges for the Count." Her eyes charmingly lifted toward the magnificent ceiling of the residence painted by Paolo Veronese. "I understand the Duke de Bourbonne is a difficult man to do business with. We, of course, residents of our beautiful city, understand that our wealth is the consequence of our long distance trade with the Orient. We know how to negotiate," she elegantly asserted.

"Please, Fionna, don't make us drool with inconsequential details," one friend quipped.

"Well, my dearest friends, my advances were not even considered! When the butler announced my arrival, I perceived through the half open gilded entry doors a pair of lovely feminine legs, naked and dangling from what appeared to be a fainting sofa. The Duke and the Duchess were engaged in a very heated romantic interlude. Their impassioned, muted voices left nothing to the imagination! The *fait accompli* did not match the words of the humiliated butler who showed me back to the door. Pardon me, Madama, the mortified butler responded, the Duke is apparently quite taken . . . a most pressing nature . . . in conference!" Hysterical laughter burst out from behind one of the Corinthian marble columns that enclosed the vast and beautiful mirrored ballroom. The ladies gathered much closer to the Countessa to hear the final tidbits of the encounter.

"Truly, my friends, she was negotiating for the formidable pearl necklace clasped around her tender neck this evening!"

the Countessa scoffed, although quite amused by the turn of events.

"I understand that they have a monogamous marriage, and that his jealousy is redoubtable," another friend of the Countessa, Maria di Peroni intoned. "In addition, I understand that while in Paris, he takes time to visit with her in the Jardins and he dines with her daily." Delighted that she had the undivided attention of all in her circle, she strolled away from the crowded dance floor toward a more secluded alcove. All strode gracefully behind Maria.

She closed in on her friends to confide a more risqué scandal—one that supposedly had rocked *le Grand Monde* in Paris. "And I heard from the best of sources that he had taken her in the *Bois de Vincennes*—and even more perverse in his own loge at the opéra in Paris. The curtains had been partially pulled."

"They both have such disdain for niceties. I feel ashamed that she has Italian blood in her lovely bones—and of good lineage at that!" the old dowager Countessa di Scalia replied in a most offended voice.

"How vulgar and colonial. It is hard to believe that he was bred so dutifully in the world's most distinguished capitals."

Another much younger woman, who wore a resplendent tiara encrusted with rubies, diamonds and emeralds, sighed. She fanned out a parchment and lemony voile fan covered with oriental motifs and started moving it nervously a few inches away from her voluptuous breast.

"How lucky to be married to someone you love and to be fully loved in return," observed young Celina Amaretto, who was soon to wed a man thrice her age.

"Bella Celina, you are terribly young and immature, dear child. Please recall that once you fulfill your duty, that of giving your husband a male heir, the freedom of loving whoever pleases you will be yours—in the constraint of discretion, naturally. You have been raised well, my child. A wonderful life filled with merriments awaits you."

"Besides, do not cling to the varnish of romantic nonsense!" Countessa di Verona retorted reproachfully. "I understand that the Duke controls her every move. You can see it in his demeanor. I hear from a very good source who just left Paris, that he struck her unmercifully and inflicted wounds! She had to cancel all her activities for two full weeks just to hide the marks he meted out. The reason was even more outrageous. She'd kissed her cousin—Cardinal Thornsen! I also hear that he has refused her singing lessons although she is a splendid soprano who was revered on stage. For heaven's sake, this was the reason why she came to France—to study and to hone her opéra skills with myriad legendary Maestros. You see," the Countessa purposely explained to Celina, "I believe that her singing gives her a great deal of independence—that independence, he will not tolerate," she concluded as she walked closer to Celina and reached for the young girl's hand. "So you see my dear Celina, life is never as sweet as it seems. Her life is not as dreamy as she would like us to believe," the Countessa finished forcefully.

"We are living in modern times, after all," the pretty Fionna Masaretti, the older of the three, started the conversation once more, "why can't a woman have as many lovers as our husbands have had and continue to have? Personally, I could not see myself with just one man, especially one who will not allow me any personal decisions that could aggrandize my potential. *Vive l'independence!*"

"Fionna, the warm plum *eau de vie* that you're so fond of must alter your thoughts of freedom and self-reliance. What have you been sipping lately? What independence do we have besides choosing our *toilettes*, our wardrobe? Think carefully, your husband sends you as a diversion—a gift to another man. The reason—a political tactic to obtain diplomatic and commercial favors for his own political end," the dowager replied innerved by the ever effervescent and very flirtatious Fionna.

"Eh bien, do not think that he is the ever faithful husband. Marino shared with me, just this morning, that one of the Duke's mistresses accompanied him to Toulon—just a few days prior to the couple's departure! It is my understanding that the Duchess was delayed in Paris."

An overwhelming expression of sadness flashed across the young Celina's face.

"Celina, my dear Celina, do not fret," the dowager exclaimed as she noted her favorite niece's distraught glance. "You'll have a beautiful and very social life. The most acclaimed painters and sculptors will decorate your home; your portraits will hang in famous museums across our cultured land. Your dresses and jewelry will be the envy of every woman present this evening, my dearest heart. Please, please, a grand smile, Celina! Life will shine upon you, my dearest child."

Elegantly, Celina brushed the red satin straps of her décolleté with her gloved hand. She heaved a long sigh and glanced to the finely carved ceiling as she raised her teary doe-eyes to the heavens.

"In my opinion, save all the gossips, I found Gabriella de Pleyssis to be most fortunate," another splendid young woman with long blond curls drifting across very feminine ivory shoulders echoed. "Besides, he is young, virile, and handsome. I would forgive him all indiscretions just to be held in his arms and spend a night in his bed!" exclaimed the young wife of Count Vintellina-Cavetta. Dreamily she clasped her bejeweled, pearly-white hand to her swan-like neck, clearly oblivious to the heartache imposed on the young Celina by an overly ambitious and land hungry aristocratic family.

Jean-Louis-Pierre de Pleyssis re-entered the vast foyer. He spotted Gabriella in lively conversation with an intimate group of very influential men and their spouses. She clearly enjoyed conversing in Italian. From the fleeting glimpses of her captive audience, he implicitly recognized that the enjoyment was mutual. He marched to the circle of acquaintances and possessively placed his hand around Gaby's narrow waist. He gazed down at his wife and subjected her to a relaxed appraisal.

"Your glass requires attention, Madame," he murmured in her ear. A smile tugged at the corner of his mouth.

"I would much rather dance with you, Cher Duc," she replied coyly.

"Eh bien, Ma Chére Duchesse, the pleasure is mine." He nodded to the crowded dance floor. A lazy grin swept across his face. Both took leave of their hosts and they slowly paced across the room to the dance floor. All eyes focused on the powerful couple. A path was cleared for the de Pleyssis. She stepped into his arms. He molded her to the full length of his body and leisurely he began to whirl her about in a leisurely manner to the sweeping music. His brazen gaze settled on her voluptuous breasts peeking through a low vanilla white lacey décolleté. Unabashed, and totally oblivious to the local culture, he bent down and posed a kiss on her lips.

"Happy?" he murmured in the crook of her neck.

A *frisson* shook her curvaceous body from head to toe. "Immensely," she replied with a grand smile.

"Remarkable," Fionnna Masaretti observed pensively, "I will try my best to win his favors. Any bets, my friends?"

All the ladies, greatly amused, laughed heartily as they re-entered the ballroom and filed obediently toward their respective husbands. The ball had started. They would commiserate later.

Chapter 10

Months later, the discussions between the parties were at a stalemate. One early morning, Gaby and Jean-Louis sat on a large velvet burgundy settee—he wore a long dark grey satin robe; she was resplendent in an ivory, frilly, French Valenciennes bobbin lace négligé.

"Eh bien, Gaby, these past few months we have achieved a great deal with both the Vatican's delegation of Pope Pius IX and their counterparts—the intimate advisors to Victor Emmanuel II," he stated as his gaze strayed to his wife's exquisite assets.

Gaby giggled and winked. She gracefully stood and sauntered close to him. Placing her two fingers below his chin, she raised his manly face to hers. "Up here, darling!" she admonished amused. Agile as a gazelle fleeing danger, she escaped his wandering hands and returned to her side of the sofa. Her hand to her throat, she glanced down and lifted the flimsy voile over her knee.

"I understand from Philippe that most of the attending ecclesiastics are bent on keeping the last vestiges of the Papal States, Jean-Louis. The once uncontested temporal power in the former Papal States is now reduced to the Eternal City, its Cathedrals and most important, its port. Have you heard that Victor Emmanuel's royal intent is to confiscate it all?" A subtle hint of indignation sounded in her melodious voice. "The Pope is counting on the French troops to protect these last assets. Don't rest on your laurels quite yet, Jean-Louis. Your work is far from over," she concluded.

An arrogant sideways glare greeted her not so subtle deduction. "The French delegation and I are here to convince

Pius IX to accept the loss of Rome and its port. Furthermore we would like for Him to be satisfied with the Vatican, the Lateran Church, and its Cathedrals across the world," he shot back. "If we accomplish this negotiation cleverly, I believe that peace will be justly achieved in Italy. The Italians have suffered greatly throughout the years. Many wars throughout the ages have been fought on the Peninsula."

"*Les Français*, your compatriots, Cher Jean-Louis, have wreaked havoc on the City States and Rome throughout the ages. Napoléon I, the uncle of your cherished Emperor is not well loved here," she pursued, her tone sarcastic.

He lifted his shoulders and acquiesced. "Incidentally, I am quite pleased that cousin Philippe passes on his thoughts on this most pertinent subject to you. And when, may I ask, did you last see the great prelate?" he solicited, eyebrows raised and jaw clenched. "He's mostly silent in conference. Perhaps you should be included in the negotiations!"

"A couple of days ago," she replied unmindful of his pointed reply. "I invited him for a *déjeuner*. Philippe questioned . . . " She hesitated a moment. " . . . Venice as the premier location for the negotiations. He indicated that Rome would be a safer venue for all concerned."

"Did he explain why?" Jean-Louis countered irritated.

"Well, yes, he pointed out that many in the Kingdom still feel very passionate about an Italian Republic."

"Yes, Philippe is partly correct. To this very day, old followers of the great Garibaldi still do not understand his alliance with Emmanuel II."

"What about the great turn about in 1859 by Charles Louis Napoléon when he allowed Venice to stay under Austrian rule, even though Austria had been defeated?" Gaby continued.

"You're far safer here, Gaby. Philippe is just plain wrong. Venice is far removed and your sojourn in Italy will be much more agreeable." His gaze remained disturbed. Philippe had raised a point of concern that he had mulled over prior to his decision. In essence, in 1849, the principality of San Marino had sheltered Garibaldi and many of his Red Shirts soldiers, as they'd fled the Pope's army and the Austrians on their way to Venice. Instead, Jean-Louis changed the subject.

"Interesting, Gaby. I'm one of the few in the government concerned about Bismarck's sight on France. All in Paris are so flippant about the wily Prussian. It appears to me that if a war should erupt between the two countries, the French troops stationed in Rome would be called back to the front."

A knock at the door ended their conversation.

"Madame," the butler respectfully announced, "your hairstylist and seamstress have arrived." He quietly stood by the door and waited for an answer.

"Thank you, I'll be right up." Gaby lifted the lace away from her legs; she fastened the four white satin covered buttons from the peignoir closer to her breasts and stood.

"I'm so terribly happy, Jean-Louis, I have not sung with such a wonderful entourage since our departure from Paris. Wish me luck, Darling!"

"No luck is needed, Gaby. You are simply the very best, ma Chérie," he assured her.

Quickly, she ran to him and kissed him. She lingered. "*Je t'aime.*" Then, she spun on her heels and darted like a schoolgirl out the door.

He sauntered closer to the large fireplace and leaned on its marble mantle as he stared down at the smoldering logs. The conversation that had just transpired had given him pause. Philippe was correct. Many Italians were still absorbed with the idea of a Republic—an Italian Republic. The silent third party, the remnant of the dedicated followers of the great Italian hero of the Risorgimento, Giuseppe Garibaldi, gave him some trepidation. He sank his large frame into a blood-red, mahogany-framed smoking chair. They had reached a plateau, patience, the essence of the moments ahead.

Undeniably, Gabriella's beauty, intelligence and, most important, her fluency in her ancestors' native tongue, had softened many jagged edges. She loved Venice and she enjoyed all of the amusement at her disposal, which, he conceded, somewhat pleased him. He had had to adjust to the great love she shared with her cousin Philippe—Cardinal Thornsen. Fortunately, the Cardinal was on his way back to Rome. He couldn't be more delighted. He hated to share Gaby with anyone. He heaved a long sigh, missing Paris and the infinite time they shared in each other's company.

Less than an hour later, his carriage departed the Palace, and Gaby waited impatiently for the arrival of the Maestro of the Teatro La Fenice whom she wanted to receive privately. He had conceded—not happily but accepted, nevertheless. Gaby understood him so well and she pleased him even more. Unconsciously, the Duke tapped and pressed to his heart the medal of the angel Gabriel she had given him on their wedding day. He smiled as her pretty and expressive face flashed in his mind. He never complimented her. Rarely, he confided how delighted he was that she'd agree to share his less than harmonious life. Gaby needed very little reassurance when it came to her accomplishments but still . . . he truly enjoyed it when she complimented him. Why was it so hard for him to acknowledge her incredible talent and supportive nature? Why had he not told her how truly formidable she had been during the negotiations last week—a fabulous support, a brainy and smart ally. He would tell her tonight, he promised himself. After an artsy and splendid afternoon, his acknowledgment of his love and admiration would be the high point of her day! A smile tugged at the corner of his mouth. All was going well today. He relaxed his head on the deep crimson velvet squabs and stretched his long legs onto the seats across from him while he took in his daily agenda.

Earlier today, he'd eased the security. Since their arrival, she'd been anxious to meet with Maestro Darionelli-Vita, the famed Director of the Teatro La Fenice. He had not wanted anyone to think they lived in a fortress, and he wished to give Gaby a bit of ease and courteous living. The famous director had graciously agreed to visit with Gaby in the palazzo. The guards outside were on alert. Maestro Darionelli-Vita was a well connected and much admired Italian Maestro. The man, Jean-Louis concluded, likely traveled with high security, as well.

Elated, Gaby had practiced her voice with her personal Parisian vocal coach, Bernard, who journeyed with her. She was thrilled about the meeting. Last week, she had heard that the Maestro would travel to Paris the next year, in order to engage with Garnier's architect. Louis Napoléon had commissioned the new opéra de Paris. It was the talk of the art world. With any luck, she might entice him with a generous contract to work in her theatre in their home in Paris.

On a beautiful Venetian day, at ten in the morning, the much-awaited artist finally arrived.

Right from the start, Maestro Darionelli-Vita appeared uncommonly tense in Gabriella's presence. Questioning his bizarre demeanor, she glanced at Melba. The famous soprano had recently arrived in Venice for the season. Sensually, the diva lifted her shoulders towards her ears. The implicit non-verbal shrug was appreciated.

Gaby smiled at her illustrious guest. She escorted the silver-haired older man with the elegant stature through the many halls of the awe-inspiring palazzo. An uncontrollable quiver shook the maestro's fingers as he reached for his golden-rimmed monocle. The spec attached to a burgundy satin sash, hung low on his rotund belly. He averted her gaze, fixing his dark brown eyes on the gilded double doors at the far end of the corridor.

The art of the Italian Renaissance covered the walls from one drawing room to the next. The Queen of the Adriatic, as Venice was called, owed a lot of its late Renaissance art revival to the Bellini family. Jacopo Bellini, *The Madonna of the Cherubim*, held the place of honor at the entrance of the music room. Gentile Bellini, *Procession in St. Mark's Square*, lined the hallways leading to the ballroom. The Byzantine influence in Venice was grandly displayed in the foyer. Large silver iconic plates were displayed in alcoves along the halls. Some were partially concealed by heavy golden *tentures, wall hangings,* swept to one side along the vestibule. A splendid representation of the Christ flanked by the Virgin Mary and John the Baptist executed by Italian mosaicists never ceased to astound those who walked up the impressive marble staircase. Gentile Bellini had painted Sultan Mahomet II while he served as Ambassador to Constantinople. For his services, the Sultan had conferred upon the talented artist the title of Bey. There was a fascinating history behind every work of art in the palazzo—one that recounted through mythological renderings and religious paintings the history of humanity.

Gaby observed closely the Maestro and his entourage as they walked down the halls—proud and silent. All, strangely, ignored the large framed paintings of Titian and Giorgione that ornamented the walls. Rare were the guests who passed through these magnificent corridors, not dazed by the artistic splendor displayed in the magnificent sitting rooms, galleries, libraries and vast ballroom.

Gaby blamed it on Italian culture. One should not bestow overt compliments—a clear assertion that the patron was not accustomed to such niceties. In essence, it was considered to be admittance to one's artistic milieu.

As they reached the theater, the butler and a few other *domestiques,* followed them inside. Refreshments were offered.

"Two cognacs," the Maestro almost shouted.

Gaby's expressive eyes must have shown surprise as Melba beamed. At ten in the morning, even in Italy, that seemed a bit unusual. Courteously, she followed his lead and ordered the same.

The portly dark-haired man with the piercing black eyes approached the fireplace and gulped down his cognac. Abruptly, he flipped his head back and gawked intently at Gaby. Pearly white beads collected on his forehead. She cast a skeptical glance back. The Maestro heaved a long and tense sigh. His head fell on his chest. His body jerked and slid downward. Only the wide, cream and gold satin spine of the sofa next to him averted a full headfirst drop onto the parquet floor. An ominous silence confounded all . . . and . . . pure hell broke out. The three violinists, who had accompanied the Maestro into the theater, lifted their multi-layered draped capes, revealing guns aimed at Gaby. A manservant standing close by attempted to fling the gun away from the assailants. He was stopped in his steps by a hand that draped over his mouth and a knife blade punctured his lungs and heart. The dead man was caught before he could thunder down onto the floor. Silently, like a well-rehearsed ballet, the two 'musicians' carried and hid the body behind the velour draperies. The 'harpist' standing by the two double doors dropped the instrument on another thick carpet that was thrown over highly polished wooden parquet. He removed his hat. A bronze gun slid down from the straw *canotier*. Without much ado, he pointed it at the Maestro.

Time stood still. Gaby ogled all the participants. A nightmare unfurled right before her eyes. She was not going down that easily. She straightened slowly, gained her full height and lifted her chin defiantly.

"You will not go far. The palace is surrounded. Let us go, I will keep quiet," she calmly told the men in Italian.

A man with beady, piercing brown eyes, an elongated Cyrano de Bergerac nose and very thin lips advanced toward her. He spoke bluntly.

"We have been told, Madama, not to overlook your keen intelligence and quick analytical mind. I am pleased to announce that our task will be much easier than anticipated. Not very cerebral that response! Do you think we're choirboys, *Mia Cara*? I can see that your non-existent intelligence was aggrandized as well by proponents of the coalition movement. Another reason why the Duke, your husband, listens to intellectually incapacitated idiots! They are willing to sell our civil rights to a King who does not seem to pledge allegiance to the Italian Peninsula. Garibaldi said years ago "Italy to the Italians," that means all of us, rich and poor, Madama. I know that Rome, our Eternal City, is the last bastion, but we will fight to the death for our freedom against Vittorio Emmanuel and against the Pope and his collaborators and protectors—the French. Furthermore, we will annihilate the forces of Vittorio Emmanuel II. The aristocrats' intent is to continue the privileged practices of the old City States. We want and will have no less than a Republic! No, this time, the populace will rise, and we will govern ourselves without the help of a Monarch! A Republic, Madama! We'll rally around an administration that will give us our rights, our freedom and our financial recompenses. We will not let ourselves be led by one arrogant power-grabbing aristocrat! Let the Italians be led by Italians. Why should we trust the French? Tell me Madama?"

A knock at the door prompted the revolutionaries to conceal their guns.

"Dismiss them. You move or say the wrong thing, and the palazzo blows up," the leader of the group said menacingly into the crook of her neck, as he brutally rammed his gun into her ribs.

Gaby stared at the Maestro's pale and petrified expression. The men were not to be taken lightly. She lapsed into silence. The servants were politely received as they passed collation to the men. Haughtily, she dismissed them with a simple wave.

"Leave the trays on the table. We will serve ourselves." Stunned by her arrogant tone, Augustus, her favorite manservant glanced uneasily at her and then at her guests. He inclined his head and he walked backwards to depart the room.

All stood silent for an interminable moment. Fear accrued; an inexplicable sadness overwhelmed her as she grasped the enormity of the situation. She was at their complete mercy. Maliciously, one of the *music men* closed in on her—the barrel of his gun thrusting deep in her side. Two men positioned across from her, near the Maestro, displayed weapons partly covered by the heavy lace cummerbunds that hung down from their waist. She could not extricate herself from this situation. The bandit with the hooked nose nodded to the Maestro and pushed her forward with the tip of his gun.

"Now, my dear Duchess," she heard the Maestro's feeble voice. "I will take you to the *Salle De Concert* right here in Venice. Your voice is a gift from God; the full orchestra is awaiting your arrival at the Teatro . . . " he finished exhausted, tears flooded his heavy-lidded eyes.

Gaby stared at him. Then, she directed her gaze to Melba. The singing legend appeared livid. She sagged across the sofa. Unfortunately, Melba feigned fainting frivolously when her wishes were ignored. Her swoon alarmed no one. Pulled from the divan, she was forced to join the ranks.

Gaby followed the Maestro and the 'violinists' out of the salon.

"Mr. Cunnan," she sternly called out, "tell the Duke that I shall return a bit later this evening. I have been invited by Maestro Darionelli-Vita to attend a performance at *La Salle De Concert*. I will meet him at Count Pellegrino's soirée this evening." She stated with a curt nod.

There had been no please, no thank you. Momentarily, Cunnan stared at her, astonished by the arrogance in Gaby's tone of voice. As she strode out of the foyer, she shot him a sideways glance. He detected terror in her immense, expressive green eyes. The fleeting, terrorized gaze was inculcated in his brain. He vividly recalled the sheer panic it revealed when he'd found her inside the ship's trunk on the crossing to France. Something was terribly wrong. About to spring into action, he caught the deadly stare of the men that framed the dear child. The man who strode directly behind Gaby, held a gun. Protruding from his black satin cape, it pointed at his little Duchess. How had he not grasped the oddness of the situation? The Palace where they resided had a music chamber deemed the gem of Venice. Why would they have wanted to convene anywhere else? Cunnan nodded to the butler. A shot rang out. The man who stood behind Gaby fell dead on the floor. She rushed sideways and bolted back toward the theatre. Her freedom was short-lived; another caped man darted forward and seized her arm. Violently he rolled her back to him. A cloak was thrown over her head. A gun touched her temple, and in this presumably secure environment, Gabriella de-Conte-Townsen-de Pleyssis was whisked away.

The butlers came alive as they barred the music impresario and his captors' exit. One gunman fled. Another was shot dead. A shot fired from the upstairs balcony had taken the life of a third kidnapper. He fell to the marble floor, gurgling blood that stained the mosaic floor.

Melba snapped out, awake for a moment, and then returned to her unconscious world. Sadly indeed, in the unfurling chaos, the Duchess had been spirited out of the palazzo. French securities followed the carriage, but were thwarted. Once more, dreadful mischance struck. A religious procession with hundreds of pilgrims moved towards the basilica of San Marco. It covered the traces of the impostors who had been planted in the religious *défilé* amongst the ranks of the pious. In a black carriage attached to six rested horses, the revolutionaries only had to wait for the Duchess to be handed over.

Jean-Louis and his security entourage arrived on the scene. He now knew the identity of the abductors. They expected him to let his emotions take over. "That will not happen," he shared with Cunnan. "Their tactics are worrisome. These rebellious citizens will not think twice about murdering Gaby if her death served their purpose. They want the French out of the equation. Whether it is for the protection of the Pope and of Rome, or a covert cooperation with Emmanuel II or most probably their goal is an Italian republic."

Cunnan nodded.

Jean-Louis predicted that Gaby was more precious to them alive. There was not a person in Venice, Rome, or Paris, for that matter, who did not recognize that the pretty American

Duchess was the Duke's weakness. This fact alone would serve her well.

Chapter 11

Sheltered for some time on a fish-stinking, hooded gondola moored on one of the piers across from St Marco's Piazzetta, her abductors had waited for the cover of night to flee. Two horse-drawn carriages had been brought on the embankment—her surreptitious transfer immediate and swift. Soon, the black coaches bore down on the cobblestones away from the island. In the campagna several riders on horseback rejoined the group. They'd provided new garments for Gaby— a light, long, white chemise sewn haphazardly with a coarse thread, was flung her way along with a knotted sash. They'd wrapped a dark brown cloak around her shoulders and they'd covered her eyes with a multilayered hood. A man's hand pressed against her back, forced her bosom down against the rigid spine of the galloping horse. It was a bumpy, hilly terrain. With every thrust forward, her back and legs splayed on the animal sent ghastly spasms to her neck and shoulders. Displaced from the galloping hooves, flying grains of sand burned her cheeks and throat. Her survival skills were failing. She sensed that she could no longer endure the torture. Suddenly, the gallop slowed to a trot. She suffered palpating hands on her buttocks, as a man thrust her legs down on the horse's flanks. Fear of rape or worse immobilized her. They had reached a field, or perhaps they were entering a village. She heard distant voices—Italian voices, bells, bleating sheep. A strong, acrid smell of manure choked her. The horse stopped abruptly. Two men pulled her down from the horse's back and threw her down on a patch of brown dying grass near an old grey stump. Pushed against the tree trunk, they slipped a large braided cordon rope around her waist and tied her to it. Sand whipped across her face. They slid the hood of the cloak away from her face. Fierce-looking men surrounded her and stared. All looked as if they had been in battle. Some wore bandages over their eyes, others looked wounded. Gaby wondered if Cunnan and the force had inflicted the injuries to these men as they fled the palazzo?

With only the thin chemise covering her, she shivered. Her well-being was insignificant to them. The men appeared to be waiting for someone. They spoke a *patois* that she could not understand.

Shortly thereafter, horse hooves clattered on the stone path that bordered the fields. The rider slowed to a stop. She turned her head. A tall, strapping man draped in a black cape slid off a black stallion. One of her captors threw a coarse brown potato sack over her head. She heard another voice. This one seemed to be in charge, and he spoke Italian. "Bring her to the village," a harsh and imperious voice commanded. "I understand that the French bastard has already been alerted and he's on our trail! The Commandante will be here shortly, and he will decide what to do with her."

"She is a most precious possession," another man posited, "there is nothing he won't do for her. He'll accept our demands."

"Good job! Take her in. She will be treated civilly. Remember she is an American, but her mother was Italian— good lineage to boot. If he does not bend to our will, we will have to rethink our position. Right now, do her no harm," the fellow who had just arrived on the scene said sternly. His tone of voice spoke volumes. No one questioned his orders.

Once again, she was placed facedown on the same old mare to be taken to a nearby village. They rode along a path bordering a dry riverbed. She took note of the eroded rocks. Faint voices sounded now and then. Peasants walked by, they spoke of how the weather would affect their fields. Closer to her, women lamented about the long distance they had to walk, in order to find a clean pump and steel trough to wash their clothes. She could hear their footsteps on the tiny white pebble stones. Children's laughter comforted her. A bright red ball rolled toward them. Quickly, the rider pulled back on the reigns, shouted at the child and turned the horse into a tight left turn before he urged the fatigued animal into a lounging gallop. Perhaps she'd miss her chance to call for help. No, she concluded distraught, there was no use. Her captors were armed. After a great deal of terrain covered, the group finally stopped. A woman driving a wine cart filled with stacks of hay pulled alongside of Gaby's mount. Torn from the saddle, Gaby was hurled into the moving cart. Her nose bled from the force of the shove. She moaned and rolled onto her side. Another body was nearby.

"Don't you dare cause trouble," a man's voice ordered in Italian.

The bumps on the road hurt her arms and legs as the cart stumbled on the road's imperfections. Her hands were tied behind her back and the cord cut deep at the fold of her wrists. The carriage stopped. A foul smelling man dragged her out of the cart, and rolled her onto his shoulder. She turned her head sideways. They stood behind what could have been the remnants of an old fortress. Tall dry reeds in a field of overgrown olive trees hid many of the square stone houses of the small village.

Gaby discerned the steeple of a church. Dusk had fallen. Quietly they hurried through narrow streets. Deserted homes with no sign of life removed the last bit of hope. One of the captors, who trailed close by glared at her maliciously. He traced his neck from ear to ear with his knife, making clear what he would do to her if she cried for help. She nodded. The sack was replaced over her head once more.

Transported to a very dark place, the man who'd carried her let her slide down to the ground. She stumbled on the unevenness of the floor, a stable perhaps. She was forced up spiraling stairs. A sense of disbelief struck. Distinctly, she heard voices—men's voices that sang drunken ballads, accompanied by women's high-pitched intonations. Heels banged hard on a wooden surface to the rhythm of an accordion. A tavern, she deduced. She attempted to slow her ascent but was shoved forward. The stench was horrific and fear enveloped every fiber of her being. She recalled that she still had her gun in her boots—the only vestment they'd let her keep. Real comfort it gave her now, she thought cynically. Be strong; don't give up, she repeated to herself. She had heard that Jean-Louis was already on their trail and that they would use her as a negotiating tool. Falling apart now was not an option. She prayed. It always worked. It would work again. Jean-Louis and Cunnan would rescue her.

A door opened at the very top of the narrow and swirling staircase. "Here she is. Keep her safe. Orders will follow shortly." That was all that was said before she was shoved down against a wall—her hands still attached behind her back, a checkered dishrag covered her mouth and another crude strip of fabric secured over her eyes. Helpless, she lay there terrified, curled in a fetal position. She questioned if her last hours would be spend in this hellhole. Total darkness surrounded her. No one came for her. She succumbed to hunger, dehydration, and exhaustion.

* * *

Meanwhile, the French delegation arrived near the village where the Duchess was imprisoned in a closet. In conference, a lot had been placed on the indiscretions of a known member of the opposition. It had, however, come to a dead end when the man had feigned utter contempt for the abduction. Less than two days later, a miracle astounded all. The man was very religious. In a rare moment of weakness, he confessed his sins to his priest. After much mental conflict, the young prelate had revealed the crime to Cardinal Thornsen's valet. Events unfolded rapidly after the revelation. The traitor was soon convinced to expose the rest of the rebels' plan.

As they reached the village, Jean-Louis and Cunnan were the first to access the tavern. Jean-Louis entered alone. He sat and waited, wondering if Gaby was still in possession of her pistol. Overjoyed by the Maestro's visit, she might have forgotten to slip it into her boot. After all, he had relaxed security. If the pistol was still hidden in her boot, he had taught her well. She would know what to do.

An old wooden door screeched open. A tall and extremely heavy man in peasant garb walked straight to him and sat across the table. His only discernable characteristic was a red shirt, which hung down beneath his black coat. Still and serene, Jean-Louis sat. Wine was ordered. It was brought quickly to the table. The tavern's owner jerked his head to the side, dispersing the last of his customers. The men pushed aside their glasses, slid off their stools and slowly ambled away— eyes focused on the seated men.

Gaby's release was in play.

"Where is my wife?" the Duke inquired.

The man shared that he possessed no authority to start the negotiations, but he indicated that the Commandante would arrive shortly.

Jean-Louis stood.

"For your sake, he'd better arrive soon," he said loudly for all to hear.

"We have something you want. If I stood in your shoes, I would not be so arrogant." The unkempt man smirked.

With composure, the Duke stood, rounded the table and advanced on the man. He grabbed a clump of his grey peasant shirt, lifted him off his chair and delivered a hard blow to his stomach. As the warrior peasant dangled from the Duke's hand, he slumped before being slapped down to the hard stone floor. Two men rushed forward to aid their compatriot, and to pacify his anger.

"Wait," they countered with authority, as he drew the knife attached to a brown leather belt and charged toward Jean-Louis, "remember the orders, the Commandante is on his way. You'll have plenty of time for revenge."

The Duke turned his back, and stepped outside to await the arrival of the Commandante. He swept the area in an arc-like gaze. Some villagers lazily leaned on trees, others chatted while seated on wooden benches, others played with life size chess pieces, and others brushed down their horses. He knew them all—his dedicated security force.

An hour later, the Commandante had not shown. Jean-Louis feared a secret passageway below the inn. There were many in these small villages—exit from far away castles and citadels into the deserted campagna. How else could a Duke, Baron or Count escape if their castles were under siege? He shared his thoughts with Cunnan. The only unknown was the number of rebels who had rejoined the deadly party. All could have been smuggled through a secret passage.

There had been at least ten abductors at the palazzo. Four had accompanied the Maestro, three had waited outside, and a second trio had been in the carriage. Without doubt, many others were party to the intrigue. But the rooms in the tavern were too small to accommodate more than a few men. Jean-

Louis had twenty-five "villagers" with him, some already inside the inn and all ready to strike as soon as Gaby was safe.

The Commandante arrived on horseback, with six men. He stepped inside and motioned to Jean-Louis to follow.

"Alone!" he shouted.

Jean-Louis nodded to Cunnan to stay outside.

"I want to meet privately to discuss the exchange," the Commandante stated.

Jean-Louis already knew what they would propose. It could not be granted. France required a strong leader in Italy, one who would agree to coalesce its resources on the many *modernity* projects envisaged by the Empire. Victor Emmanuel was such a leader.

Both men sat down in the dancing hall. A ceiling to floor fireplace held a black cauldron within its hearth. A mixture of pungent odors reached all corners of the dining area.

"Where is my wife? I want to see her. Talks will not start until then," he declared.

The chief looked at him in disbelief.

"You love her that much? Weakness for a female has destroyed more than one great man, my Lord!" he replied, a smirk widening his thin-lipped mouth. "Excellent for us. Very well, I understand from your tone of voice that the pre-condition is to be met first. You're an intelligent man. We will comply after you hear me out."

Jean-Louis listened.

"The French Empire is bent on our demise. You are willing to sell our civil rights to a King, who does not pledge allegiance to the Italian Peninsula. Garibaldi said years ago: "Italy to the Italians!" That means all of us, rich and poor, Monsieur. I know that Rome, our Eternal City, is the last bastion. The French are stationed in Civitavecchia for the protection," he gagged, "of the Pope. In reality, you like

Vittorio Emmanuel on the throne of Italy; you even want to deliver Rome on a silver platter to the monarch. It would suit you traitors just fine!" the man accused with blazing eyes.

Jean-Louis kept silent.

"I know, you're not fooling us, but we will fight to the death for our freedom, against Vittorio Emmanuel and against the Pope and his collaborators and protectors—the French. We will annihilate the forces of Vittorio Emmanuel II," the man struck his fist on the table. "It is the aristocrats' intent to continue the privileged practices of the old City States. WE WANT and WE WILL have no less than a Republic! No, this time, the populace will rise, and we will govern ourselves without the help of a Monarch! A Republic, Monsieur! We'll rally around a government that will give us our rights, our freedom and our financial recompenses. We will not let ourselves be led by one arrogant power-grabbing aristocrat. Let the Italians be led by Italians. Why should we trust the likes of you?"

Jean-Louis braced his hands on each corner of the table. The town's people had already been paid off. All needed to be away from town in the nearby fields for the rest of the copious reward to be paid. Jean-Louis' *villagers* needed access to the tavern. A quick glance toward the windows put him at ease. He recognized his men. They'd stealthily surrounded the drinking hole, dressed in peasants' clothes. Poverty was rampant in these small towns. Money talked. It did not solely apply to Italy. England, France, and Germany—all were in the process of redressing the financial divide of their societies. Meanwhile, the lower echelon of the population lived in utter misery. The only alliance the populace possessed was to their immediate families and to a bowl of soup!

Security knew what to do once Gaby was in sight.

"I want to see my wife," he countered staring into the man's eyes.

The stocky leader jerked his gaze to his allies. He nodded.

"Bring the Duchess to us!" he ordered. Tension dominated.

Men at the bar dispersed quickly. They abandoned their wooden stools and slowly began to drag the two remaining drunks crouched on the floor toward an opening to the right of the hidden staircase.

Jean-Louis stood and straightened up to his full height. The chief stood as well, along with six of his revolutionaries. All guns pointed at Jean-Louis. From under the staircase, a door opened. Gaby was shoved down on the floor. Immediately, the leader grabbed her under the arm and lifted her battered body, his knife pointed at her throat.

"Well, well," he scoffed, "here is the exceptional Duchess de Bourbonne, the Duke's jewel. You have good taste, my lord. I wouldn't mind tasting your wares," he continued in broken French as the knife started its descent, cutting its way down to what remained of Gaby's thin chemise. Dried blood smeared down her nose, across her face and shoulders, her dirty and disheveled hair hung down her back, the only glimpse of a former privileged life were her white leather boots that tied high above her ankles. The razor-sharp blade continued its slide down the middle of her garment, the cloth ripped open and it allowed the men, a full view of the Duchess's splendid body.

"I can see why you have a smile on your face, de Pleyssis." the man groped Gaby's voluptuous breasts.

She flinched at the first touch. Suddenly, her composure returned and her eyes blinked oddly.

Jean-Louis starred at her, hypnotized. In effect, her blinking revealed the number of men secreted in the rooms above. Fifteen. Jean-Louis noticed that Gaby's boots had not been removed. He hoped to God that she still had her revolver hidden in it. He remained immobile, showing no emotion. The knife angled closer to Gaby's throat.

"Both of you are a bit too calm," the leader sliced. "What will it take to persuade you to hand over money and sign the documents? A little blood perhaps from this pretty lady?" He returned the knife to Gaby's throat, pressing the blade to her white creamy neck. This time, a thin red line streamed down her breasts and she moaned in pain.

"Let's deal, de Pleyssis. I'm a gentlemen, you know that, but my goal is immovable, so cough it up now and we will spare the pretty lady if you . . ." his verbal threats cut short, the drunks dragged behind the staircase fired the first round of shots. Gaby seized a moment of opportunity to attack her captor. Frazzled by the impromptu, her assailant turned his head to look back. Shoving her body backward, she kicked his patella. His leg cracked at the knee. Without respite, she stomped on his feet with the steel heel in her boots. The concealed captors in the staircase ran to their leader. It was too late. Shots rang out from all directions. Windows shattered and doors were kicked in as the Duke's 'villagers' converged on the scene and commenced battle. Gaby's captors were taken by surprise, many falling dead on the floor. Invincible, Gaby freed herself, ducked down and grabbed the pistol out of her boot.

Naked except for her boots, she shot the Commandante at close range. He moaned, covered in blood, his left arm dislocated at the shoulders. A wide, bloody groove split his face. She emptied her pistol into his head; his half blown, twisted face and dangling flesh formed a thick pool of blood that oozed down the wooden planks. Running on adrenaline, she bolted toward Cunnan and snatched the gun he always kept concealed, under a brown leather vest. She returned to her dead captor and shot him in the heart. Dead bodies were scattered atop tables, on wooden benches and in the staircase. The smell of blood, sweet wine and urine permeated the room. Standing alone, near her dead tormentor, Gaby looked haggard. She began to tremble uncontrollably. Jean-Louis ran to her. Swiftly he covered her body with his jacket, wrapped her in a blanket and whisked her away. Out in the open fields, as gunshots continued to blast through the windows, he lowered her to the ground and covered her with his body. An eerie silence reigned.

Cunnan and his men had killed all the revolutionaries. They'd finished off the ones lying in pools of blood on the soaked red planks. No one survived. No one needed to know.

Outside, terrified peasants peeked through the windows of their shabby houses, horses neighed wildly, and frightened farm animals meandered in all directions.

Deeply ensconced in Jean-Louis's arms, Gaby's eyes darted left and right as she surveyed the carnage. Her spirit distressed by the emotional impact reacted violently. Because of her daily training, the physical response had been immediate. Now, a rattling and uncontrollable shudder convulsed her limbs. Cold sweat dripped down her face, and vomit gushed out of her in spurts. The latter uncontrollable thanks to the cramps in her abdomen, so intense were the pain that she lost consciousness.

Jean-Louis uncurled her body, shifted her and forced her head in between her knees. An exhausted Gaby regained consciousness and opened her eyes. She batted at the salts Jean-Louis swayed under her nose. A gentle smile cracked her husband's face. "All is well, Gaby," he whispered to her.

Down the valley, a woman from a nearby village offered clothing. Jean-Louis helped Gaby into a coarse, grey skirt and tucked in a white peasant blouse. Without delay, he gathered her to his chest and kept her there for a few precious seconds.

"Oh, Mon Dieu." He gazed absently toward the horizon. "All is well, Gaby, all is well, Chérie," he brushed his lips to her mouth. Without more ado, he lifted her on his horse and mounted effortlessly behind her. Once more, he held her close. It was unnecessary to stay behind. His men had finished the work. No revolutionaries had survived. No need to encumber his mission any further.

They rode all night. As dawn set in, all were back in the palazzo. Many of the men who'd rescued her, those she'd previously thought were servants, approached her. Congratulations were in order. Her courage, *présence d'esprit,* and quick response had been formidable, they all asserted. It made their mission easy, she was told. She accepted all with grace and humility.

She was not about to shame Jean-Louis. Inside, however, fear rattled her every bone. Anxiety would lessen, she told herself. She prayed hard and she thanked God for his protection. But . . . she clung to her husband and would not leave his side.

Once everyone departed, Jean-Louis took her in his arms. His emotions surfaced. All he'd ever wished he'd shared with her before the abduction, he articulated now. He did not stop at how impressed and proud he was at the courage that she'd displayed, but whatever came to his mind, he declared. He also professed his undying love.

"I simply adore you Gaby, I appreciate your succinct intellect, your passionate nature toward your music, your considerate demeanor toward others of lesser means, your wit and simplicity." He heaved a long sigh and disclosed his insurmountable fear when faced with the possibility of losing her. "I would have shot myself, Gaby, had you not survived."

Finally as he pursued his out of character tirade, she burst out laughing.

"Jean-Louis, tell me, since I am so splendid and gifted and beautiful and fearless, do you feel that Louis Napoléon chose the wrong person to negotiate with the King and the Vatican?" She looked up at him, amusement in her expressive eyes. He gave her a tap on her bottom. "Perhaps, my beautiful, and impertinent wife. I love you so, Gaby." He spoke from his heart, still shaken by the thought of losing her.

"Upstairs, my Lord!" she responded.

He lifted her into his arms and carried her upstairs to their private apartment. She wrapped her arms around his neck and kissed him, not once, but twice and all the way up the staircase. After closing the doors to their room, he gathered her close to him for a long time. He looked down and saw passion in her expressive green eyes. Swiftly he ripped apart the peasant shirt that she had been given. His mouth swept down to her breasts, as he slid his hands down her hips to release the skirt. He lifted her naked body onto their bed and filled with sexual madness, he let his body fall on hers. As their passion for each other mounted, the thrill and rapture of the moment offered an escape from their tormented world.

The couple slept late into the afternoon. Their meals were brought upstairs. Jean-Louis sent out a note stating that all negotiations would be held in their residence for the subsequent two weeks. Gaby needed to recover from the ordeal. Furthermore, security would be reinstated to his specifications.

Philippe, who'd arrived two nights earlier, insisted that it was time to reconsider their location. "Venice was a grave mistake, Jean-Louis," he hissed, unapologetically.

Two weeks later, Jean-Louis resumed his habitual schedule and Gaby went into seclusion—in their apartment when her husband needed to be absent from the residence.

Chapter 12

Gabriella's dreams of working her voice with the top maestros from the Fenice Teatro were gone forever. She admitted that much to herself. When Jean-Louis was absent, anxiety attacks surfaced with mounting severity and her concentration waned.

"Enjoy Venice," she confessed bluntly to Bernard, her vocal coach. "I have no desire to practice anything."

Before Philippe's return to Rome, the cousins spent an afternoon together. She concealed all of her horrific fears from him. In return, he persisted that Rome should be the seat of the negotiations. "The *Castle Di Angelo* or the *Palazzo Farnese*, of all places, Gabriella, the Bourbon held on to it for years. Both would be appropriate and safe residences. You love the arts, Michelangelo worked on the main feature of the façade; its frescoes *Cycles* of the *Love of the Gods* are unequaled. Convince the beast, my dearest Gabriella!"

The great disdain that both Jean-Louis and Philippe held for one another was no secret.

"I would like to return quickly to Paris, Philippe. I feel safe and loved there," she confided. "Italy is a magnificent country. I hope to return here someday to partake of the fabulous artistic scene; you know how much I loved it in Paris. Edgar Degas and Claude Renoir shared the thrill when they studied the great Masters at the French Académie in Rome." Philippe nodded. " I want to experience it all again, Philippe, the awe-inspiring sculptures, the music, the interesting and kind people that I have met. Now, though, I ache for Paris. Please, dear Philippe," she murmured as she rested her head on his chest, "I have never asked much of you, but today I beg you to facilitate the negotiations with the Pope. I know now that

Jean-Louis's life is in great danger. My insouciance has vanished. Imagine Philippe, my life was placed at the top of the spire."

The Cardinal did not respond. The very idea of losing his dear Gabriella turned his stomach.

For the first time in their lives, she was in dire need of his help. He collected her close, kissed her temples tenderly and then gently pushed her away. He could not and would not intervene in the manner that she demanded of him. The Holy Father had been quite clear on that subject.

"I will do my very best, Gabriella, my very best, my dearest cousin," he lied as he crossed himself.

* * *

Since the abduction, anxiety filled her days. Thoughts engulfed her that something horrific threatened. No comforting words from either Philippe or Cunnan dissipated her distress. All rational thoughts evaporated when she thought that Jean-Louis, the man she adored and for whom she had given up all her personal dreams, could be the next target. The mind is a furious clown that will strip your will and strength of character if you let it, she would repeat to herself. Nevertheless, obsessive thoughts transported her back to the narrow closet, the scent of cheap wine, the firing of guns— the killings. Since their return, she had not wanted to betray the love, the passionate words of immense pride that Jean-Louis had bestowed upon her—now, however, she was losing the battle.

Cunnan had been sworn to secrecy, but for how long? How would Jean-Louis react? Willingly, he had fought in bloody wars and countless skirmishes. He thrived in these settings. Yes, of course, the Civil War had been horrific! Yes, she had survived. However, by coming to France, she had hoped to leave all the horrors behind. Her only wish had been to grasp her fate and to accept the challenges of a famed opéra singer on the world stage! Now all had vanished.

Feel sorry for yourself, Gaby. You deserve it, she whispered to herself. Cry, please cry, Gaby, she supplicated. Yet, she was incapable of shedding one salty little tear. She clenched her fists in self-disgust. Every morning, upon Jean-Louis' departure, she'd snatch up her skirts and calmly climb the stairs back to their apartment. She remained ensconced in his large burgundy fauteuil. Fear and hopelessness encompassed her every moment until his return. This morning was no different. Eight more hours and Jean-Louis would return.

Chapter 13

The carillon struck six times. Six o'clock, she glanced backwards, Jean-Louis slept soundly. His leg lay heavily across her hips. She reached for the satin eiderdown that lay at the very end of their canopied bed, drew the covers over her shoulders, and reclined back in his arms, shivering. She moved closer to him and caught his curious stare from the corner of her eyes.

"What is wrong, Gaby? Are you ill?" he questioned anxiously. He brushed his knuckles along her chin and quickly palmed her forehead.

"I must have caught the flu while riding under the heavy downpour," she reminded him.

He looked suspicious. She smiled sweetly.

"I'll be home early. I will bring the delegation's physician with me."

"No need, Jean-Louis, really, I'm absolutely fine, but . . . I would love it if you returned early. You know how much I miss you."

She rolled closer to him, and he gathered her snugly in his arms.

"I can't wait for these negotiations to be over, Gaby. I wish it could have been different for you, Chérie. Have you gone out at all this week?"

"No, I adore the music room in the palazzo. This crazy cough, however, is annoying. Perhaps I'll venture out next week."

* * *

Hours later, while on his way to the *Palazzo Ducale*, Jean-Louis pondered Gaby's clinging behavior when he strolled in their apartment. Now that he thought about it, she rarely waited for him downstairs. When they sat down to dinner, she pulled her fauteuil closer, practically touching his. She even followed him into his dressing room—just to talk. Not normal behavior for his beautiful wife. He had thought that the passionate lovemaking that she spoiled him with every night, since her abduction and rescue, demonstrated a renewed love for life and all that it had to offer. At the moment, he felt less convinced of his theory. He wished they could spend more time together. It was unrealistic to even entertain such ideas presently. She knew it, as well.

"Have a fun day, a good day, think of me." She had blown kisses as his carriage passed by to take him to the nearest canal. Then again, something in her eyes had betrayed her cheery mood. He observed how she'd turn around, straightening up to her full height as she heaved a sigh. She'd shaken her head from side to side as if to sweep away some awful thoughts. He had noticed that very movement of her head, the first few days after their encounter. Gaby had these 'black clouds', as she called them, which momentarily terrorized her. She had attributed those to some unknown events that must have emotionally scarred her during the Civil War. But, he curiously mulled over now, he did not recall these fleeting moments of immense sadness in Paris.

A flash of clarity burst into his overly politically oriented analysis. Gaby's distress became crystal clear.

Damn it all! How could he have been so callous? He'd complimented her brave spirit, her swift response, her selfless comportment, but he'd overlooked the inner terror that she was much too proud to recount to him, now. His high praise had been a curse! Beyond his wildest imagination, he had been remiss. Gaby still felt terrorized and too ashamed to share her dread. The woman was so damn complex. Would he ever unravel all of her secrets? He doubted it!

The delegates would have to wait. He sent his valet with a note to the Palazzo and returned immediately to the residence. Striding urgently the few stairs that led to the dining room, he ran into Cunnan.

"Where is Gaby?" he questioned.

"Upstairs. She swore me to secrecy after the incident, Jean-Louis-Pierre. 'I'll get over it soon, you'll see Cunnan, please don't tell Jean-Louis. It is just absurd. I know it. I have to evaluate the situation and come to terms with it. I will. I will, she proclaimed.' A week later, she locked herself in her room. She pretends to be immersed in her music once more. Bernard told me otherwise yesterday."

"Why didn't you say something?" Jean-Louis fumed.

"I was going to this evening. She's emotionally injured, Jean-Louis-Pierre. When you're gone, she does not budge from the room. Her maid rolls out her dining table, untouched. The poor girl has been sworn to secrecy as well, although she broke her vow last evening and revealed a Gabriella that I hardly know. Thank heavens, she recoups her appetite at night. She loves good food. How she stays so tiny, that is anyone's guess. Another wonder of the magnificent Duchess de Pleyssis that only the Almighty can answer!" A sad smile hung down from the old sailor's lips.

Repentant, Jean-Louis stopped by the side bar and reached for the crystal decanter leveled to the very top with whiskey. He topped his glass to the brim.

"My reaction is abominable. How could I have been so flippant? I thought all was well," he admitted sourly. "Our adventuresome lives did not prepare me well for Gaby's current reaction." He swallowed the liquid quickly and lapsed into silence. He'd expected a great deal of her.

"She needs you, Jean-Louis-Pierre. Go to her," Cunnan advised. The Duke nodded. A charged silence fell between the two men. Both stared at the Persian rug, beneath their feet. "Yes," Cunnan repeated sadly, "go to her, Gabriella needs you."

As he opened the double doors that led into their apartment the Duke found his wife under myriad of blankets. A closed book was placed on her lap and a distant, fearful stare greeted him. Almost immediately, upon recognition her innocent smile flashed.

"You've returned early, Jean-Louis? Have you forgotten a document?" With hopeful eyes, she solicited a response as she tossed aside the blankets and stood, shaking her tousled mane. It took a couple of long strides before strong arms encircled her shaken body. His mouth opened over hers and parted her lips softly. For a long while, he held her close as he provided the secure environment she needed and deserved.

"I'm sorry, Gaby," he candidly murmured. "I'll never leave you again until we leave this forsaken place. Get dressed, Chérie, we'll talk in the carriage."

A tug on the satin sash summoned his manservant.

"We'll need the larger carriage to be brought to the entrance," he ordered as he reached for Gaby's hand, and winked at Cunnan.

A grin swept across the old man's face. He grabbed two warm croissants from the silver basket and tucked them into a white linen napkin. He offered the sweets to Gaby. A happy grin flashed on her pretty flushed face as she pivoted on her heels and followed Jean-Louis into the carriage.

The old mariner understood Jean-Louis' implicit scheme. Unknowingly, his sweet Gabriella had just turned a corner. Soon, she would become an active player on the European political theater. Just as well, Cunnan thought. Gabriella spoke fluent Italian. Without her music, she needed something cerebral to provide a diversion for her active intellect. She'd be involved in the last stages of the negotiations. All's well that ends well, the kindly sailor thought as he sat down at the table to munch on breakfast.

Chapter 14

Upon their arrival at the *Palazzo Ducale*, the delegates observed the couple with great curiosity.

"*Continuez, continuez, Messieurs.* From this point forward, my wife, the Duchess, will be amongst us. The Duchess speaks Italian fluently. She also understands the value that Charles-Louis Napoléon and his ministers place on these negotiations. She will prove to be an excellent and trusted translator, in the oral contexts and in the written documents."

Ironic glances and knowing smirks greeted the statement. It was none of his concern, Jean-Louis thought. Gabriella had a photographic memory and a remarkable gift with languages. Much had been settled. Although, the curia still questioned Venice as a venue. In essence, communication with the Pontiff took time. Unlike Vittorio Emanuele's delegates, who had marching orders and who knew exactly where they wanted to take these negotiations, Pius IX was not even lukewarm to the idea of a Roman unification to the Kingdom. Romans within the Aurelian walls wanted to be Italians. The Pope resisted the movement. Gaby doubted that he would willingly agree. However, she kept her evaluations private.

The Duke's novel ways and complete lack of aristocratic etiquette shocked the Italians at first. Soon they came to expect a novel approach to many conflicts. His directness, and analytical nature moved the talks forward. Many did not like him, but all respected him. Consequently, they rode the tide. Clearly, the Duke was a minimalist.

At times, annoyed delegates questioned Gabriella's role in the Conference.

"It is their lives. Why a man would want his wife to be in his presence from morning to night is beyond comprehension!" Count Pellegrino, an avid supporter of the King, would exclaim while he raised his arms to the heavens. "Then again, the Duke's influence is enormous. If he can unite all sides and form a willing coalition between the King of Italy, the Vatican, the former supporters of Giuseppe Garibaldi, and the Empire of France, the more power to him! Besides the young Duchess is a beautiful sight to gaze upon."

At the beginning, Gaby sat beside Jean-Louis every day. They went to coffee together, ate their *déjeuners* together; discussed privately the many issues presented in the special conference rooms provided to him. And then, as the weeks passed, the Duchess ventured out more often—by herself. Many members of the Italian delegation befriended her, and many depended on her for her exacting translations. At first, she'd noticed the pursed lips, half-smiles and blatant smirks. It had not taken long for the sarcastic remarks to be transformed into pointed statements and questions. On several occasions, she listened to members of the delegations repeat the very same observations she'd purported.

Jacopo de Castriodrianni had become a good friend of Gabriella. The Count was a member of the King's delegation. Large numbers of aristocrats were named as delegates, only a few attended all the meetings. Jacopo was one of them. Instead, he made her discover the wonders of Venice—its long history tied with the vast trade markets of Asia. The art history fascinated her. He shared succinct anecdotes on the great Venetian painters—the Bellini brothers, Gentile and Giovanni, and Nicolò Bambini, who had decorated many of the palazzi and villas in the Bellissima. One artist adored by Gaby was

Rosalba Carriera. She had begun her career as a portrait artist and then found a wonderful new medium—painting with chalk. She worked mostly with pastels. Gaby remembered admiring her many works while in Paris. She now learned that Rosalba had been admitted to the Académie Royale de la Peinture while in Paris in 1720.

There were, as well, the intimate restaurants along the *Piazza of San Marco Basilica*. Jacopo had taken her to *Caffé Florian in the Procuratie Nuove of the Piazza San Marco*—a coffee house that permitted women. It was said that the illustrious lover, Casanova, had spent a great deal of his time in this sumptuous establishment. Many rooms had their own names, the room of the Illustrious Men, the room of the Senate Halls, and the Chinese and Oriental rooms. Her favorite was the Hall of the Seasons, where beautiful paintings of women represented the four seasons. To boot, the coffee was absolutely delectable!

A private visit to the *Teatro La Fenice* had been arranged, as well. The pain was still too vivid, so she declined. Great melancholy would at times take hold of the pretty soprano— not solely from the immense fear that she'd experienced in Murano and the Campagna, but for her musical dreams gone awry. Better not think about it. She'd always been quite capable at compartmentalizing her life. Now more than ever her will was tested. On a happier note, most of her days were pleasant. She even had doubts about a return to Rome now.

Jacopo filled her days with fun adventures. Although the Count's reputation was less than stellar, a wicked libertine she'd hear often, she knew him to be very much in love with his long time mistress Roseanna Gullienderess Alberti. Consequently, she took in her stride his flirtatious manners. Often she had extended an invitation to Roseanna.

"Roseanna is a dedicated lace-maker. That is her passion," he'd countered promptly. "She sails every morning to Burano, still the center of the most sought after lace in the world, to work with a great master. Burano represents horrific memories for you, Gabriella, I am so sorry." He heaved a long sigh and gazed absently. "Like your great passion for singing, needle lace making is Roseanna's other love." Stunned, she wondered how he had learned of her abduction. She would have to ask Jean-Louis. On second thought—perhaps not! He'd be livid if he knew her whereabouts and the company she kept. Besides she would not be too surprised if some members of the delegations knew. Jean-Louis despised Jacopo. They had had words over him. Therefore, she kept her cool and reserved demeanor in the conference rooms. She knew better than to make her husband jealous. The thought alone of him reciprocating made her shudder! She was getting more confident and for that Jean-Louis was grateful. He had told her so during times of arduous negotiations to which she was not privy. Meanwhile, she enjoyed the city—with Jacopo.

Jean-Louis knew that trouble lurked with the introduction of the Count. He was ready. Jacopo was a thorny and demanding negotiator whenever he decided to participate— which was rarely. He opted instead to spend time with Gaby. A dashing aristocrat and a brilliant supporter of Louis XIV's philosophy—*diviser pour mieux régner*! Divide and Conquer. He still administered vast provinces. Naturally, his allegiance was with the crown King, but Jean-Louis was wary.

'The man is not playing his cards well, Gaby," he'd warned her early on. "He's a divisive force."

She's a bit too 'chummy with the fellow' as his British friends Rimbaud and Luke would say. Recently, however,

Jean-Louis pondered, Jacopo was more involved than ever. Why? Had he been a conspirator in the botched kidnapping? Jean-Louis would not put it past him. After all, if the remnants of the Revolutionary Republicans became more powerful, once the French had decamped from Civitavecchia, the conflict between the Monarchy and the Republicans could fire up the Peninsula once more. Accordingly, the Count would be left in an envious position—the return to a fairly united Italy to members of the former aristocracy *sans* the Pontiff! Quite a few Italians were not overly pleased with the Sardinian Monarch. Most had wanted a Republic without Papal intervention. Playing all sides, the Count now required new contacts to re-enter the scene. Notwithstanding, if his intuition proved correct, a traitor operated within the Conference. The intrigue needed to be monitored closely. If the negotiations turned sour, preparations for the eventuality of conflicts needed to start now—with as little fanfare as possible. The Conference of Vienna in 1815 had lasted a full year. He hoped that would not be the case in Italy. And then again, perhaps he was just jealous of the well-spoken Count de Castriodrianni.

Gaby had regained her confidence and *joie de vivre*. Jean-Louis was hesitant to curtail her liberated demeanor. He would let her escapades last a while longer. The treaties needed to be signed and a fast exit was imperative. Danger lurked. He would surmount it. However, Gaby's temerity showed signs of distress. Poor Gaby. She had traveled to Europe to sing and to be merry! Upon their arrival back in Loire, he would involve her in all the womanly interests ever present in that part of France. Numerous aristocrats spent their summer months in their castles. Women enjoyed it greatly. She would, too. No need to draw her back to Paris. He would manage for a month or two without her. The lighter side of a Duchess' life could be immensely enjoyable. Suddenly, the most beautiful woman in Venice—certainly in his eyes—marched in.

"Hello, Beauty, you look stunning in yellow!" he admired candidly.

"Thank you. It just arrived from Paris! Look, Madame Gabriotte also included the latest slippers," she sensually spun on her heels as she uncovered her anklet, "the heel is a bit higher, but it matches splendidly." She snatched up her dress, and revealed the latest fashionable item.

He nodded. "On you, Gaby, rags could become the next fashion item. Your style is followed all over Europe. You are beautiful, my darling, and I love you more with every breath that I take." She approached his chair, touched her lips to his and kissed him passionately. Nonchalant, she fell onto his lap and stayed there. She stared into his eyes.

"If you miss me so, spend more time with me!"

He caressed her hand. "Soon, darling, soon."

* * *

It was nearly two o'clock; the couple had just finished their meals. Gaby, gathered in her husband's arms, read. He loved having her near—just the two of them like in Paris. A knock at the door interrupted his thoughts.

"Come in," the Duke said. A butler appeared.

"Le Count de Castriodrianni, Le Count Pellegrino, Monsieur." The rod-straight butler formally announced in heavily accented French.

"Let them in."

The two men strode in. Jean-Louis still held Gaby in his arms, as he perused the documents. She, in turn, reviewed the notes she'd translated earlier.

"*Buon pomerriggio*, gentlemen," Gaby declared as she removed herself and her notes from Jean-Louis's lap. "A cup of your fabulous café?" she solicited. "Everything is magnificent here in beautiful Venice, the people, the soirées, the palaces, the arts, the sights, the food, and the café, " she declared gaily.

The men smiled but declined.

She walked to the rosewood rectangular table where an ornate silver coffee pot, creamer and sugar bowls rested on a massive silver tray. She poured two cups of the strong brew. One for Jean-Louis—she brought it over herself. Expertly, she poured some milk and added two spoonfuls of sugar to his cup. She then stirred the black liquid. She drank hers black.

The men looked at her, amused. A Duchess who poured her own café? These two never ceased to amaze.

She smiled and came to sit next to Jean-Louis.

Jacopo smiled back. His dazzling white teeth appeared even more brilliant against his tanned skin. How could this gallant, friendly man entertain such evil thoughts! Jean-Louis was surely wrong on his account, she thought. She continued to read her notes for a while. Bored, she excused herself and left the room while the men continued to converse.

"Where are you going?"

"On the terrace to take in a bit of fresh air. Most of the delegation is out there," she replied as she left the room.

Soon after, Count de Castriodrianni terminated his business with Jean-Louis. Count Pellegrino glared at the departing Count but remained silent. He moved his seat closer to the Duke and continued the discussion.

The 'God', as Gaby referred to the handsome Italian Count, walked down the long corridor leading to the main conference room. As she turned the corner, they almost ran into each other.

"Gabriella," the Count called out, as he got closer to her. "It appears that both of our partners have extra dilemmas to explicate to each other. Would you like to have a *patisserie*?" he asked in French. "The finest baker in all of Venice is just minutes away from the palace, my gondola is nearby and it is quite comfortable, I must say."

"No, thank you, Jacopo," Gaby answered. Jean-Louis would be irate, if she even left the building without his permission. Never mind if she was accompanied by the Count himself! "But I'll walk with you to the restaurant down below, if it is companionship you seek."

"You have read my mind, Madame. It will make my day."

The exquisite restaurant was below the main floor, down the staircase, quite somber and tucked into a mysterious corner of the Palazzo. She looked out and saw myriad gondolas gliding by, under a bridge on the Grand Canal.

Jacopo was an intriguing man who'd traveled much and spoke six languages. His command of the French and the English languages was impressive. With cunning affinity, he used his considerable vocabulary to charm anyone in his circle. Actually, she found Jacopo quite appealing—along with every other woman in Venice.

Seated in a massive fauteuil, she could not reach the floor. She scooted forward, closer to the table. She sank her elbows into the burgundy velour tablecloth, trimmed with Burano lace and she rested her chin in the palms of her hands. The glasses along with a magnificent crystal vase in the middle of the table had the insignia of Murano's world famous glass factories. She picked up a delicate dessert knife holder, set across from her plate, and closely examined it. She rotated it between her elegant fingers several times.

"Stunning art work on such a miniature object," she exclaimed, astounded at the intricate carving of a young woman observing a school of fish on the banks of a lake. She admired and observed as she swiveled the object on all sides. The pastry for Jacopo had turned into a plate of fresh grilled langoustines and mussels served over pasta. He'd asked for a glass of white wine.

"What happened to the *patisserie,* Jacopo?"

"Later, later, Gabriella, when in the presence of a beautiful and brilliant woman such as yourself, one would be foolish not to make every moment last to infinity!" He subjected her to a leisurely appraisal.

She held his gaze, and shot back a most sensual intent glance. He stiffened for an instant and quickly grinned. She smiled back.

Jacopo's compliments centered on innate and feminine traits displayed in a woman. She had noticed his flirtatious nature with many of the aristocratic women they'd encountered at balls and soirées. It was not flattery, but actual traits sought out. Once he discovered the quality—he would remark favorably on it—often. She liked that. Jean-Louis was not the most complimentary fellow. He expected her to be perfect.

On their way back to the conference room, he'd recounted the sadness that the Venetians had experienced under the almost seventy years of Austrian occupation. Essentially, Napoléon I had practically handed it to the Austrians. She knew that it was also a pun aimed at Charles Louis Napoléon, no doubt, who had not honored his promises to the great minister Cavour. After a sound Austrian's defeat, the Emperor had accepted the Savoie and Nice as the fruits of war, but he'd declined to press for Venice. She kept quiet and she changed the subject. After all, she was here to represent France with her husband. She knew well the impasses that the French had to surmount in order to have the Pope acquiesce to the demands of Emmanuel II. He picked up on her reticence and centered instead on her great gift.

"Tell me, Gabriella, your singing—it's heavenly. Why not sing here, of all places, the Italian language is the sole venue for opéra!" he scoffed in heavily accented Italian. "Why have you stopped singing? Roseanna and I attended one of your performances at the opéra in Paris. We were so enthused by your voice; we stayed in the capital for another week, just to attend another of your concerts. You conquered the stage at the Opéra de Paris almost immediately?"

"Yes, it was immediate," she responded with melancholy. She let it go at that. Jacopo had done his homework. He knew about her acceptance to the Académie de la Musique, prior to her chance encounter with Jean-Louis. Not willing to discuss her life, she questioned the history of myriad islands in the lagoon. Burano and Murano stood out, but there were dozens of small islands with their own *artisanal*.

The Opéra season in Venice was about to start. She heard all about Verdi. Since her arrival, Jacopo was by far the most interesting person she had met. Avidly, she listened to his tales. Artistic conversations were always titillating, and the Count delighted her with the culture of the City.

"I wish I could roam around the other islands of the Lagoon and learn firsthand of their cultural, artistic and historical grand times. However, we will have to return in more clement times," she remarked sadly after the Count recounted myriad stories of the excitement she longed to experience.

"The Duke should take you to one of these performances, Gabriella. Verdi likes the Teatro de Fenice. You are aware that the first performance of *La Traviata* was performed here in the city in 1853."

"Yes," she responded. "I would like that very much. I'll talk to the Duke."

Jean-Louis would be making his way back to the conference room. Somewhat reluctant, she politely took leave of the handsome Italian to rejoin her husband.

Her outlook had changed these past few weeks. She had been thankful at first that Jean-Louis had made the decision to involve her in his work. Challenged by the political adversities, she was fascinated to be at the heart of a changing world. Now, however, her role was destined to be one of an interpreter.

Many delegates became acquainted with her. Her great beauty intimidated. At first, it worked against her. In her homeland a very pretty woman, one who liked fashion and beauty was often considered less than cerebral—for no other reason than men and women failed to imagine a great beauty could also have been given a brain! In Europe, it was singular, if a woman was beautiful, she was credited with more intelligence than she actually possessed. Either way, the pressure was intense to accept life as a wife and a mother.

In Italy, she did not know how she was perceived, most probably as the pretty and now intelligent wife of the Duke de Bourbonne. The few that were aware of the kidnapping had a newfound admiration for her. Warm smiles showered her when she walked through the halls with her security.

Already seated, Jean-Louis shot her a disparaging glance when she entered. She strolled close to the table and pulled up a chair next to him. She covered his fist with her hand, and shifted closer. "I went downstairs for an apple tart," she whispered with a smile. She made no mention of Jacopo, who inadvertently trailed behind her.

Darts in his eyes, Jean-Louis glared at the Count. At times these piercing blues eyes could pass as ice shards. So severe, Gaby thought.

The rest of the afternoon, Gaby and Jacopo continued to work in the ante-room.

"A bite to eat, Gabriella, and a bit of fresh air to rest our minds," Jacopo asked in English with his sensual Italian accent and appealing demeanor.

Jacopo made her laugh often. Her crystal-like laughter could be heard in the conference room. Amusing anecdotes were recounted. It made her feel young, pretty and interesting again. She was well aware of her gifts, but sometimes a woman needed to be reassured.

Since their arrival in Italy, Jean-Louis had been most serious—far too serious. He was a changed man. He loved life in Paris; he enjoyed friends, parties, the opéra, and the theater. All that had changed. He'd become serene, overly possessive, and all business. Consequently, in effect, the days that she spent working with the charming Count uplifted her daily life.

Jacopo fascinated her with his knowledge of the Italian Renaissance and amused her greatly with his less than polite and irreverent remarks on the political situation in Europe. They would sneak out often for sweets in a small café nearby that once had tended to the Doges and their advisors. Jacopo was carefree and Jean-Louis deeply engrossed with the situation at hand. She needed a little amusement so as to keep her sense of wit and playfulness, she reassured herself.

That was good for Jean-Louis, as well. It was her duty to give her husband support and comfort. To appear light and cheery in the darkest hour was what the Cardinal had recommended. She was doing the right thing and enjoying it— immensely. Absolutely nothing to be ashamed of, she assured herself. That was one of the things she loved about the French—polite banter. It never meant anything more than curiosity about the true nature of the individual they were having fun with. Nothing less, nothing more. Often people in America interpreted this sense of polite interest, of polite mockery, as sexual innuendo—a desire for a sexual encounter, a fantasy.

The French certainly knew how to be direct about their sexual fantasies if such were their desires and their final intent. No deviation there. Prudish they were not.

Back in the conference room, she sensed that the negotiations this afternoon were more complex. It appeared that, every time they neared a point of agreement, the opposition countered with a point of contention. If it continued, they'd be here forever!

Chapter 15

Soon after concluding that their imminent departure would not occur, Gaby decided upon a *grande soirée*—a masked ball in the Parisian tradition! Security had struck it down. Nonetheless, it would be a grand ball. The preparations were extravagant, reminiscent of the regal extravagances of *François Vatel*, the great French chef of *Nicola Fouquet at château Vaux-le-Vicomte* in the 17th century. The food, the entertainment, the right guests, all were significant to show the grandeur of Jean-Louis's French aristocratic background. The night was upon them. She had chosen to surprise all and sing one or two arias from Verdi. After all, the composer was beloved in Venice.

In the foyer, she stood with Jean-Louis and greeted their guests. Among the *invités*, the Count Jacopo de Castriodrianni and his mistress, Roseanna Gullienderess Allevitti. The Count was wealthy and influential and he was a most trusted member of the King's inner circle. During the nine years of the reunification, he had not been opposed to curtail the Pope's power and to return most of the land owned by the rich Counts of the Papal States to Italy—as long as his lands and those of his brother's were kept as large landowners' estates.

Jean-Louis had already warned her on several occasions to steer clear of his charming presence.

She on the other hand liked him very much. He worked hard at making her life pleasurable during the negotiations. The well spoken, amiable man unabashedly flashed his pearly whites at her. Jacopo was one of these remarkable specimens—not unlike the Greek sculptures exhibited at the Louvre. Women scattered around him like the petals of a rosebush in a rose garden after a whirlwind. She snickered at the irreverent comparison.

Jean-Louis had some competition, she thought amused, as she continued to greet her guests.

Well aware that she made her husband's life miserable because of his possessive nature, the counter-balance effect with Jacopo pleased her immensely. The Italian Count's magnetism was no secret. She now was well aware that he was an avid philanderer. Personally she did not care. It did not affect their relationship. In her view, women accepted too readily the advances of the Italian Apollo! Women—rare specie, she laughed knowingly. There were also gossips about brutal behavior toward Roseanna and with many of his previous paramours. Scenes of jealousy, Gaby had heard were attributed to his flirtatious nature with her. God forbid, she mused, if Jean-Louis even heard of these rumors—her private outings with Jacopo would cease immediately. These insinuations were unsettling. What if the rumors were true? No, there was no denying the Count's great love for the beautiful Roseanna. Consequently, Jacopo was not a threat to her marriage. In essence, it was perfect. She could enjoy his flirtatious company without the fear of an importune advance.

Jacopo loved a seemingly smart and beautiful woman. If she paid no heed to his flirtatious nature, she could enjoy his sunny and humorous personality, as well.

The story went along the following lines. During one of Jacopo's expeditions to Argentina, he had fought alongside the men of her small Patagonian village. Jacopo had purged single-handedly, she'd been told by one of the ladies in her circle, the deadly thieves intent on bringing chaos and despair to all. True or not, it added to his appeal. Women had a tendency to adore a warrior with a charismatic flair; the danger was too attractive to pass up. Jacopo possessed the same aristocratic haughtiness displayed by Jean-Louis. Apparently, if the story was correct, his sense of adventure rivaled her husband's as well.

In the weeks after her abduction by the rebels, Jean-Louis fully involved her in the intricate negotiations between the nascent Italian kingdom and the rich merchants of the former influential City States, along with the Prelates and Counts of the Church. She'd worked as hard as many of them. She had been a devoted and very knowledgeable figure in the negotiations. Her fluency in the language was of great service since she was her husband's sole confidante. But her achievements were rarely acknowledged by most in attendance. She was treated with deference and respect because of her station in life, but the divide that separated the great male ego from the innocent female was inculcated in the spirit of all present. The sole exception was from the Count Jacopo di Castriodrianni. In effect, Gabriella thought, her friendship with Jacopo might serve the negotiations well. Jean-Louis would not hear of it. She needed to tread carefully.

"One should not discount, Gaby, that Victor Emmanuel has many enemies in Italy. The charming Count might very well be one of them. No matter how conciliatory he appears to be." Jean-Louis reminded her countless times. "Gaby, do not divulge anything that you may know. Remember whom you are working for. Often Jacopo has asked to work with you personally. Why?" The Duke could not quite let go of his earlier premonition.

Flippantly, she rolled her eyes to the heavens.

"I comprehend your objections and concerns. However, I find it insulting to be reminded of my allegiance. I think that I have proven my loyalty more than necessary." Gaby responded miffed.

He arched one of his brows and stared at her questioningly.

The real issue lay with his possessiveness—not with the Affairs of State, she suspected. A little jealousy should jolt his consciousness. He had a young wife to attend to as well.

Jean-Louis stepped away from the receiving line for a short time. A missive had just been handed to him.

"Gabriella," Cunnan who just stepped out of the shadows, murmured into her ear, "your guests are at hand. The Count is looking intently towards you and you seem to be returning his prying glance. Be aware, my dearest." Knowingly he sauntered away.

Quickly, she lifted her chin defiantly, and smiled grandly at the arriving dignitaries.

An hour later, Jean-Louis wrapped his arm around her waist. A frisson of sensual awareness spread along her spine. "Our glasses need attention, Chérie," he said as he smiled.

* * *

Jean-Louis and many of the men took refuge in the ornate salons of the Palazzo. Not Jacopo. He invited Gaby to dance a few times and brought her back to mingle with his circle of friends.

French dignitaries sent by Charles Louis Napoléon and Principals in Venice that had just arrived from Rome were in attendance. Philippe had not responded. She wondered why? The weather had been inclement these days. He would come and visit soon, he'd promised Gabriella a few weeks back. Certainly, Jean-Louis would not take offense to her dancing two waltzes with Jacopo.

"Don't invite him if you dislike and distrust him so much!" she'd snapped earlier while they dressed.

"We need to have him here," Jean-Louis had hissed, incensed. "You know very well, Gaby."

"Don't patronize me," she'd remarked haughtily. "The Count makes life difficult for you. When I personally loathe someone, I don't purposely seek his or her company in a social setting. Trust me, none of the merchants I dealt with on the plantation were invited to the gatherings that Philippe and I had from time to time. I didn't court them."

"You know damn well how the Count is intricately involved with some unsavory members of the opposition." Jean-Louis replied, annoyed by her tone. "Don't let his light nature fool you. Be polite, but reserved toward him. I don't trust the man. His goal is not peace. He likes conflicts in a most unnatural way. Measure your words in his presence." Jean-Louis ordered.

She sensed the animosity he felt for the man. Gaby knew better than most women the chameleon nature of many of the political *Grands* they were dealing with. She inculcated Jean-Louis' words. He was right.

She had seen another side of Jacopo when she listened to his remarks while he spoke to his delegation.

He could accept the status quo, if the Pope could not be convinced of the inevitable loss of Rome. He did not see the future starting now. "The populace is too uneducated to take on the role of modernization," he shared with her. "Wealth and power for the educated elite can still be accumulated," he declared in a rare moment of clarity.

Here lay Jacopo's position. Unlike Jean-Louis, he was not willing to give away what he considered to be rightfully his on the sole merit of his birth. Not yet, anyway. "I am deeply troubled by the power the Sardinian King has acquired, Gabriella," he confided. "I want to insure that the Monarch keeps the Italian Peninsula for the educated and the intellectual elite. Modernization will arrive sooner or later. My sole purpose now is to keep the populace free of wars and invading armies." She thought of the French garrison in Civitavecchia. "Poverty—that is a known entity. It is not a new concept. We need the poor! The next generation will have to struggle with it."

Gaby understood well that aspect of the Count's philosophy. Slavery was not called 'slavery' in Europe, Gaby posit silently. Sometimes it was hard to differentiate.

Nevertheless, she liked the Count. He was a distraction and she was confident that no one would make her divulge, in her playful moments, information consequential to the negotiations.

She had dealt with some unsavory characters on her plantation, *La Justine*, and she never forgot that weakness in her character could and would ruin her. She learned early on in life to deal from a position of strength. She was in a position of strength now, and she opted for amusement at her *soirée*. She was too emotionally happy with Jean-Louis to destroy everything she had ever dreamed of! She missed him so. Paris could not be too far ahead. They would regain the French capital, their habits, and their sensual lives soon.

She nodded to the group of men and turned on her heels, to socialize with the well-heeled women who'd been invited. She was a woman, and the hostess of this grand ball. Act like one! She admonished herself.

A grand smile on her pretty face softened her features. She circulated amongst the pillars of feminine society. She surprised herself. After avoiding these women for quite some time now, she enjoyed the lightness of their conversations, the artistic expressions that the women seemed to feel rather than just employ to impress.

Her obsessions, her fears of being left alone, had robbed her of that feminine touch that she surely would have developed had she not been kidnapped. She enjoyed herself thoroughly and felt more secure than she had in months.

Charmingly, she strolled toward Roseanna, Jacopo's mistress. Her goal was to make the mistress feel secure. Surely, the Argentine must have heard the rumors running rampant, about the Count's flirtatious banter with the Duchess. Gaby remembered the painful moments that jealousy had caused her. Jean-Louis had never given her reasons to be green-eyed.

She looked for him again. This time his gaze leveled squarely on hers. She placed her forefinger to her mouth and blew a kiss. He did not appear too pleased. This political ordeal was a nuisance! Such a damn nuisance! She just wanted him in her arms.

Ready to spread her benevolence to Roseanna and the women surrounding her, she quickly turned and caught a sinister glare from one of the dignitaries who seemed to constantly trail the Count. It struck her as odd at first, but then again, security was intense—not solely on the French side. She stopped a butler and reached for a flute of Champagne.

Why couldn't people be more like her? She expected smiles and compliments from these feminine circles—on her looks, her dress, her hair and her husband. Heavens, she was the hostess of this *grande soirée*. What ensued floored her!

Roseanna, Jacopo's *maitresse attitrée* looked stunning in a red satin gown that *placed en valeur* her splendid, bronzed complexion and large dark brown eyes. Insolence and hatred stormed in her fierce stare. She glowered at the Count first, and then a stare of cold revulsion directed at Gaby caught all by surprise.

The Count had complimented the Duchess while in his mistress's presence. The South American goddess knew that she had to endure many outrages for the 'cause' but the open flirtation had gone too far.

Ready to compliment her on her magnificent gown, Gabriella smiled at her as she tried to assuage the jealous feelings she knew the woman harbored.

Courageously, the dark-haired beauty inculcated the detrimental consequence of her demeanor, but the hatred she harbored toward Gabriella could not be contained. She stepped toward the Duchess.

"Gabriella, your flirtatious remarks and incessant outings for café and déjeuner with the Count are deeply disturbing to me. I ask you to stop," she emphasized in a heavily accented Spanish inflection. "I wonder about your idyllic romantic marriage that all in Venice envy? Have you forgotten, my dear, that you have a husband? A most handsome and sensual one at that."

The little peasant from Argentina left Gaby speechless! Flabbergasted, she staggered backwards as she desperately attempted a proper retort. She recovered her smile.

"No, I have not, Roseanna. The Duke and I have a most passionate and endearing love. Please do not take my light and flippant comments to the Count as anything other than a lack of knowledge of the Italian culture. I thought that my mother had taught me well, but she left this beautiful country at an early age. She must have forgotten to teach me the most rudimentary etiquette when one deals with Affairs of State. In her days, there probably were none! My sincere apologies if I offended you and the Count," she informed Roseanna with a curt nod.

The mistress, shaken and flushed, took note of the taut set of the Count's jaws immediately. She took in the immensity of her rude comments as she stared at the stern expression on Jacopo's face.

How dare this impolite *effrontée* humiliate her so? At her elaborate ball, in her residence no less! Astounded at the gall of the woman, Gaby was incensed. She jerked her gaze away.

Yes, sometimes she enjoyed flirting with Jacopo. Every woman in Venice was of the same mind. After all, he was a charming God. But, she would never, in a million years, entertain thoughts of a romantic interlude. To laugh heartily with this most astute and charming fellow was great fun. Italian men, in general, with their infatuation with the opposite sex, certainly had a most desirable effect on the feminine spirit! Now, however she had been placed in a most discomforting position—to suffer the public insults from Jacopo's cherished mistress!

Gaby presumed that she had bounced back in her court by admitting to a cultural faux pas. Surely Jean-Louis would hear the sordid remarks that had passed this evening. She'd rather not think of it. The situation had been diffused diplomatically, she reassured herself. The nerve of that little peasant from Argentina! She had saved face in front of her Italian guests, but . . . how would Jean-Louis react?

Talk of the devil; she caught his icy blue glance from the corner of her eye. Courteously, he walked behind her and reached for her waist. Did he pretend not to have heard, or had he been too busy with the other men to pay much attention to the tension that had just mounted in the ballroom? She hoped for the latter.

Impatience and jealousy had surfaced these last few months. The tension he was under was insufferable, and it affected their union in a most inappropriate manner.

Tonight, however, she'd engaged in a most inappropriate behavior. She had forgotten how pleasurable it was to banter with a man other than her husband in a playful manner. Well, all that playfulness had a price.

The ball continued late into the night and finally the last guests bade farewell to their hosts in the early morning hours. Jacopo and Roseanna departed earlier than anticipated.

"The early departure does not fare well for Roseanna," she overheard another woman say in the powder room. "The Count is not an easy man to contend with when angry," another one of his former lovers shared. "Brutal," they'd whispered.

Well, serve her right! Gaby noted, inflamed, as she slipped out of the boudoir. What did Roseanna think she would accomplish by embarrassing her hostess?

As she slipped down the carpeted stairs, an overwhelming sadness revealed a sense of loss. She stopped for an instant, and watched an exhausted servant, who stood half-asleep at the entrance to a small dining room. Life was hard for a large number of the population. Often she passed in front of these men and women who attended to her needs as if they were inanimate objects, here on this earth to serve others. She noticed a small Louis XVI satin settee placed in a shadowy corner. She ambled toward it and held on to its spine for a long time, before she rounded the chair and allowed herself to recline in it. Her dismal reaction to the rumors this evening shocked her. In reality, she had lost perspective and had joined the ranks of the worthless aristocratic women she had met upon her arrival in France. Would she return to the stage or would she sink into nothingness like so many before her?

She'd imbibed a bit too much this evening. She would pay for it tomorrow! Gossip ruled in her new world.

Chapter 16

The Count di Castriodrianni had been given the title of Cardinal—Nephew. The family's title had been purchased from the Curia.

Upon their arrival at the magnificent palazzo, Roseanna sadly experienced the consequences of her intemperate conduct. The Count had taken her upstairs to their apartments and had struck her savagely.

"What were you doing?" he'd screamed as his brothers and compatriots downstairs hung on his every word.

"Trying to undo what we have been working on for close to half a year? I have Gabriella eating out of my hand. In a few short minutes, you unravel weeks of my hard work. We are too close to victory to allow you to destroy the sovereignty of our principalities!" he shouted. He beat her down to the carpet once more.

"We are a team, Roseanna. Don't ever forget that. Our friends down below expect me to beat you or worse. You have deceived and disappointed all of us, and you have endangered our goals with your stupidity!" he declared cruelly in the crook of her neck, as he held both of her hands tightly into one of his. "You will do as I say from now on and this correction will teach you to know your place and to follow my orders during these times. After I'm finished with you, you will not show your face in public until this sordid affair has come to a just ending. Our ending!" He slapped her hard, once more. This time Roseanna did not cry out for mercy. She took the pain he inflicted like a warrior.

"What, Roseanna, no retort now, my love? Do you feel you have to atone for something you have done that has displeased me?" The Count shouted to impress upon his comrades downstairs that his love for Roseanna would not unravel the affair of State.

"I was thinking," she gasped, unable to resist the impulse, "that it is you, Jacopo, who is searching for an excuse to display your brutality!" She had gone too far. "Please, no more, I was wrong, I understand now," she interjected immediately. "Confronted with jealousy, I forgot about the mission. My feminine side re-emerged . . . I know that I was wrong. Shocked and pained at what I was made to endure, I could not tolerate your amorous and gallant remarks to the Duchess." She lowered her eyes and winced, submissively. "I am so sorry, Jacopo."

He stared down at her and relented for a short pause. Alas his anger took the best of him once more. The viciousness of his attack surged. He dragged her bruised body, curled up like a beaten dog without resources, onto a red satin chair.

"I want a letter of profuse apologies to the Duchess—on my desk—first thing tomorrow morning. Is that understood?" he shouted livid, as he headed to the door.

She nodded and glared at Jacopo, her face streaked with blood and tears.

Torn by pains that radiated down her long sensuous body, she summoned enough strength to rise and crawl into bed. Her eyes lifted to the painted ceiling. She stared at Mars and Venus, the Roman mythological Gods. Courtesy of the open window, the white-lace glass curtain flew in and out of the room. Suddenly, she heard muffled voices and Jacopo's shouted call for his carriage.

Where was he going? Beautiful Roseanna knew. Even now, she could not bear to think of the Count's nocturnal infidelities!

Gabriella De Pleyssis rattled her nerves! How could she have been so obtuse? She had let the movement down. She would make it up to him, Roseanna promised herself as she burrowed under the down coverlet. In a most atrocious way, she now expiated for her foolishness, but he did not have to be so cruel, she sadly pondered.

Years ago, her mother had opined that women were the prime targets of men's cruelty when they lost control. "Not unlike old men who send younger men to war, knowing only too well that defeat is inevitable," she'd recounted. Her younger brother had died at the hands of roaming bandits. A dagger, a mule, and a week's worth of food had been given to him at the tender age of eleven before being dispatched with not much older comrades to search and hunt down the rebels hiding in the surrounding hills.

Chapter 17

At the Palazzo Gritti, the residence that the Duke and the Duchess de Bourbonne had called home for the past year, the sordid remarks uttered by Roseanna's inflamed voice had not been taken lightly by Jean-Louis. The Duke played his role of perfect host well. He'd been amused at first by the female gossips describing his magnificence . . . the most romantic and heady husband . . . at her side constantly as he gazed lovingly into his wife's eyes while they waltzed. But the rumors of a flirtatious rapport between Gaby and the Count enraged him.

It had not been easy for him.

Instinctively provocative, she stepped into his arms for the last waltz. "I love it so when you display your sweet and loving charms to me," she remarked candidly, "I feel like I'm the only one in the world who matters to you."

"You are, Gaby," he retorted softly.

"It reminds me of our dreamy lives in Paris. I miss the attention sometimes, no, most of the time, Jean-Louis. You have been so busy, and this collaboration, as you call it, has been more difficult than I anticipated." At the end of the waltz, she lingered in his arms longer than protocol permitted. Without the least embarrassment he kissed her and sent shivers down her spine. No one missed the intimacy, especially not the women present on the dance floor!

As the last guests departed, Jean-Louis walked straight to the library and reached for a well-appointed cognac. Gaby followed, waltzing without a care in the world inside the vast mahogany paneled room. He stood with one elbow propped on the mantle of the fireplace and glared at her. He'd salvaged the soirée all right, but was incensed. How dare she flirt with one of the principals of the opposition? What was she thinking? The real issue, however, was his overwhelming jealousy. The courtesy and theatrics that he'd displayed for society riled his inner self. Unaware of his seething fury, Gaby approached and encircled his waist. She lovingly posed her head to his chest.

Inhaling the strong brew, he gathered her small body and he stroked the long dark mane flowing down her naked back to her waist. Her passionate nature always touched him. But suddenly, the sensuous gaze she'd graced on Jacopo earlier in the evening flashed in his mind. He swallowed hard. None too gently, he grasped her hand and drew her toward the marble staircase.

Gaby had imbibed too much champagne. Her usual astute intuition jaded, she obediently followed him upstairs and entered their apartment. Nonchalantly, she walked in and paused before the warm hearth. Extending her fingers to the burning logs, she absorbed the warmth and rubbed her hands together. Jean-Louis stood by the door and watched his pretty wife. For a moment he wanted to join her in the boudoir, make love to her, and then share that the Emperor had ordered the French delegation back to Rome. Then, he would reveal that he thought it best for her to return to France.

"The ball was fabulous, Jean-Louis. We were the perfect hosts," she sang happily in her crystal clear soprano voice.

"You think so?" He clipped as he advanced on her.

She nodded sweetly, before she took note of the taut set of his jaws.

He flung his black velvet coat and grey vest on the chair and unbuttoned and loosened his shirt collar. Fury surfaced once more as he clasped her shoulders and glared down in her eyes. "What in God's name were you doing? Have you lost your mind?" His grip turned steely.

"Stop it, you are hurting me!" she shouted. "Have you gone mad?"

"If I ever see you flirting with Jacopo again . . ." he heaved a long sigh, "God help me, Gaby."

She lapsed into silence.

Jean-Louis glared down at her as he tried to summon self-restraint.

At that very moment, Gaby saw in Jean-Louis' eyes what she had seen on that horrific day in Paris—the day she'd met Philippe in front of Notre Dame. The threat of menace horrified her. Shaken and flushed, she promptly moved out of his reach and bolted to a spot behind the great desk near the windows. Pure revulsion registered in her horror-struck eyes.

He jerked his gaze away, inhaled deeply, and he strode away toward his dressing room, leaving Gaby half hidden behind the roll-up desk. When he reached this level of anger, departure from the scene was primordial. He remembered the drama in Paris far too well. His toilette finished, he returned to the bedroom. Gaby had not moved a centimeter. Without a glance, he threw himself on the bed. For a long while he lay still, his hands folded behind his head as he stared at her. Then he sat up, his mood mollified somewhat. Silently, he gazed at her again—for a long time.

"Come to bed, Gaby!" he finally commanded after his emotions calmed.

"No," she whispered, "I'm frightened and horrified. You turned from a loving, passionate husband into a demon, just seconds after we entered our room. You must have presaged this scene all night."

Tears flooded her eyes. It did not soften his demeanor or his speech.

"Absolutely, I dislike immensely having my wife called a harlot!" he shouted. "Maybe I should have made another spectacle of our private life and killed Jacopo, at least that would have served some purpose. Eliminate the competition both politically and emotionally. You would have preferred this last option?"

She did not answer. She could not.

His accusation left her speechless. Twice tonight, a jealous woman had alluded to her loose nature. Now her husband had articulated the unimaginable. She swallowed hard.

He rolled out of bed, strode to the door, and locked it. Then, systematically he snuffed out all the candles in the room as he usually did every night when she was already in bed. Her tears froze in her eyes.

He slipped into bed, knowing that she was terrified of the dark. "Come to bed, now" he said ominously.

Instead, she fled the room from her boudoir, and she ran into the hallway to her dressing room. He did not pursue her. Good, she thought, she was in no mood to listen to his absurd allegations! Finally, she relaxed, sitting tranquilly on the long sofa that faced the hearth; the many-lit candles in this room served her well when Jean-Louis was out. She did not dare to fall asleep now. Many large homes had succumbed to great fires as well. They had dismissed the servants upon their arrival. Normally, they slept together every night, rather than disturb the sleep of a domestic. Their securities were paid for that particular service, the servants were not. Tonight, she wished the servants were present. She was tired, very tired now. It was still a bit chilly; she was pleased that the fireplace had been tended to.

Warm and ensconced deep in the golden velour pillows, she reviewed the last hour. How cruel Jean-Louis could be when angered. He had turned off the lights to frighten her and to force her into bed. The champagne must have given her the strength to cross the dark spacious room and hallway to reach her dressing room.

In her mind, she tried to reconstruct the *soirée*. How could he have known? Well, that was the foolish question of an inebriated woman. Jean-Louis knew it all—always.

This sordid episode was caused by his jealousy of Jacopo. Had it been with any other portly merchant, he would have laughed and congratulated her on her politically savvy retort. But with Jacopo, Jean-Louis imagined an attraction. He had mentioned it once to her, and he'd been less than polite at every encounter he had with the dashing Italian. He'd even gone so far as to find an inexcusable pretext when invited to attend one of the aristocrat's balls. He was 'tired', he had his secretary write on the response to the invitation. Well, so be it, Jacopo was devastatingly handsome and charming. He never missed a chance to compliment her intellect, her beauty, her accent, her perfect, fluent Italian, and so on. During the translations, and more than once at several of the *soirées* they'd attended, the Count had joked that he'd never enjoyed work so much. "How could I," he had concluded with a chuckle one early afternoon, "with such a beautiful and brilliant woman at my side?"

"This is love at first sight, *Signora*." The Count had the gumption to assert in a private late afternoon meeting in front of many of their colleagues. "It is just not fair. Ah, Captain," he had said, ignoring Jean-Louis's title, despite the Italian custom to show respect to those who held titles. In Italy, there were many. "Your wife, the Duchess leaves me weak . . . in my negotiating skills, naturally," he'd smiled sensuously at her. "I'm afraid that I will give far too many concessions to the opposite side."

"In doing so, Jacopo," she'd retorted heartily laughing, "you will bestow upon your beautiful country an enormous financial boost. Commerce is returning to your part of the world. Remember Venice in its pre-Renaissance days, before the Portuguese decided to bypass the Mediterranean routes to Asia? A fabulous legacy indeed." She had given no thought to Jean-Louis's reaction on that particular afternoon.

A grave error, she now realized in retrospect!

Upon their return to the residence that day, Jean-Louis had entered their vast apartment at the palace; he'd coolly removed his grey overcoat and unbuttoned her satin cloak before he tore it off her. With one hand, he'd clasped her wrists and turned her around, tearing her dress and silk underwear from her body. He'd lifted her onto their bed. Tears had streamed down her cheeks as he'd taken her forcefully. No caresses. No loving gestures. Minutes later he'd rolled out of bed and had strode to his dressing room and down to the library.

"I expect you downstairs in a quarter of an hour!"

"I'd rather die than to dine with you, as if nothing has happened just now," she'd retorted in a voice replete with resentment.

"If you continue your sordid *badinage*, you will be in over your head. I am not the one who caused the awkward scene this very afternoon. What were you thinking of, Gaby?"

Prior to descending the staircase, she'd walked to the side bar and poured a healthy amount of brandy and consumed it. Dinner had been silent. The lobster bisque, her very favorite, she'd hardly touched.

"Do I have your permission to return to my room?" she'd questioned, arrogantly. Then the paradox of the situation had paraded in front of her eyes; she'd terminated the sentence with venom in her voice. "I believe that I have accomplished my wifely chores in more ways than one!"

The icy stare that he'd posed on her had turned from fury, to pain, to adoration. She knew well that the anger he felt towards her burned hot. His heart told him otherwise. He adored her. She was in his blood. She was also well aware that he was in hers.

Italy was testing their will.

He'd stood and had come close to her, towering over her, so much so that she had had to bend her head backwards to look up at him. She had seen passion in his eyes. At that moment, she had taken her sweet revenge. She'd returned his gaze disdainfully and slowly strolled out of the dining area.

He had not come to bed that night. Instead, he'd stumbled into the room well past midnight—smelling of cognac. He had kissed her tenderly on her lips and reminded her of the party at the Pellegrino that evening.

Jacopo once again had been the lightning rod. Well, there was no rhyme or reason in his behavior. It was not her fault. She was constantly left alone. And no, she did not want to hear that he had done her a great favor by the mere virtue of bringing her to a foreign and very exciting land. "You have the chance to be immersed in the great conflict of the century."

To hell with all that! She had come to Paris to study music, to be an artist, to follow her dreams; she had not asked to be known as an influential political figure! The Duchess de Bourbonne, they would say with awe in their voice. Look where it had taken her. She'd given up her singing, she'd left the country she had chosen to inhabit, and, furthermore, since their arrival, she'd endure the infrequent attention of her husband. She needed affection. She had almost lost her life, for God's sake! And now, Jean-Louis was furious with her for socializing with Jacopo? At least the man was gallant and amusing. The Duke was wrong. She would not relent—nor forgive him this time. Apologizing for spiteful behavior was too easy. She would not endure another bout of his jealous nature. She would let him suffer. And suffer, he would. He loved her more than life itself!

Still settled in the sofa for the night. She ruminated on all the evil ways he'd put her through. She wished she could come to terms with her disability. The kidnapping had fed into an already well-developed obsessive behavior, all types of uncertainties and fears.

Obsessive people were terrific workers if they were placed in a setting in which they felt passionate about. She felt passionate about Jean-Louis. God, how she loved him! She hated to admit it at this time, but he truly was her ultimate in all things. Without him, her life would have no meaning. She also liked working with him. His dreams of a modern, peaceful, united Europe titillated her—well, somewhat. She'd never thought that she would become jealous of his work. At least she was included, she conceded.

Her other relentless passion was her singing. But here again, she could not devote herself fully to music. She needed teachers, maestros, and music doctors, as she liked to call them. She needed the entire hospital! She smiled sadly. It had started well here in Italy, but the abduction had caused a temporary end to her music lessons. Security did not allow anyone not directly related to the French delegation in the surrounding terrain of the Palace.

So why was she so unhappy? Clearly, her life was in a simmering mode. In her eyes, it was easy to be perfect, even easier to be bad, painless to be mediocre, but to walk on the cusp of the good and the bad, the middle line as she liked to call it, and be happy with the results was perfection. That she would not tackle now, could not.

She surmised that both of her passions were on a temporary decline. She felt like she was at the base of a mountain, helpless in her quest to climb to the top. Actually, maybe that was the wisdom of aging—accepting the downtimes while waiting for the great ones to return!

Lost in her melancholy thoughts, she did not hear Jean-Louis enter her boudoir. His naked presence made him appear twice as powerful, intangible and surreal as he stood before her. She jerked in surprise. Her first impulse was to sit up but instead she reclined deeper in the divan. He looked like Michelangelo's sculpture of David, an invincible giant glaring down at her.

Non-threatening, he approached the sofa. He stood silently for a moment. Then he bent down, picked her up, and brushed his lips over her ear.

"I can't sleep. I need you, Gaby," he murmured in the softest of voice, as if embarrassed to disclose such a lack of emotional restraint.

Stunned, she turned her face to her husband. He had told her lots of lovely things in his time, but 'need'—that was a new one!

She allowed herself to be picked up.

"You need a whore? How could you, Jean-Louis?"

"What?" he questioned in English.

"A harlot, as you called me, Jean-Louis!"

He did not answer. He pulled her tightly to him, walked back to their room, and slid into bed with his wife still held in his arms. He kissed her neck, her breasts, her stomach, her hips, and returned back to her cheeks and lips. His mouth opened over hers passionately. "I adore you, Gaby." He held her close as if he wanted to absorb her into his pores.

She felt his manhood swell on her stomach, but she did not budge. He could rattle her sexuality instantly, if he wished, but he didn't attempt to sway her to his will. He wanted her to come willingly now, and by George, she would not give him the satisfaction—even if she wanted nothing more than to feel his strong arms around her, sexually arousing her, loving her. Instead, she turned away from him, forcing herself to lie quietly and suppress the urges that mounted uncontrollably. Instead she willed herself to sleep. She was safe in his arms. She could let everything go.

Earlier than usual, the Duke got up to prepare for the day. He stopped to watch her sleep for a moment. Italy had really been most difficult on their relationship, he mused. He would make it up to her.

Now, however, he left her in the large bed and tucked her in with lots of blankets. Upon leaving the room, he lit a few candles just in case she awakened. Gaby was always cold and she hated sleeping alone. He'd suffered for having turned the lights out last night. It was a real nightmare for her. She should have come to bed. The stubborn little brat, instilling a little fear in her would probably serve her well. Then he felt awful again. Her fear of the dark was real. In his fury, he had used it last evening to try to bring her to heel. She had stood her ground! The champagne must have worked its magic! In the past, even after an argument, she would curl up against him. She gave him all of her personal conflicts consciously or unconsciously. He never pushed her away. Tonight, he had gone over the line of sensibilities. She would forgive him in a day or two. Right now she posed a temptation. Better run downstairs and work.

He marched down to his study, which was located next to the library. This second time around, he continued to peruse the documents. The Emperor had given a direct order. Return to Rome! The Tempête was ready. Perhaps he should send Gaby back to France. She would be safe in either Villefranche or in the Loire. He sensed a note of urgency and settled down to read once again.

The Italian negotiations were not going as well as he would have liked. Perhaps the Emperor was correct. Venice had been an error. He had thought that perhaps Gaby would enjoy the city and its art. She had suffered an incredible ordeal, instead.

It was primordial, he deliberated, for most of the Italian lords associated with the Vatican and the rich merchants in Rome and the surrounding hills, to understand that the drive toward nationalism was important not solely to satisfy the egos of the great Europeans leaders but for the financial well-being of a rising untitled class. All of the clerics and lords, those who divided the political structure of the country caused a devastating impact on international commerce. Everyone danced to his or her own lyrics. To enrich themselves, they forgot that the masses could one day rise up against the aristocrats and wealthy merchants to cause political instability and havoc throughout Europe.

War was never good. The mark of a true leader was in his negotiating skills. Old men sent young men to war to give up their lives when negotiations could no longer endure the test of time.

He wished he could remember who was the writer of an inspiring prayer that often came to mind. The many prayer books that he had been obliged to read and heard as a young man had often gone in one ear and out the other, but that particular one had been fitting. The gist had been to keep on treading on the same path although one could no longer see the light and to never give up. At the end of that righteous path the light reappeared and it still shone bright. With the spirit of peace at the very core of any political debate, one could win on all fronts if he persevered.

Understanding people's cultures, their histories, their backgrounds, their popular financial and religious needs were primordial lessons in humanity and power. Perhaps, he pondered, in a hundred years from now, children will be raised with children of different backgrounds, will receive great public education and earn enough money to travel and learn about the magnificence of the world. The human race might be less inclined to accumulate titles, lands and riches for the sole purpose of competing with their peers. In the world he and Gabriella occupied, the responsibilities of the advancement of the human race relied on people like himself, wealthy, educated and powerful with clear and definite goals for the advancement of human rights through political negotiations that hopefully led toward more democratic venues.

He used his wealth and influence well. There was still a long way to go. He would not give up. God was good. People of all nationalities and creeds were inherently good. The United States had accomplished great strides in this endeavor. If men like Washington, Adams, Jefferson and Lincoln had given up, he would not be doing that type of work himself. His own aristocratic roots would have taken over his enthusiasm. Today he would probably be in France, living the high life in one of his castles with a pretty wife with good lineage, in a loveless marriage and with mistresses and many friends. He would be involved in inconsequential verbal conflicts on how hard it was to manage all of his wealth notwithstanding the trouble that came from growing his wealth.

"A true leader needs to be a good man," Gaby had told him. "Jesus said in the Lord's Prayer, the one he taught to his disciples, to forgive others as you would have them forgive you." She'd smiled her sweet smile. "Try to live by this quote, darling, we will then never forget our humanity."

Jean-Louis-Pierre de Pleyssis attempted to live by this quote. Forgive past actions of despair and constantly strive for the good in the present and the future.

He normally tried not to hold a grudge against people. He wished he could extend this grand *geste* to Jacopo! When it came to Gaby, his emotions were not in order. But usually, he did not carry a chip on his shoulder, like his American friends commented. It was not hard for him. He did not forget anything and that was good. A weather vane he was not. He believed in preparations. For all that was good happened after a momentous time in history. In the event that good leaders were there to ensure that the population of a nation grew in financial and cultural well-being, the chance that these nations would coalesce with others to foster the advancement of an educated freethinking populace might prove viable. Individuals would be more likely to prosper in a modern, enlightened world.

At this time, Europe needed a united Italy in order to renew trade with the Middle East and Asia. Although the Spanish bypassed the Mediterranean routes by hugging the African coast, around the Cape of Good Hope, and into the Indian Ocean, the use of the Mediterranean middle voyages routes were still huge opportunities now that Commodore Preble, along with his contemporaries, had been able to sustain a successful blockade in Tripoli. It had opened new trade routes. Europe, France, in particular needed these routes. Everyone would profit in the end.

Thinking about Preble, his thoughts returned back to America. He loved America. Although his revered titles and vast estates would afford him a very comfortable life in Paris or London, essentially anywhere on the old continent, he dreamed of returning to the United States.

He had commissioned the firm of defunct Architect Charles Bullfinch to build a townhouse in the heart of Boston, in an area called Beacon Hill. The man had been an American architectural genius. Since money was no object, he knew that his new home would suit him nicely. He hoped to have offspring, although he now doubted Gabriella's ability to bear their child after her miscarriage. If not, many orphans would find a good home in his household. After all, he had adored his nanny. She had known how to love. She had been allowed to take care of him, fortunately often, because of his parents' constant social engagements and travels. She had given him all of the nurturing he had needed. If God allowed Madame Perideot a long life, he would find a way to take her with him to the new world.

He smiled, recalling how Madame Perideot had even taken his side while his own wife was recovering from the incident in Paris. She had told Gaby that 'he' needed his rest as well, when he'd insisted on staying by her bedside. This insensitive statement had prompted Gaby to tell him that no one liked her. Poor Gaby. He had really turned her life upside down.

If they could have children, he wanted his children to grow up in a country where he could presage the continuation of their intellectual independence, working in a free and advanced society. Titles or not. Gabriella would take to it easily; after all, she had been raised in Louisiana. Granted it was the South, but she had learned a lot about the reunification of the Italian States. She would apply that same concept to her homeland. He would be there with her. She would be happy.

True to the nineteen-century male vision, he did not even envisage that she might want something different. Like . . . returning to Paris to continue her artistic life, the same life she had so willingly given up for him.

He returned his attention to the documents on the massive desk. For the past hour he'd tried to concentrate on their contents—to no avail. He walked slowly to the side bar, poured a cup of coffee and carried it back to the large leather chair that faced the fireplace. Once more, his thoughts reverted to the pretty brunette, asleep upstairs in his bed with not a care in the world.

Gaby's childhood had been quite difficult, devoid of love from both father and mother with only her black governess Tita and her husband Gustav, whom she had adored. Another great nurturing story.

She had known slavery. Her father had been a cotton broker in New Orleans. He owned a large cotton plantation near Natchez and another sugar plantation with over 200 slaves before abolition, near Lafayette.

La Justine, Gaby had shared, had been delegated to her mother by her father to keep her quiet. Quiet or not, the beautiful plantation belonged to her mother. Her Italian father had given it to her. So the present had not really been a present. *La Justine* was her land. Gaby's father, meanwhile, lived a lively social life in the French quarter in New Orleans with a large family of his own. He had never expressed any interest in his only daughter. According to Tita, Gaby's uncanny resemblance in her demeanor to her mother drove him mad! Another thing they had in common, Jean-Louis thought, two emotionally weak fathers! What a lame excuse to give up their parental responsibilities, just because their children had resembled their discarded or dead spouses. Clearly, they both had done quiet well without the emotional support of dismal parents!

Gaby understood the ignominies of slavery. She understood the abolitionists' battles. Her mother had died for the cause.

Caterina de Conte Thornsen had fallen in love with a young abolitionist who had taken her to Faneuil Hall in Boston, to listen to the impassioned discourse of Mr. Webster. In the end, she had hung with her lover for the cause. After a lengthy trial, she had been accused of setting up connections for the Underground Railroad, around and to the north of her plantation on the Mississippi River.

On a rare occasion of candid conversation over dinner, Caterina de Conte Thornsen had revealed to Gaby the horrific ways of slavery. She'd pointed out with much pride, that upon her return from her first trip to Boston, she'd resolved to give all of her slaves their freedom papers.

"I may die, Gabriella, for my new found passion," she'd said, predicting her own demise. She had died for her newfound passion but not before the ink had dried on her slaves' freedom papers. At least, that was admirable. Probably the only admirable thing her mother had done in the eyes of her only daughter. Gaby loved her servant Tita with all her heart.

Caterina had been a miserable mother. She'd considered Gaby an unwanted, superfluous thing in her life. *Une chose pas voulue,* she'd decried too often to recount.

But, in her circle of friends, Caterina had become revered—her beauty, her intelligence, her witty *réparties*, always the talk of the town. At times, she'd take Gaby on short trips, namely to show the world that she was, in her own words, *une femme complete*—until naturally the affair with Ayden had ruined her reputation and had taken her life.

The only person close to Gaby's heart while she grew up, save her servants, was cousin Philippe—Cardinal Thornsen; Gaby adored him. Like herself, he had had to fend for himself, living alone in the plantation next to hers. Tita, the adored servant, and her husband Gustav had taught the young children to cook, to hunt, to shoot, to fish, to sing and to use simple percussion instruments to enjoy rhythm and movement. At night Gaby read to them and often wrote down stories that Tita and Gustav gladly narrated about their experiences as slaves under many different masters. Gustav had been one of the black men to arrive in one of the last boats that carried slaves from western Africa. In 1808, the American Congress had outlawed the transport of slaves from outside the Continental United States. Nevertheless, the traffic continued. Brazil, the shortest middle voyage from western Africa to its shore, had not abolished the trade. Consequently, the buying and selling of slaves on the Mississippi was a matter of life on the river— with no remorse and no authority to police the practice. She hated to talk about it, although he had seen it first hand while staying in New Orleans years before the Civil War.

Gaby had been most fortunate during the Civil War. Her father was of Irish descent and therefore claimed British citizenship. He'd pressed her on it several months ago.

"The plantation was not ransacked, nor was it quartered by either side. Sherman and his officers bypassed it, but they burned everything else in and around the surrounding towns. It was like a great bonfire, Jean-Louis. With the help of a lawyer friend, I placed my name on the deed. My father was way too pleased to get rid of another mouth to feed, so before *The March*, he'd gladly signed the document. He repudiated all responsibilities to his natural daughter. For a certain period of time, he could have either been a very wealthy or a very poor man! I liked and I excelled with finances. Consequently, after the war ended, out of two hundred freedmen, one hundred and seventy stayed on the plantation in my service. The question became moot. Very few plantation owners financially survived the first two years of the reconstruction era."

It appeared that Gaby did not really know her Father, Jean-Louis thought oddly. He hated to bring up the subject of her family. Every time she spoke of those times, she appeared devastated. He was not quite certain if a horrific drama had developed during the war or if a family secret was kept locked in her heart. It did not matter.

"My father lived in New Orleans with his six children from a woman of French and Spanish descent," she'd shared. Why her father had never loved her, he could not understand. "According to the other plantation owners who mostly attended the social season in January and February in the French Quarter, he was a most kind, devoted and generous father to his other children—all sons," she'd explained.

"After my mother's death, Philippe and I spent our summer in the city at the Convent of the Sacré-Coeur. We would attend our music camp in the church. I glimpsed my Father several times—in his carriage of all things—while I ran chores. He'd completely forsaken me until the day I resurfaced at the *Cathédrale* on Christmas Eve, singing the Ave Maria. He attempted a light conversation with me, but Philippe took my arm and removed me from the claws of a cruel and weak man."

What she meant by weak and cruel, he'd never really asked her. Her father had not been deserving of her love. In essence that was weak and cruel, especially for a young girl. Clearly, she had nothing in common with either of her parents. He wondered how, given her conflicted past, she had turned out so well? No wonder she had fallen so madly in love with him, he thought. She had never known real integrity in her young life. She had just followed her own delineated course, depending upon the excellent education her mother had showered upon her—mostly to keep her away from her and the plantation. Caterina could be applauded for that realization. He trusted Gaby fully. She could analyze and evaluate a situation to death. She never missed any angles in business; she'd handled her career in Paris, *sans lui*, extremely well. He hadn't known his mother, but Gaby embodied a complete, substantial woman in the very essence of the word. He would never convey these words to her, knowing how it pained her not to be able to bear children. Why women equated potential and accomplishments with bearing children was incomprehensible to him? As far as he was concerned, being childless was just fine. It suddenly dawned on him that sharing her with anyone else, even his child, would be most difficult. He thought of her asleep in that big bed upstairs and felt the urge to make love to her. How would she react, after last night's verbal trashing? He would soon found out. Let her rest. He smiled. To antagonize the Duchess early in the day was always a huge blunder.

All night, he had rehashed their lives and accomplished nothing. Useless to start perusing through stacks of documents, he decided. Later in the morning, he'd find time. The sun filtered through the heavy drapes. He stood and climbed the stairs, two by two to their apartment. Time to expiate his sins to the great lady!

Chapter 18

Meanwhile at the di Castriodinni's palazzo the following morning, the Count summoned his lover to the library. As best she could minutes later—Jacopo did not like to be kept waiting—she rolled out of bed with the help of her maid and began the long walk down to the library.

The 'Regulars' as he called his war colleagues were in high spirit. The return of the negotiations to Rome had been circulated in all quarters at the ball. Apparently, the Emperor Charles-Louis-Napoléon had decreed that Venice had been the wrong venue from the onset. The Duke and the Duchess, along with the French delegation, were to return immediately to Rome. All knew that the immediacy of the message alone had been a blow to Jean-Louis-Pierre de Pleyssis. Many questioned the de Pleyssis's apparent rebuke.

Roseanna swept silently inside.

Jacopo stared at the monument of strength that faced him. Her pained strides denoted the extreme punishment he'd inflicted.

"Have you written the letter?" he questioned. His voice had lost the cruel tone of the night before. Gazing at Roseanna, he wished at this moment that he could lift away the pain that he'd meted out. God, he loved her. He remembered last night how she had taken the beating. Some of his most trusted men would have flinched. Somehow her pride persisted under the most adverse conditions. She was a peasant with an aristocratic heart! In a perverse approach, he'd always been attracted to her steely demeanor under the most adverse conditions.

"No, I have not yet," she murmured, supple. Very slowly, she made her way to his desk, pulled up a hassock and kneeled atop it. She picked up the quill in the inkpot on the desk and began to write.

His eyes were glued on the statuesque, black-haired beauty.

Upon completion, she stood tall and proud as she handed over the missive.

He took it, read it and approved it.

"Leonardo," he called out to his secretary as he sealed the enveloped with a thin film of salt and wax. "This note is for the Duchess de Pleyssis. I want it delivered personally within the hour."

His gaze turned to her. She stood, rigid as she glared down at him. The servant passed by and offered coffee on a silver platter.

"Sit down," he ordered and quickly clenched his fist in self-disgust. He bolted up from the fauteuil, rounded the corner of his desk, and clasped her in his arms. She clung to him as he tenderly brushed her temple with his lips.

"Ask Marietta to help you," he whispered to her. "She concocts special tisanes and ointments that saw me through many horrific battles." He kissed her passionately on her lips, gathered her to him and stroked her thick, flowing black hair for a long time. And then with flawless determination he prepared to leave.

"Where are you going, Jacopo?" she demanded.

"To undo the harm that you caused last evening. I have just received a note stating not to attend the negotiations this week. That's all right. If the rumors were correct last evening, we'll soon be on our way to Rome. I'll make an entrance somehow this morning. They will need me to sign on a few documents. It is now all-out war! We just have a few more days, Roseanna."

She looked at him with adoring eyes. He returned to her.

"I love you. You have my heart and soul, Roseanna," he murmured with compassion.

"I want your body as well. Your whole self, Jacopo," she retorted as she kept him encircled tightly in her arms.

He did not answer her. A man needed change. Women, he thought—so forgiving, so fast. He would give up Nicoletta and all his other women friends for a while. Roseanna deserved it. She'd suffered. He would sacrifice a bit as well. Although Nicoletta was too good in bed to give up entirely, he smirked. The woman submitted to all vices. In his eyes no one came close to the virtues that Roseanna possessed. Gabriella, well, that was another litany. She was brilliant. He'd never met a woman like her. Not even the love he possessed for Roseanna could topple the admiration he dotted upon Gabriella. One of a kind, that woman, she did not fit any mold. He would miss the occasional banter and laughter but, surely, they would meet again. He intended her no harm. The Duke, however, had to go. No rest for the wicked!

He waived down a gondolier. Jacopo tried to place his position in perspective. The French had overstated their boundaries this time. They needed to be blocked. Why bring down all the Papal States and Rome? They could have been given to large landowners like himself and his family. The Sardinian warrior along with his sidekick, Garibaldi, had already unified all the other states into one country—Italy. Garibaldi, the great man himself, handing over all powers to a Monarch? Who would have thought? This last turn of event, he had not seen coming. There was absolutely no reason for it, he mulled. Industrialism would have worked without the reunification. Independent States worked well. Why, in this day and age submit to one ruler for the benefit of the masses? It was just one way in which France extended its long tentacles! Naturally it made sense for them. Why deal with many rulers when one could impose one law for the masses, the aristocrats and the wealthy merchants?

"Incomprehensible," he scoffed softly. All the talk about modernization, the Italian States had been at the center of the Renaissance. Who had been trading with China? Italy was far ahead of her time then and now.

Verdi and his co-conspirators should be sent back to the music halls. Let him compose scores instead of playing politics! One ruler for all of Italy was insane and unworkable. Too much was at stake. What had the French received to rally under the power of one ruler? They'd elected a President in '48, Charles Louis Bonaparte. Less than two and a half years later, he'd crown himself Emperor! The populace fared no better under Napoléon III. The rich got richer and Haussmann built beautiful buildings, but the beleaguered poor starved on the outskirts of Paris. They would reunify the last vestige of the Papal States, Rome, over his dead body!

Chapter 19

The morning sunlight suffused the entire room. Gaby awoke from a deep sleep. She opened her eyes and turned her head away from the light. She caught sight of Jean-Louis as he left their bed. Fears and anxieties returned. He might forbid her to accompany him after last night. Perhaps she could come up with something that would mollify his anger and furious jealousy. Damn her pride! After all, he'd confessed that he needed her.

As he re-entered the bedroom, she fastened her frilly peignoir and began to follow him as he washed, shaved and dressed. A smile hung from his mouth as his gaze subjected her to a leisurely appraisal, but he kept silent.

Annoyed, she left the room and strolled downstairs to the dining room. Deep breathing and a brisk walk in and around the gardens would lift her mood. She pulled on the blood red cordon next to the marble side bar to summon the butler. She asked for her cloak. When the man returned with it, she placed it over her nightwear and pulled the hood over her head. The mornings were a bit chilly. She clasped the cloak closer to her body and hastened onto the large terrace. The sky was vivid blue. Although hidden from sight behind great walls, she heard the familiar sounds of the city waking up. The magnificence of the manicured gardens facing her, relaxed her conflicted spirit. In one of the corner, behind an old and majestic pine tree, stood a *pigeonnière,* a rounded stucco tower where pigeons were kept. Years ago, she had been told, during the High Middle Ages, the size of a *pigeonnière* in a castle was an indication of the lord's wealth. Now many different birds nested inside and outside the tower. She had often observed the gardeners sort out grains for the many different species that called these gardens their home. A few grey doves skittered nervously upon sighting her. She strolled in and out of the beautiful alleys before settling on a pink veined marble bench. Tall, round and square fountains adorned every turn of each aisle. She never ceased to admire the fountains and their intricate waterworks, along with innumerable songbirds. She imagined a natural orchestra; one that could accompany her if only her passion for singing returned. Perhaps soon Gabriella . . . perhaps soon! She lingered a while longer, reluctant to return to the main house.

As she entered the foyer, heat radiated from the hearth. It felt wonderful; a flush crept up her cheeks. She removed her gloves and lifted her fingers to her throat to warm up before handing the cloak back to the butler. Apparently Jean-Louis had waited to have breakfast. He looked self-assured, powerful and handsome. In contrast, she imagined that he stared down at a subdued and submissive young girl. She stalked past him. He chuckled.

"Good morning, Gaby. Did you enjoy your walk?" he questioned, amused.

"Immensely."

He glimpsed at the beautiful young woman whom he adored. He would forgive her anything. What was it about this chit of a girl that could make him behave like a vile lunatic? He'd stopped asking long ago. As she stood facing him, he analyzed her beautiful features.

"Why aren't you dressed? We are already late," he said covering his annoyance.

"You want me to come with you—today?" Without waiting for an answer, she dashed up the stairs to their apartment.

Not quite understanding her behavior, he marched to the table, sat down, nodded to the servant for a cup of coffee and reached for the newspaper. *Mon Dieu*, he thought, news traveled fast. Talk of their return to Rome had made the front page. Less than a quarter of an hour later Gaby returned with a light grey cape and matching gloves. She had not had the time to pin her hair up so afraid that he might leave her behind in the palace. As she re-entered the room, he looked up, amused while he finished his breakfast.

"Well, here I am—all ready," she smiled coyly.

"Indeed, you are and as lovely as ever," he concurred. He stood up, walked to her, reached for her waist, pressed her whole body close to his, and clasped her head to his heart.

"Did you really think that I would leave you behind, Gaby? I may be a controlling, jealous beast, as you so often remind me, but I would never punish you emotionally. Never, ever, Gaby. You know that," he reminded her, as he brushed his lips over her temple.

What was he thinking? How could she not be scarred emotionally after the verbal thrashing she'd received last night? Men, of all people should understand about pride. To avoid another outburst, she did not respond. She refused to stay alone in the palazzo. Why were women so weak sensually? They forgave the most outrageous acts when in love? She recalled the rumors concerning Jacopo. Was it practicality when faced with reality? Laws did not protect women against the unfair physical advantage men held over them. One needed to survive. Forgiveness gave them the power to live reasonably happy lives. It also kept them in good standing with the Almighty and with the faith inculcated in their spirit from an early age.

"Croissants, blueberries?" he demanded with a smile she wanted to wipe off his face. She shook her head. "Very well, Chérie." Turning to the servant, he asked for a couple of croissants for the crossing. He fed her a few blueberries and kissed her tenderly.

"Besides, my love, you are far too valuable a translator. You saved us a good week of hard work in these highly delicate negotiations. Had you not been there, the conference would have taken a different turn!" He passed the paper to her. "We are returning to Rome next week. The Tempête will sail to Civitavecchia in the next two days. We are going to the Pellegrino's ball tonight. An invitation arrived last evening. I think that you will be pleasantly surprised."

"Why are we going to Rome?"

"The Emperor deems it necessary. We will talk later."

She recognized the tone of voice. She asked no further questions but continued to read the paper intently. No allusion to the reason for the imminent departure was given. Oh well, closer to France, she thought, just as well.

In the carriage, she said not a word. She munched on the croissant, wondering how to subdue Jacopo's flirtatious nature for the next week. Jean-Louis might send her back to France if the situation continued. She needed to put a stop to it, once and for all.

The crossing to the Palazzo de Doges was just a few canals away. Jean-Louis boarded the gondola first and then guided her down the steps. They lowered themselves into the barge's deep recumbent chaises, which were recovered with sumptuous gold and red brocade.

"Tell him to refrain from singing, lest he wants to swim in the canal!" Jean-Louis snapped out.

Her anxiety grew more acute as they approached the centuries old buildings. The Doges' palace contained myriad buildings with dissimilar formations that displayed distinctive architectural ages—from the brick building of the Gothic Age to the Renaissance edifices encrusted with large white stones.

As she lifted her eyes to the very top of the magnificent structure, she recalled what Jacopo had told her about Giacomo Casanova's escape from the Piombi prison, located at the very bottom of the Doges' Palace. He had been accused of spying for the French on commercial and trade deals, while also sharing a common mistress with a French ambassador to Venice. He'd tried to escape twice. His two previous fugues had been thwarted. Nevertheless he'd been released by a non-vigilant geolier the third time around. Jacopo had shared that saved the Venetian seducer libertine demeanor, Casanova had been a brilliant descriptive writer of the late 18th century. He'd contributed abundantly in the discipline of medicine—alchemy, as it was referred to. Oh my, she thought, chase all these interesting moments from your head, Gabriella, they can only harm your charmed life. The gondola hugged the wall. The gondolier wrapped a cord around a large wooden stake that emerged from the golden bronze waters. They'd arrived. She hopped out. They walked the short distance to the building and marched under the arches. Quickly the attendants spirited them inside. She'd have to face the music.

As they entered into the impressive Hall of the Great Council with sumptuous carved ceilings, and gloriously decorated paintings of the first seventy-six Doges who'd ruled Venice, essentially from the seventh century to 1797 when Napoleon I had forced Ludovico Manin to abdicate, she marveled over the staircase that brought them to the upper floors of the palace, to the staterooms, the Scala d'Oro. The gilded stucco ceilings, originally designed by the renowned 16th century architect Jacopo Sansovino, were breathtaking. Jacopo had also taken her to the ballroom. She'd let herself dream of entertaining a crowd of deserving opera aficionados. She shook her head to chase away her girlish thoughts as she reached for Jean-Louis' hand. The return to Rome was sound, she decided. Most certainly Jacopo would remain in Venice. To her great surprise, in the conference room she found an old corpulent man with sleeked back, brilliantined, black hair seated in the Count's seat. The man gazed intently at her. Jean-Louis had had his way once again. This time, she was thrilled. Ah, power!

Chapter 20

Jean-Louis and the delegation began to see results in the negotiations, chiefly with the representatives that resided in the enwalled city of Rome. The proletariat, it appeared, might very well accept the Monarch. They would then vote outside the walls of the city. A surprising and positive augur for Victor Emmanuel and the French Empire. The influential Venetian merchant class had been key in these negotiations. They also wanted a capital not controlled by the Church.

Quietly, Gaby and Jean-Louis returned to the palace in the late afternoon. Still vivid in her mind was the great insult she had had to endure—from her husband of all people, last evening. Gaby was intent on not accompanying him to the Pellegrino's ball. Cunnan had shared that he would retire early. Good. She'd stay behind as well. Once more, she began to ruminate over the wrong committed by Jean-Louis. Jacopo was polite and yes flirtatious and yes, she liked it. Going to a déjeuner with a man without asking Jean-Louis' permission was not, after all, the end of the world. But quickly, the idyllic years they had spent in Paris returned to haunt her. Their relationship had deteriorated in this charming country. Would they ever retrieve the light and amorous moments of their past? They had not spoken much all day. She'd coolly answered his questions.

Her plans to retire early at the palazzo did not materialize. Jean-Louis would not hear of it. Consequently, she'd obediently marched upstairs. A caged bird, that's what she'd become, and now she couldn't even sing! Weary, she ceased to care. Have a good time, she murmured to herself. She nodded to her maid to follow her.

A short while later, with a brazen smile on her gorgeous face, she waltzed out of her dressing room and into the sumptuous sitting room. Two burgundy satin sofas threaded with gold faced each other in front of a giant stone fireplace. A large mirror hung above the hearth with cameos of long gone powerful guests that had visited and been guests in the Gritti, all were tastefully inserted in the gilded frames. To the right of the entrance, magnificent tapestries displayed various pastoral scenes flaunting the affluence of the Venetian lords. It kept the rooms warm and cozy as well. Alcoves with ivory carved exotic animals displayed on crystal shelves, covered most of the opposing wall. Jean-Louis sat patiently, one leg crossed over his knee, staring at the golden flames, which crept up in crescendo high inside the black tunnel of the chimney.

Gaby's dark, long, auburn mane of curls flowed down her back. Her maids had elegantly coiffed the young Duchess and loosely, she'd adorned her locks with wide golden pins encrusted with yellow diamonds. All shone and scintillated as she twirled around the room. Jean-Louis immediately noticed the wanton glance as he let his gaze descend upon her décolleté. Nonchalantly, she raised her breasts forward to accommodate her arms that she slid sensually in her gold satin cloak lined with white ermine. Stunning, sensual and irresistible, she was all of these and much more, he thought, but under no circumstance, she would be wearing this damn gown to the ball! She could carry on for days if she so chose. He stood up annoyed and stomped towards her. The closeness was such that her breasts met his black topcoat.

"You look stunning, Chérie, but get back in there and change immediately. You are not going out in public in this lovely dress." He walked behind her, slipped off the cloak, and turned her in the direction of her dressing room.

"I will do no such thing," she assured with fury. She grasped her cloak out of his hand and began to slip it back on as she moved toward the two gilded double doors. Almost immediately, she felt a hand clamp down like a vise on her upper arm, and then another rested on one side of the dress.

"No, Jean-Louis! Stop! It's my favorite!"

"It would have been mine too, Chérie, had you been wearing it for one of our private *tête à tête*. Since you prefer to have others admire your niceties, I don't want to even see it in your closet!"

As he spoke, the lovely dress slid down over her petty coat and onto the floor.

Stunned, she glanced down at the dress and then, she let her eyes wandered to the white petty coat and lacey chemise. Fury surged as she lifted her eyes to him.

"I hate you!" she screamed with all the venom she could muster. "It will never be the same between us! Tell me, do you think you have broken my spirit? Why in the world would anyone want to be married to a person who knows only three words—as you wish. Why? Why can't you appreciate my talents, my accomplishments, and my feminine assertiveness? Why, Jean-Louis? Why? Are you so insecure that you have to control my very being, my very core? Or are you terrified, Big Man, that the love you feel for me will be your road to perdition? Tell me. Are you at least man enough to tell me? To admit it to me?" she fumed spitefully.

Subjugated, that's exactly what she was. An al dente noodle!

He stared at her. Anger flushed his handsome face. Determined that the manège had to stop, he held her gaze until unrepentant he turned her around to face her dressing room.

"Go and get dressed. We will be late. I have some final clauses I want to include in the last concessionary documents."

His calm response infuriated her.

"I have nothing to wear!" she shouted incensed.

"Oh come, Gaby, your closet is filled with new outfits you've received from Paris recently."

"Ah . . . but . . . they have not been ironed." Anything to aggravate him now, she fumed.

"You have three minutes Gaby," he reached for her hand and led her to the front of an immense closet.

His shoulders leaned halfway on a large pillar. He watched her next move.

She closed her eyes.

"And what will be my consequences, my love, if I dare to stay in my room? Will you insult me today? A very manly thing to do." She proclaimed regally, as she glared at him. "Or perhaps you'll take me again—unwillingly that is. Or perhaps I will be banished to my room to ponder how to redress my dreadful behavior to the illustrious Jean-Louis-Pierre de Pleyssis? Or maybe all of the above? I don't care anymore." Sarcasm and disdain mingled in her voice.

Her words were sword sharp. Immobile on his pillar, he stared at her, impenitent. He could not quite believe that his treatment was harsh. How many women in her entourage and society had her privileges? The freedom that he allowed her was mind-boggling. How many women traveled freely as a man's equal? Had he ever once tried to make her jealous? No! She was unreasonable and capricious! Mon Dieu, she could not have it all.

Apparently, tired of his silence, she chose a traditional green dress that matched her emerald eyes.

Derango, the butler opened the foyer doors. As she marched forward, a scornful glance darted from the corner of her eyes. She brushed by him as if he was invisible. A smirk creased his lips as he lowered his head as she passed by. The little brat, often he'd enforced his will, but for some reason he always felt he'd lost the battle. *Eh bien voila la passion!* She walked briskly outside and climbed into the carriage, silent. He followed close behind and sat next to her. With a sigh, he stretched his long, elegantly clad legs onto the opposite burgundy velour bench. His right arm wrapped around her shoulders, he tapped on the windows with his left fist. The carriage bolted out of the courtyard.

His close presence agitated her, even when she despised him as she did now. She hated it. She took a seat across from him by the window. A smile lit his vivid blue eyes. She looked away, out the window. Thank Heavens! A gondola was not *l'ordre du jour.* She gleefully would have thrown him overboard, watching as he drowned in his own fury!

When they reached the mansion, large crowds had already entered the palace. As they waited on the foyer, where their coats were taken and their names checked off a list of those guests still to be announced, Gaby heard a faint voice calling her name. A definite tug on her gown forced her to lower her gaze. Little Marco de Pellegrino whispered her name. He demanded her silence with his forefinger placed over his lips. She bent down and hugged him tenderly. Little Marco was the only son of the frivolous, socially conscious couple that hosted them that evening. Apparently, he was a very lonely little boy. Gaby had taught him how to play hide and seek in the garden during her free time. She always made sure to stop by the well-dressed tables in the French delegation's apartment. Peach tarts and *choux-à-la-crème* were his favorites. She embraced him for a long moment.

Jean-Louis followed the scene curiously. Gaby's admirable maternal instinct touched a chord. He cast a glance at his wife. She would have been a wonderful mother, he thought sadly.

"This is the Duke de Bourbonne, my husband, Marco," she said to the boy.

Quickly the little guy reached for Jean-Louis' hand and tugged on it to force him down to his level. Taken by surprise, Jean-Louis first resisted. But then, he glanced down into the child's large, dark brown expressive eyes and bent down.

"Please, please, do not take the Signora Gabriella away," the young boy pleaded. "I want to marry her." He turned his head back to Gaby, "I love you Signora Gabriella, and please do not leave!"

The candid statements took Jean-Louis aback. He knew enough not to laugh at the loving remark.

"I love her too, Marco, very, very much," he replied tenderly.

Jean-Louis' remarks were interrupted by the strident rebuke from the boy's governess. Marco released their hands and sadly pushed himself away.

"I am sorry, Madama. It was nice to see you again." He hugged Gaby before running off, scalding tears streamed down his cheeks. The governess followed closely behind the boy.

Flabbergasted by the demonstration of affection, inadvertently, Gaby lost her balance. Had it not been for her husband's vigilant eyes, the Duchess de Bourbonne would have fallen backwards on her derrière in a most irreverent fashion—ballerina training or not, there was not much elegance in a fall such as the one Jean-Louis helped to avert. She regained her composure in his arms. Without thanking him, she strolled to Marco who waited nearby while his parents greeted their guests. "I will visit soon," she whispered. He smiled back politely. Hiccups heaved his chest.

Their names were called. They were next in line to be announced. Gaby took her place next to her husband, awaiting the announcement. Thereafter, she deserted him.

It was to be a long night; many artists had been invited to perform simultaneously for guests that did not enjoy the dance. She re-joined her friends in the sitting area where many of the opera singers assembled. A ballet troop performed on a stage nearby, opera singers gathered in another smaller venue with magnificent acoustics, a play in the theater. All artists eagerly waited the midnight hour to pitch their finest crafts. Two tenors just returned from Paris. She had sung with one of the tenors on several occasions.

"Have you been singing privately, Gabriella, since your arrival in Venice?" she was asked.

"Sparingly, I'm having too much fun in this formidable city, a short hiatus is *de rigueur*," she replied as she reached for a flute of champagne. She finished it quickly and then savored a second one. The night was young, the champagne enchanting.

Tonight was a grand night, she decided.

Jean-Louis was a bit surprised not to see his wife in his entourage. In the carriage, he'd promised himself that he would let her enjoy this evening. He had assigned six more guards to her security. Assured that everything was in place, he rejoined the men in the smoking room to finish the last remnants of business.

The sitting room was decorated with dark brown, wide leather chairs with their own serving trays. A sweet scent of cigar fragranced the area while a suspended perpetual grey haze formed a cloud over the guests. Game tables in the far end displayed neat little columns of varied colored chips with no one in attendance. The gambling would start later. The men awaited the arrival of Jean-Louis. The tall French man entered and settled into a chair. He reached for a cigar and reclined quietly. Discussions began regarding their return to Rome.

Much later, a melodious aria sung by a crystal clear voice enveloped the assembly.

"Ah! That Melba! Not another like her! Listen here, she sings better and better as she spends more time in our great country. Italy, the country where opera singers are born—reborn in this magnificent art!" The old count went on about the Italian public's appreciation of opera. "It makes all the difference," he continued, "when the audience understands the music."

Jean-Louis smiled at him. "*Eh bien*, my friend, I must say that I do agree with you on the grandeur of your operatic training. However, my wife is singing. The Duchess is singing," he announced.

"Ah, we love Gabriella," the Count retorted amused, "but no, no, my friend. I could wage my fortune on that voice!"

"Well, Count, I would hate to be the one who placed you in the dishonorable position of a noble aristocratic beggar, but Gabriella is the one holding these magnificent high notes—for the last three arias, would you care to see for yourself?"

"Love is blind, but I had never heard the saying love is deaf!" The old count laughed almost hysterically.

Jean-Louis stood and glanced at his partner. He nodded toward the ballroom, and urged the amiable old man to follow him out onto the balcony, which overlooked the dancing floor.

Sure enough a look of utter disbelief covered the man's face.

"Imagine that? Little Gabriella . . . the Duchess," he corrected himself promptly. "But Monsieur, where have you gone to harvest this angel of perfection? You must have died, gone to heaven and brought her back down with you."

Jean-Louis smiled as he rested his forearms on the ledge and listened to the exquisite rendition of *Verdi's, La Traviata*. Gaby played the role of Violetta. She was admirable in *Sempre Libera*. Splendid interpretation, the little witch, the little angel, he amended. She took pleasure in every millisecond of her defiance.

At that very instant, intuition had her turned around. An arrogant, rebellious simper flashed across her expressive face. He would have loved to kiss it off her visage! With great artistry, she focused all her passion on the aria.

No longer able to resist, he left the group and strode briskly down the staircase.

From the corner of her eyes, she caught sight of him. She did not flinch. Instead, she spun forward and faced her audience. Her crystal notes expressed a depth in feelings rarely explored by other sopranos. She breathed new life in the aria and infused unequalled fire in the heroine's tragic destiny. In a *frisson* producing delivery, she electrified the ballroom. A sense of awe suffused the audience. The lush *roucoulement,* sadly for all, concluded ever so passionately. Many surrounded her, but Jean-Louis hastened to a spot behind her. Her waist and shoulders enveloped by his embrace, he brushed a sensual kiss to her temple.

"Magnificent, Signora de Pleyssis!" Another long kiss landed on her neck. "Bravo, you are splendid, Duchess," he exclaimed louder than protocol allowed. Finally, a passionate kiss opened on her lips. Pretending to be amused, she sweetly pushed him away. "You defy all rules of proprieties!" she murmured as a gracious smile greeted the applause of the other guests. Very much aware that the kiss aroused in her sensations she refused to feel, he chuckled and kissed her rosy lips once more.

A waiter stood nearby. The Duke seized two flutes of champagne. He offered her one, and nodded to the orchestra to continue their musical program. His arm curled around her waist as both strolled onto the dance floor. She stepped into his arms. Jean-Louis whirled her around to the harmonious sound of the Polish composer Frédéric Chopin's Minute Waltz. The magnificent music in D flat major had been written for Delfina Potocha, the poet Zygmunt Kransi'nki' muse, lover and confidante and a great friend of Chopin.

All her anger dissipated as promptly as a Southern shower in her beloved New Orleans. How could she? She questioned her treacherous emotions. The Champagne must have assuaged her wrath. She sensed his delight and she recalled joyous memories of their life in Paris—the balls, the plays, the salons, the operas, *la vie bruyante*. How wonderful it all was! Jean-Louis was vital, virile, and great fun. She surrendered to his gaiety and giggled at the comical stories he shared with her.

Tired and breathless later that night, she took a leisurely walk on the balcony in search of fresh air.

"It's beautiful from this vantage point. It overlooks the bay," she contemplated mostly to herself. Jean-Louis stopped by one of the deck officers on the Tempête and frowned. "I'll re-join you in a while, Gaby," he clipped with ill-conceived annoyance, as he began to walk in the opposite direction. She nodded.

She observed with surprise the illumination onboard the Tempête. Jean-Louis had had the ship brought into the bay. Their departure was imminent then. Few people knew when and how they would leave. Better to keep it that way in the treacherous world in which they lived. It dawned on her that she didn't even know. Jean-Louis had spoken about the return of the Tempête to Rome. She naturally understood that they would embark on the ship with a grand fanfare, signaling the positive turn of the negotiations. In Italy celebrations were a way of life, very much like the siestas in Spain. She liked it immensely.

In retrospect, she'd experienced great joy in this country— as well as numerous anxieties and fears. She had matured as a woman—and as a wife. She now looked at her husband as a man, not as the God she had married. The funny thing was, she loved him even more now than ever before, if that was even remotely possible.

Muted noises behind her made her turn her head halfway as her elbows rested on the peach stucco balustrade. Jean-Louis was returning to her. Instead of the ship's officer, Jeans-Louis ambled slowly toward her, but he was now engaged in conversation with the beautiful, and talented wife of Count Gaillardia. Gossips had it that she was also one of Jacopo's many mistresses. The woman travels about, Gaby concluded. It was hard to keep track of the affairs in Europe; maybe it was the same in the United States. As a young girl in New Orleans, she'd befriended many groups of adolescent girls, but she understood very little of the emotional and sensual lives of the adults around her. Why should she be so shocked? she reflected. She only had to look at her mother, her father and Philippe's family. Enough said for the sanctity of the Southern families. She caught Jean-Louis' gaze. Without so much as even fully turning her body, she nodded her head to call him back to her side.

Astounded that his wife had not even noticed that a woman accompanied him, he determined to stay away a tad longer—to test her reaction. So confidant was she that he adored her, that she'd become oblivious to his appeal to women. Gaby was a bit too accepting of his faithfulness. Minutes later he still spoke to the very appealing Countess Gaillardia. He'd never ever attempted to render his wife jealous, but tonight was different. He was in a flirtatious mood. He laughed. What a charade! What Gaby had reduced him to! He guided the Countess toward the opposite railing, in full view of his wife, and listened intently to the beauty facing him.

He was good at that. He had had years of training—of looking interested but yet oblivious to the words uttered.

Madama la Countessa now permitted herself a few graciousness. The Duke subjected her to a sensual appraisal. She smiled a devastating smile at the tall striking man, who smiled back appropriately.

The exchange was not lost on Gaby. A glare of utter disbelief spread across her face—and then fury.

What was he thinking? Shock immobilized her. The gorgeous woman was flirting with Jean-Louis, and he returned her attentions? Distress turned to melancholy. Was marriage weighing heavily on his shoulders, as well? There had been far too many altercations these past few weeks. She heaved a long sigh. These conflicted moments would pass. She left her corner to rejoin Jean-Louis and the Countessa. At that precise moment and without as much as a backward glance, Jean-Louis begun the short walk back to the ballroom, seemingly entranced by his lovely companion.

Astounded, hurt and angry, Gaby trailed him. None too gently, her hand darted toward his as she reached the group. She tugged at it sharply. Without a care, perhaps even expecting it, Jean-Louis grinned and clasped her waist, bringing her small body close to him. He kissed the long mahogany waves. She was mortified. How dare he leave her alone on the balcony while he returned to the ball room with a female companion—not on his arm, but still too close for comfort.

Hours later she had forgotten the incident. She had been asked to sing several more times, and she'd brought the house down after every aria. Her husband adored her. She wished this night would never end.

Chapter 21

The departure from Venice was a formal affair. Many dignitaries had stood on the Piazetta as the Tempête sailed away. They, however, along with a large number of the delegation, chose to take the inland voyage. Philippe had already secured a magnificent High Renaissance Palazzo in Rome. Palazzo Farnese with its incomparable vaulted ceilings by Annibale Caracci. It had been in the Bourbon family for close to two hundred years. The Commandant of the troops in Civitavecchia and the Emperor had approved it.

The trip began quite nicely. A large convoy had started south along the Adriatic route through Bologna, across the Principality of San Marino to Assisi, where they had stayed for a few days, and finally further south to L'Aquila and then on to the Abbey of Monte Casino.

Jacopo and Roseanna also reappeared on the scene. He had been asked by Victor Emmanuel to travel to Rome with his delegation. Grudgingly, Jean-Louis acquiesced. At night, the accommodations tended to be in villages in close proximity to the others in the party, but never in the same inns. Essentially, Gaby had only had one interaction with her former colleague. Jean-Louis retrieved his cheerfulness and carefree spirit during the trip. She enjoyed the beauty of this idyllic land with him. She recalled often her first few days on the old continent in the South of France after her crossing. There, as well, she'd bathed in complete happiness with the love of her life. Here, they spent time exploring or riding up and down the hills at breakneck speed. Endless olives groves and colorful vineyards dotted the rolling hills between the valleys where they traveled. Late for the season, she'd noticed large raisins that still adhered to the remaining vines left to grow wild on certain terraces. She'd eaten truffles near Spoleto, before an old farmer had explained how they sought out the subterranean fungi. In the mist of these wonderful trips, a dreadful accident—a calamity for Gaby—transpired.

Near a small medieval village not far from Bevagna, in the spectacular Umbrian's rolling hills, a band of horse bound bandits threatened the many carriages that essentially traveled as a convoy on their way to the Eternal City. While they hugged the banks of a verdoyant valley, with gaping death threats, the brigands had descended on the convoy from both sides of the hills. Traumatized, the kidnapping still vivid in her mind, Gaby had found herself hanging on to Roseanna for protection as Jean-Louis and Jacopo, on their horses with their security in tow, engaged the bands of thieves. The raid lasted less than one hour. Two of Jacopo's security guards had been injured, one gravely, but all the bandits had been dealt with. Most had been killed and six more had been placed in stock to fry under the Umbrian sun. Gaby held onto Roseanna for dear life. None too gently, the Argentine had pushed her away. "Gabriella, this is not *the ruée vers l'ouest*, the rush westward!" she'd haughtily exclaimed. "Salacious thieves, these are. They've gotten what they deserved." Gaby felt mortified, and she did not disclose her interaction with Roseanna to Jean-Louis. The woman was a hardened warrior. Next to Roseanna's steel composure, Gaby felt like a scared songbird.

Less than a week later, they reached the Abbey of Monte Cassino. The Abbey was perched high on a rocky hill—to secure the Abbey as a center of higher learning—and was far removed from the populace below. It was the very heart of the Benedictine Order and held within its walls libraries and museum collections of considerable importance for western societies. An informative tour of the caves, museums and libraries collections of the Abbey was given to the few top members of each delegation.

Philippe had arranged for the visitation. It had been the first time since her arrival in Italy that she had the pleasure to be the honoree. Her guests were allowed in the Abbey because of her familial ties. Once more, Philippe was her knight in shining armor. His position in the Vatican and his succinct knowledge of the Papal response to international politics was invaluable.

Within a day they were back in Rome, established in the magnificent Palazzo Farnese. The Palazzo was an architectural wonder. It had been the residence of Pope Paul III in the mid 16th century and Michelangelo had executed the exterior walls of the three-story palace and its interior courtyard. The back façade overlooked the Tiber. As she strolled through its many corridors with her French guides, the frescoes in the barrel-vaulted ceilings of the Carracci Galleria overwhelmed her. Mythological love pictures told stories of how the human soul can be transformed by divine love. Jean-Louis had to gently take her elbow, as she stood mesmerized, her eyes lifted, staring at the masterpiece.

Chapter 22

Meetings and conferences were once again pursued. Jacopo also resurfaced. At first, she had been most formal with him. They worked on the translation and interpretation of the manuscripts for the Pontiff. Quickly, however, Jacopo reverted back to his gallant and gracious self. Less than a fortnight after their arrival in Rome, she joined him for coffee.

"A bite to eat and a bit of fresh air, Gabriella," he'd asked sweetly in English, with his sensual Italian accent and demeanor. She'd agreed. He entertained her with his amusing anecdotes and she liked his attention. Her crystal clear laughter resounded in the conference room.

In stark contrast to Jacopo, Jean-Louis was grave and serious once more. He loved life in Paris; he always enjoyed friends, balls, the theatre, and operas—all that had changed in Venice, and now again in Rome. Instead, he'd become very possessive and controlling. Consequently, Gaby looked forward to the hours spent with the charismatic and very appealing Jacopo.

Today, she'd asked an aide to pass on a note to Jean-Louis. She'd accepted Jacopo's invitation for a short déjeuner at the local eatery. "Would you like to join us?" she'd written to her husband.

The irate Duke, who sat at the head of the long conference table, glared at his wife and at the Count as they re-entered the room. His brilliant blue eyes followed the aide who walked briskly toward him. He snatched the note from the man and read it. Without lifting his eyes, his ominous voice resounded so powerfully that everyone looked up, first at him, and then at Gaby.

"Don't you dare walk out of the room!" he commanded.

Mortified, she pretended not to register the anger in his voice.

"But . . . just for a short bite," she replied sweetly with a devastating smile, "we'll return promptly, Jean-Louis."

"No!" came the forceful answer.

She knew not to force the issue. Jean-Louis was livid. She politely turned to Jacopo. "Thank you ever so much for the invitation, Jacopo, but I'm afraid my husband needs me here."

The Count nodded. He gallantly kissed Gaby's hand and he promptly left her side.

"I will see you soon, Madama. Very soon, I hope," he pronounced with a hint of sarcasm. Because of his flirtatious nature, he was a natural at it. Jacopo nodded and left the room; very much aware of the tension he'd purposely created.

The men seated at the table stared curiously, flabbergasted by the verbal altercation between the two lovebirds. Promptly, the chief of Vittorio Emmanuel's delegation stood and strode out behind Jacopo. Outside of the doors, they spoke briefly.

"The political process should not undergo any more major changes," came the angry statement from the Chief. "I wonder whose side you're on, Jacopo?" the Chief continued.

"Don't be absurd," the younger man replied, feigning indignation. "I have been a most reliable ally to Victor Emmanuel."

The Chief stared at him. For a moment, he appeared to question whether he should divulge the latest development to Jacopo. The news would be released soon enough.

"The Pope is as stubborn as ever in public. The Prussians are intent on humiliating the French Emperor into a war. I believe that now, the Pope is beginning to understand that a great demise is at hand. We have heard from those close to him in the curia. His emphatic denial of the eventual loss of his temporal power over Rome resounds clearly within the Roman walls. But if the new development stirring between France and Prussia comes to pass, soon France will declare war on Prussia and the French soldiers and the garrison in Civitavecchia will be called back to the front. This scenario might bode well for our king. Without much ado, Rome would be his capital. Think about that and act appropriately." The Chief turned on his heels and regained the chamber.

Gaby reclined in the red velvet wing chair and stared at her husband. It was lunchtime; they would take a break soon. She could not wait to share with him—in no uncertain terms—how humiliating his response to her note had been. She heaved a long sigh and gazed at the very end of the conference table. Jean-Louis stood straight. Fury in his demeanor was easily recognizable. Perhaps not now . . . she would wait until a more auspicious time.

The chief of the Vatican delegation had been signing documents. Jean-Louis stared at her, his gaze leveled coldly, in between signatures. She wished Philippe had attended the meeting. They would meet for dinner tomorrow.

At twelve thirty sharp, the clergymen stood and took their leave to proceed to their own private salons.

No, definitely not. This was not the time to aggravate the situation. Jean-Louis had a pronounced jealous nature. Long ago, she'd resolved never to exacerbate his anger. To soothe the incident? Yes. To face his wrath? Not a good idea.

All the diplomats had left the large conference room. She observed Jean-Louis gather the necessary credentials. She smiled but did not expect any acknowledgment. His nature was so unpredictable. Across the room, his blazing eyes spoke volumes.

Documents were slipped into a brown leather, boxlike case, with a dark brown velour handle. Jean-Louis circled the table and proceeded to where she now stood. He clasped her elbow and led her down the hall through the breath-taking hallways. Large Masters paintings, Da Vinci, Michelangelo, Raphaël, architectural drawings from Bramante, more religious paintings from Raphael decorated the sumptuous large halls. Wherever the eyes rested, fabulous paintings and countless sculptures and Venetians mirrors that decorated the villa's walls and ceilings charmed the viewer.

Perhaps she should ask for educators to guide her through the wonders of the Eternal City. Surely Philippe would know several academicians from either the Vatican or the French Académie de Culture of Paintings and Sculpture in Rome. The *Prix de Rome* was coveted. The negotiations could be terminated without her. The Italian heartbeat, she had learned to appreciate more. A tendril of fear gravitated from her heart to the very tip of her toes. I guess not, she concluded. All and all, she knew she was not quite ready to visit alone. Anxieties still tortured her very soul. She felt safe only in the knowledge that Jean-Louis was close by. Maybe one day, she would return and truly enjoy this splendid country and its age-old traditions of beautiful craftsmanship. She lifted his hand away from her elbow and slid it into hers.

They passed the salons and the small conference rooms set up to accommodate the negotiators to brainstorm in privacy.

Jean-Louis had instigated this mode. Long ago, his father had lectured while attending the Congress of Vienna of 1815. After the French Emperor Napoléon I had been defeated at Waterloo, the four formidable diplomats, Metternich, the coachman of Europe, Tsar Alexander I, Viscount Castlerey from England and Talleyrand from France instituted an agreement between the great powers. The negotiations had lasted almost a year, in the midst of balls, banquets, operas, with hundreds of diplomats with their families, and Chargé d'Affaire and their mistresses. In effect, it had been a formidable agreement that still stood to this day, Jean-Louis had told her. Although regional revolutions and skirmishes had occurred throughout Europe, the great European powers had not fought a major war against one another. Jean-Louis hoped that this format would serve him well.

"Because of his constant illnesses, Charles Louis Napoléon listens too closely to his generals and the Empress. Prussia is about to invade France. I am convinced that Bismarck will find an excuse to incense the Emperor." Jean-Louis shared with Gaby.

"While we were still in Paris, you had told Cunnan and I that the man was not to be trusted. Why is it that others do not follow your advice?" she questioned.

"The Emperor's advisors are convinced, falsely in my view, that a war would weaken Prussia's influence in European politics, once and for all. An arrogant and idiotic position, I am quite certain. The Pope's incitement of the French Catholics is now secondary, Gaby. When the treaty with the Italian Monarch is ratified, His temporal power will be minimal in the new political arena." She had not replied. Philippe thought otherwise.

"The French Republican spirit has caused many conflicts for the Empire. Some believe that a war might reunite all parties under one flag. Religion has taken a back seat. Like it or not, the Papal States have united under Victor Emmanuel II with the blessing of Garibaldi. The rich central city of Rome will align with the Italian State sooner rather than later." Jean-Louis stated.

Time is no longer of the essence, Gaby concurred silently. Jean-Louis has given the curia sufficient time to ponder the problems—to understand and appreciate what they would have to give away and what they would receive in the negotiations.

The Vatican and the Lateran palaces would be given to the Pope. But Rome would fall to the Italian Monarch, if the French troops were removed and sent to the front to fight the Prussians. Dear God, she prayed that her husband's analysis was false! He'd be taken away from her again.

As they were about to enter the salons of the French delegation, a butler handed him an official note.

He let her go for a minute.

"Have something sent up to the room!" he ordered curtly.

Angry at being treated so impertinently, she replied just as sharply.

"I hate it when your talk to me in such a flippant tone. I'm quite certain we can discuss our misunderstanding like two reasonable adults. Your problem . . ."

He gripped her forearm so hard, she thought it would break. Her ashen face must have indicated that she was about to faint. He quickly let her go. "I'm sorry," he murmured as he caressed the area. A pretty pink blush returned to her face. She tore free of him and bolted down the corridor. He watched for an instant, and then turned on his heel to return to the conference room.

She entered the room, had a bite to eat with the delegation and took refuge in her office. Instead of picking up the documents she had been working on, she pulled out her music books. She'd begun to work her voice while traveling to Rome. Why not? She hated translations and the hours spent commiserating in this room. Staying close to Jean-Louis was really the only reason why she was involved. She stopped a secretary and asked him to recopy the document. Her music books in hand, she returned to the Conference room. As she prepared to re-enter, she caught a glimpse of Jean-Louis. His glance was as inflexible as when he had left her in the corridor minutes earlier. He had not de-charged! On the contrary, he appeared angrier. What had happened to the man she loved? She no longer recognized him.

Back from a midday déjeuner as well, Jacopo did notice her sudden cool demeanor. Openly flirtatious, he'd brought her a cup of hot chocolate and black licorice candy.

This was a most unfortunate gallantry. To the son of a French aristocrat, no matter how liberal his ideas might have been, *la tasse au chocolat* was in the court of Louis the XIV, a gracious way to suggest to the King's duchesses, countesses and favorites to expect the favors of the Monarch on that particular evening.

Jean-Louis did not miss the connection. She needed to return quickly to the salons. She regained the French rooms, waiting for him in the presence of other negotiators, generals and secretaries who called cabinet meetings at regular intervals.

They paid no real attention to her. She was part of the décor! She could not help thinking that her presence in these decorated halls was unusual. Most of these powerful men did not notice her feminine nature. They treated her like an equal with great respect—quite certainly because Jean-Louis demanded it. Whatever he willed, he received.

Brilliant, forceful, and brave, Jean-Louis was a force of nature. Nothing disarmed him—except perhaps his wife! She was his weakness. She must have had a slight grin on her face as she reminisced. Suddenly, his impressive stature and presence forced her to turn toward the double doors where he stood. It was about two in the afternoon. All in the room stopped their routine, expecting orders and changes in the documents. No such things occur. Momentarily, the Duke scanned the room and focused on his wife.

"Meetings are over for the day," he announced without any further explanations. "Back here tomorrow morning at eight o'clock. Meanwhile, if there are any changes—no matter how insignificant—I want to stay informed. Send notification immediately. Members of my immediate circle will reach me."

Immediately, Gaby dreamed that he'd realized how bored she'd been. He was taking her somewhere fun. They would do something special just the two of them. Perhaps an opera? The season was coming to a close. She would apologize. After all, she would have been furious if he had chosen to go out to lunch with another woman. Although . . . she'd invited him. Oh well, she would assuage his jealous nature. She smiled grandly.

He glanced back and nodded to the door with authority.

"I'm ready." She elegantly stood and walked toward her husband. As he moved sideways to let her pass, she felt his icy gaze. This ordeal was going to be more difficult than anticipated. They walked silently out of the palace.

"I'm so very pleased you took the afternoon off just to be with me," she graciously spoke.

He did not acknowledge her statement. He kept on marching.

"What have I done that is so distasteful? You appear angry. Are you dissatisfied with the way the negotiations are playing?"

"No," he retorted without further explanation.

She kept pace with him. He'd come around.

"What a magnificent city. There are challenges, loves, romantic intrigues, a very charged social life, indeed, I hope we will be able to return in more favorable times. I'm utterly happy when we are just the two of us. It reminds me of Paris." She rambled on, as he kept silent. "Do you recall our nightly sorties when we had no social obligations, just strolling the cays at night, hand in hand?" She slid her hand into his. "Do you remember what fun we shared?"

He stared down at her, clearly touched. She reached for his upper arm and pressed it to her cheek. The icy glare softened. She did not wait for an answer. Her husband had not been the most joyous individual to live with recently. A tremendous pressure had been placed on him, this past year and a half, both in France and Italy. How fortunate he was to have had her with him, she was about to speak aloud. Instead, she modified the statement.

"We are so lucky to have each other. With all this beauty around you and me . . . my world is complete. I know you feel it, too." She concluded confidently.

"You think so, Gaby?" he sliced back. Shocked at his response, she nonetheless did not miss a beat. "I know so, Jean-Louis. I'm your world, as well."

A faint smile cracked his lips.

She knew she possessed a special gift that forced him to face his feelings. "Yes," she concluded with a sideways leer. They took a carriage to the pier.

"Where are we going?" she questioned as the carriage stopped by one of the barges. She noticed the Tempête moored in the bay. Jean-Louis did not answer. Instead, he waved the fisherman to him. Once more the white barge lined on its concave flanks with a double red and green painted ribbon came closer to the pier. Jean-Louis picked her up and lifted her into the ferry. They changed boats on another pier where a French navy vessel was tied up. The Captain met Jean-Louis halfway. They spoke for a few moments, and Jean-Louis returned. She observed her husband as he scanned the horizon. Had he received disappointing news? Strange that he would not share his thoughts.

Another boat with a fisherman at the wheel tied up close to the fleet landing. No words were spoken. He seemed to know where to take the couple. Now heading toward the Tempête,

Jean-Louis edginess amplified. Anxious, she moved her body closer to his. She knew not to ask questions.

"The Tempête? I love it at sea. I'm happy we have this time together. Do you recall the fateful days during the crossing?" She placed her gloved hand on his thigh. No reaction to her affectionate gesture. Her head inclined to his chest gently. She lifted her eyes to his face. Deep in thought, he stared at the horizon. Intent on altering his disposition, she reached out and caressed his cheek as she gently forced his chin downward to meet her gaze. What she saw, she refused to acknowledge. She let go of him but kept her head pressed to his heart.

The barge hugged the ship. Jean-Louis stood up. Up the gangplank, he helped his wife.

At the sight of the Captain everyone came to attention. Surprisingly, shouts and insults traveled from the bow of the ship. The first officer tilted and nodded his head toward the cacophony. In one swift motion, Jean-Louis flung his dark frock on the deck; he loosened and tossed his formal white foulard on the rescue barge, with nimble fingers he unbuttoned the top four buttons of his shirt and removed the large cummerbund around his waist. He gave a missive to the first officer and checked his gun at his waist. "Follow me," he ordered. No one paid much attention to her. She chased behind, too.

On the deck of the Tempête, a man was being held down . . . two others or perhaps more, she could not see clearly, were tied to one of the masts. Jean-Louis turned to her.

"Return to the cabin, Gaby." The tone was authoritative and harsh. It did not allow for any questioning. She began to pivot to obey his command, but quickly stopped, frozen in place. The cutting swish of the lash followed by a man's painful shrieks immobilized her. A man hurled insults in Italian

. . . once more, the crack of the whip landing on flaccid flesh screeched. Unfolding events kept her on the ladder. She placed one hand on the bulkhead and one hand on the overhead for balance. Her husband walked towards the first lieutenant of the ship, and grabbed the pistol handed to him. A sailor handed him a lash.

Mesmerized she did not budge. Jean-Louis strode toward the man who still churned out insults. He pushed a sailor out of the way, averted a foot meant to trip him by one of the men who was restrained. He lassoed and sliced the lash across the face and chest of the tripper. The man buckled down onto the deck. Simultaneously a shot was fired. Gaby's gaze went from the gun held by her husband, still spewing smoke, to the falling body of the man who had been shot. Out of nowhere, a man rushed to the scene brandishing a shiny dagger, his arm ready to ram the knife into her husband's back. As if he had eyes in the back of his head, Jean-Louis pivoted on one foot, his full torso twisted to the side, in a flash another body tumbled onto the planks. The intricately carved silver dagger slid across the bloody deck. Silence reigned.

Jean-Louis had shot two men dead without any explanations. Shocked at the sight of her husband reaching for his gun and shooting a man held down by two mariners, Gaby's stunned glance traveled from Jean-Louis to the lifeless body that lay dead on deck. Then, she lowered her gaze to the still body, whose blood still gushed out of the stomach forming a pool of blood that stained the rolled up anchor chain. "If anyone would like to join these vermins—blink an eye. I would love the opportunity to do away with all of you cowards!" Jean-Louis's ominous voice exclaimed. There was complete silence and very little movement from the invading impostors. She knew of Jean-Louis's exploits in Asia, Mexico and the Civil War, but this warring man . . . was a total stranger!

Cunnan was the first to walk to the dead man.

"Should we return the bodies back to the authorities?" he asked Jean-Louis.

"No, have you searched the ship?"

"Yes, we have." Cunnan responded. "These guys walked on board with the night watch and galley workers. So close to the French fleet. Our sailors have been working night and day. I think our security slacked off when we sailed into Civitavecchia."

Jean-Louis nodded.

"The prisoners will be kept in the brigs. We will keep our crew as is. No new mariners on this ship for now. We'll make do until we reach Toulon. Until then, no one leaves the ship until further notice. They should have known better."

A cloud lifted for Gaby. Their voyage back to France was imminent.

"No one is to leave the ship," she heard her husband's thundering command, "until I get to the bottom of this new attack." He approached Cunnan, taking his Commanding Officer aside. "I think this latest incident might be related to Gaby's kidnapping," he told Cunnan. "The bastards know damn well how to get to me. They're trying to influence the last steps of the negotiations. I am certain that they are aware of the new development between France and Prussia."

Cunnan nodded.

"What are they thinking, going against their Monarch? For what? The return of the status quo *sans* the Pontiff? Rich landowners with a Republican heart, enjoying the finest while the populace starves under the title of a Republic? Garibaldi was correct in ceding the reigns to Victor Emmanuel. Ten years make a difference. They'll fail. One thing is certain; they want us out of Italy. They might get their wish sooner rather than later. Keep the ship ready to sail at a moment's notice. I just spoke to Captain Guiderbeau. He will cover us. We might be forced to leave before this ordeal is over. The Pope is not budging. I want Gaby's safety ensured above all else. Let's try to find out the identity of the insurgents. Have you had time to question any of them? How many of them were there? Do we have any sympathizers on the ship? How about the galley workers that came on board? Question the new sailors we picked up in Venice. Keep them on the vessell! I'll return for the questioning later. Have the ship searched and forbid anyone to return to shore. We will work harder upon our return, but it will be safer. We will pick up a few extra sailors in Toulon. Right now, I want everyone identified and questioned. Prepare a summary."

"Do you really believe that it is the same group that tried to capture Gaby?" the old seaman asked.

"I don't know, Cunnan. There are two or three staunch groups that were against the reunification under Emmanuel. How can we know for certain? But they will fight anything French. We will just have to trudge forward with great care and caution."

"Very well, Jean-Louis," Cunnan responded as he walked back to the main deck where the officers and sailors awaited his orders.

The Captain turned around to march back to his cabin. He faced his wife. Gaby had not moved a millimeter since the killing. Paralyzed, she was glued to the last rungs of the ladder.

Furious at first by her disobedience, he quickly noticed terror in her communicative eyes. She'd witnessed the whole episode. "Go to the cabin and wait for me, Gaby," he instructed calmly.

Although his voice was serene, the authority in its tone did not warrant a question. Shocked and horrified, she turned and walked down the two steps that led down to their cabin, situated close to the bridge. The man who'd spoken these words was a man she did not know.

The pleasant smell of their scent surrounded her as she stepped in the dark cabin. How many days she had spent at sea with him? She longed for the day when they walked back onto it together . . . sailing toward France for good.

What is happening to me? She questioned her confused mind. I'm a woman with two heads, rattled by a mountain of emotions that swing me from total bliss to the depths of fear and despair. The horror of the killing confronted her.

Her thoughts returned to her ordeal—that fateful day when she had been forced onto a dark closet until Jean-Louis, Cunnan and the force had executed her assailants. In this emotion-drenched moment, she'd emptied her gun into the fiend's heart and genitals. Revenge and contentment had swathed her entire being.

Thank God that's all they had done to her—keeping her captive. The man had torn her clothing from her body in front of the security forces and her husband. While she stood stark naked in front of a male crowd, the Commandante had fondled the most sacred places of a woman's body.

She had not lost her wits then. Good heavens, no! She'd pushed backward suddenly against her captor's body. A second of inattention had cost him his life. The feel of Jean-Louis's arms around her to this day calmed any fearful situation. It was still the reason why she wanted to stay nearby. She would unravel in his powerful arms—in the security she longed for.

The door of the cabin opened. Jean-Louis backed in, still in conversation with one of the officers. Something told her to stay motionless.

He strode closer to her—the gun still in his hand.

After the episode this afternoon, his anger had subsided. The fear for her safety had erased the last remnants of jealousy.

But then again, it had returned full blown, when he'd realized that once again his directives had been overlooked.

"Why didn't you obey?" he questioned.

She nearly told him to tone down his attitude. But . . . she quickly changed her mind. "I don't know Jean-Louis. I was mesmerized, paralyzed by the events. I could not move forward or backwards."

The pistol still in his hand frightened her. He walked past her and asked if she remembered the rules on the ship.

"Yes," she whispered as his voice trailed off her neck.

"Then why didn't you get down below when I told you?"

"I'm sorry, I heard the shot, I was frightened, and I froze. I did not know if it was directed at you." She quickly strode to the door that led to the deck. He caught up with her and clasped her arm as he kicked the door closed with his booted foot. She hated him with a passion when he shouted. Furthermore, the Venetian ambiance had changed him. He was not the same man she'd known in Paris. Perhaps that was the way he handled himself outside of France. After all she had never met him when he was fighting in the United States. The proof was that, although admired and sought after by the opposite sex, no one liked him much, except Cunnan, and herself, and Madame Perideot, his governess.

She knew that a major altercation would ensue if he let his fury take over his rational temper. This afternoon he rendered himself jealous of Jacopo—and now this new development on his ship. Traitors had infiltrated the crew. God only knew what would have occurred if they had not been thwarted.

Unfortunately, she was in no position to let him rage and vent. The incident up above had not touched a chord. He'd responded with a militaristic mind. But she remained the object of his madness.

She watched him walk over to the side bar. He poured a hefty shot of whiskey.

The calm before the storm, she pondered. She walked closer to the door again, some help that would be. They were in the middle of the Mediterranean Sea!

"Come here, Gaby," he asked much more calmly.

"No, you frighten me when you're angry," she whispered.

That last statement did not appear to calm him.

"Look, Jean-Louis, I'm sorry. I was mesmerized by the turn of events, immobile. I could not move, darling. I am sorry." Her eyes then settled on the gun. "I am truly sorry, darling," she repeated in her most repentant tone of voice as she watched him return from the side bar with the gun still in his hand.

"Jean-Louis, please put the gun down. You are angry with me and accidents do happen, please," she shouted, voice filled with terror.

Surprised by her horrified expression and panic stricken intonation, he carefully placed the gun on his desk.

"Gaby, you couldn't think I would do you harm?" he asked in disbelief.

She had watched while he'd killed a terrorist at point blank, and now she thought that he would turn it on her. The ordeal was too sordid to even give it credence.

To clear the air, he returned to the reason why she had angered him.

"Should I be angry with you, Gaby?" He thought back to the incident earlier that day and of her flirtatious behavior with Jacopo.

Gaby did not answer. Instead, she took the gun and placed it in a drawer.

"Well, should I?" he persisted.

"No, of course not, but I could not obey anything, not even for my own survival!"

The little brat, he fumed. She had forgotten her laughter, her intolerant statement, "we are going out to lunch . . . we will return promptly" while he worked. Instead of lending support, she was going to have fun with a fellow who liked himself when he was still single had a reputation of being a dreadful rake. His anger recovered some of its momentum.

"Come here!" He walked toward the door and before she could recover, he gathered her shoulders and pressed her to him.

"Jean-Louis, don't please, let's talk."

Fear in her voice made him pause. He gazed down at her. She seized the moment. Ever so gently, she stroked her hand alongside his waist. She joined her fingers at the base of his back. For a second he waivered, and then he crushed her against his chest.

"I love it, Jean-Louis, when you respond to my touch." She softly kissed his bloodied starched shirt.

Now completely overtaken by her sensuality, Jean-Louis-Pierre de Pleyssis let his wife control the moment. She took him in her sensibilities by lifting his shirt and stroking the middle of his back. Huge knots of tension twisted the thick muscles—hard rocks under a prodding drill. In this case, under her nurturing hands, she raised the lower edges of his shirt out of his pants and bent down to kiss his stomach, his waist . . . she caressed his backside.

"Jean-Louis," she whispered, "love me, darling, I love you, I love your body, I love everything about you." She soothed him sweetly.

Desire surged into his body. She felt it. His buttocks in her soft and warm hands, she slowly rolled his pants down his long muscular thighs. Her lips lingered on his stomach. Striking out of his pants, his engorged manhood searched for her body. She lowered her head and pressed her lips to it. Filled with passion, he swiftly, unfastened the leather belt around her waist and flung her skirt, petty coat and white lace underwear across the cabin. He slid his hand beneath the silk blouse, the tiny pearl buttons popped, her nude body lay willingly open to his needs. She rubbed her naked breasts against the inside of his thighs. Filled with tension and desire, she felt his hands press her head deep in his body while he caressed her long, graceful neck; a sudden spasm cramped his body. Brutishly, he pulled her hair back and forced her face away from his body. In one swift motion, he lifted her off the floor, his mouth opened over hers in a violently sensual kiss. He cleared away maps, documents, and pens from his desk and he laid her down on the hard surface. Her arms held above her head with one of his hand, he tore the remnant of her clothes and placed his lips on her breasts. He pulled hard on the engorged rounded buds that arced to him. She sensed the sweetness of passion as his gigantic body fell on her small stature. He pushed her thighs open and thrust into her sweet feminine womb. She held on to him—tight, shaken, and flushed.

Up on deck, Cunnan had sent one of his mariners down to the Captain's cabin. He needed an answer to his request— namely what to do with the two dead bodies that lay lifeless on the deck? In actuality, he was intent on disturbing Jean-Louis. He had not liked the anger in his face. Poor Gaby did not need to always assuage his anger.

"Well, Sir," began the embarrassed mariner, confused, whether he should disclose what he had seen.

"Get back down below and get an answer immediately," came the curt command from Cunnan.

"Well, Sir, impossible, Sir. The Captain is screwing his wife—on his desk, Sir," he replied disgruntled. Everyone close by broke into a roaring laughter. Ridiculed, the sailor stuttered and even Cunnan, who had gotten quite impatient with the fellow not following orders, smiled.

"Well, sailor, stand by. When conversation starts up again, knock and follow up on my order."

"Yes, Sir." He saluted and returned to his duty. The red-faced sailor was terrified. What could he do but follow orders? He now hoped that his comments would not get back to the Captain. The man had no compassion. What he had seen from his vintage point, perched up above at the very top of the mast, had not reassured him. The sailor had descended the ladder at the most inopportune moment.

He had seen the Captain walk on deck, kill a man who'd appeared to be calm, and then turned around as if he had eyes behind his back and he had killed dead another fellow who had gone for his boot. The episode had happened so quickly, he did not know if the sailors were part of the crew or impostors. Why had he climbed down at such an inauspicious moment? Let the deck guys be the meddlers, he did not want to be involved with the Captain—or his wife. The Captain was not a very nice chap! After what he had seen on deck and in the bedroom, he was now sure that the man was evil. Seriously, he murmured out loud, taking his wife on his desk? The bed was positioned a few meters away. While the mariner pondered his future life after the incident, the Captain walked out of his State Room. Should he relay the message or remain quiet? The decision was not his to make. The captain passed right by him.

"Get back to your post!" he shouted.

The sailor nodded. "Yes, Sir." He scampered up the ladder and followed the order to the letter. He liked it up there on top of the sail.

Gaby fell asleep. Jean-Louis walked away from the bridge on his way to interrogate the remaining prisoners.

Later the pretty soprano woke. She rolled, and reminisced the location of the act. In the large bed, she had been carried. She lifted her head and searched for Jean-Louis. Gone again. She remained under the cozy eiderdown a while longer as she recollected the exciting hours she had had in that very bed. It was almost five before Jean-Louis returned.

"*Eh bien, paresseuse*, are you ready to return to the Villa?"

"No, let's leave, let's return to France, Jean-Louis—now. I miss it so. All these intrigues are too devastating to me, darling. I'm an artist, remember, not *une aventurière!*"

He smiled, stepped closer, and brushed his knuckles along the side of her cheek.

"Our return is imminent, Gaby. You are right, ma Chérie. It is a crazy world. I'm looking forward to our life in Paris as well." He sat on the bed. "You are une *femme formidable*, Gaby. You have handled yourself admirably well, in the worst possible of situations. I'm sorry I have placed your life in such a turmoil." He spoke plainly and candidly as he caressed the long fingers peeping out from under the duvet.

"You have." A half smile graced her sensual lips. "I would not have had it any other way, you know that," she replied as honestly.

"One of our men was killed. First Lieutenant Arnaud—a fine officer, Gaby," he said dryly. "Traitors infiltrated the Tempête."

He helped her out of bed and kissed her lips.

Chapter 23

Gaby walked out of the cabin shortly after Jean-Louis.

Already seated in the small yellow barge, Jean-Louis gazed at Gaby as she descended the ladder. He explored every curve of her delightful body, recalling the day on which she'd disembarked from his ship in Villefranche. Still clothed in an oversize mariner's outfit, she'd caught his glance and winked. The impertinent brat, he recalled with an indulgent smile. So much had passed since that faithful day. His love for her had grown encompassing. He could not imagine life without her.

As she reached the bottom of the railing and stepped onto the concave bottom of the boat, Jean-Louis gripped the sides of the barge and rocked the craft from side to side. She lost her balance. Terror registered in her facial expression as the certainty of a plunge in the Roman murky water while clad in a weighty grey suit, flashed across her mind. Thwarting disaster, Jean-Louis pulled her back to safety, and encircled her body with his arms. Incensed, she turned to glare at him. Faced with his familiar sheepish, sensuous, amused grin, something she rarely enjoyed these days, she smiled and kissed his lips.

"Yesterday morning, Signora Cassandra brought me the most beautiful leather belt—hand made with myriad colors of leather straps woven in and out of the strap. Tonight you will be the first one to experience its feel, Chéri!"

"Hmmm, I shall look forward to that!"

She reclined fully in his arms. She jerked her gaze toward the upper deck as they turned back toward land. Cunnan smiled. A grandfatherly expression flashed on his wind-battered face. She loved him dearly and trusted him with all her soul. When she felt lonely, he always stood by her and kept her reassured, hopeful and entertained. He treated her as the daughter he never had. Going so far as to assuage the impact of Jean-Louis's anger, when he ran out of patience with her antics. Cunnan always forgave her youthful carelessness.

In comparison, all the mariners hated Jean-Louis. He never tried to understand humanity and its many faults, although he was fair and admired by others. Early on, he had taught himself to be as perfect as he could be and he expected perfection from others. If they fell short, they suffered his wrath.

Nestled in his arms, she enjoyed the warmth of his breath on her neck, remembering his demanding kisses. She wanted to be nowhere else in the entire universe but here in his arms, on this dingy little barge that would deliver them back to the villa.

As usual the French delegation waited on the embankment.

Of course never a lost moment, she thought. Wasn't there a place in Rome where they could get lost for a day or two? Nevertheless, they soon were back on land. Jean-Louis spoke to his security and quickly returned and clasped her hand. "Let's get a quick meal at the Cercle," he said as he mentioned a club where many French men and women socialized while in Rome.

The city was not the safest. Poverty, intrigues, debauchery filled the city streets, especially at dusk. Dark-caped figures jumped out from the covered path that lined the Tiber. One needed to walk down the streets, in an alert state or accept disaster as the consequence of inattention. George Sand and Alfred Musset, the prolific French writers and ardent lovers, had lived in Venice and in Rome. Both searched for answers to their troubled lives—he as an opium addict, her as his dedicated lover—dear Musset, as she liked to call him, had almost overdosed. She had written about the joyous merriment of the cities and of her extraordinary love for Alfred, who'd wasted his genius on alcohol, women and drugs.

Gaby walked carefully, aware of the people and movement about her. Her gun kept in her right boot or reticule was never far from her thoughts. She'd learned how to visualize an attack and how to respond to the visualization. She remained aware and confident. Jean-Louis shot her a look of admiration. He squeezed her hand, as he placed it on his thigh while he continued to walk the streets. He wanted to talk.

"Darling, you appear to have accomplished everything that you have come here to accomplish. Why do you look so morose?" she questioned.

"I can't wait to leave this city, Gaby. I long to be with you in Paris and to forget about this damn conflict! I have second thoughts about nationalism. Mostly about the way, I presume, it will be handled for the next generation—at the very least. There is a lack of understanding on both sides of the aisle. I assumed that the poor could be dispensed of while the wealthy and powerful managed the economy and the future to their liking and advantages. Revolutions have plagued the century. It should be a reminder for those who trample on the lowest echelons of humanity. And perhaps that is what is needed now to forge a better, freer future for the next generation. But financial gains acquired by some new members of an emerging class are rarely passed on to redress the needs of the proletariat. France should have stayed out of Italy's conflicts. Yes, a member of the Hohenzollern on the Spanish throne was frightening. But I doubt that protecting the diminutive last vestiges of Pope Pius IX's domain was necessarily a clever diplomatic shift for France. We should, instead, have strengthened our armies for a sure to develop conflict with the Prussians."

"Why Jean-Louis? It appears to me that the voters within the Wall will vote for inclusion to the Italian Kingdom. The people will be the better for it and, frankly, the Church as well. All things considered, they have no choice. You are only here to assuage the parties and to establish some diplomatic relations with Victor Emmanuel II. Church and State should be separated," she said. "This is how it works in my country, Jean-Louis. I trust that the United States of America will be the next force to be reckoned with. Our Constitution demands that our entire citizenry have a say in governing."

He smirked. Slavery had been abolished in the United States a little over five years ago. How soon does one forget!

"The will of the common man must be taken into consideration," she continued well aware of his thoughts. "The orders of an all-powerful Church or of an autocratic King are not mentioned in the document! Our government is made up of simple people who believe that their lives are as notorious and blessed as any aristocrat or clergyman. A government that is made up by the common man for the well being of the common man!"

"I hope that you are right, darling," he answered tiredly.

"You accomplish the right things, Jean-Louis—not by war but through diplomacy." I hope that the Emperor will appreciate your dedication—and mine!"

He smiled at her assertiveness. In reality, Gaby had given a lot—her life as an artist and, furthermore, the kidnapping that evoked in her fears that she had long forgotten. He intended to make it up to her tenfold.

"Surely, Jean-Louis, it is impossible to accomplish a lot toward modernization when everyone here in Europe has their own narrow interests in mind—not at this stage, I think not. Small gains last, however, and you've achieved your goals. You did it well and ..."

"I really do not want to do it, Gaby, but I also know that upon our return to France, I will be faced with much greater dilemmas. I'm not sure that I want to sacrifice five or ten years of our lives together to politics. I do not know that you would allow it, Gaby." He stopped, sat on a little marble bench, and pulled her down to sit beside him. He kissed her jaw playfully.

She kissed him back with tenderness, understanding his frustrations but not yet willing to accept a life in the political world of Paris. She evaded an answer and continued to speak about the American concept he had proposed.

"We have had our conflicts in the not-too distant past. Our civil war was devastating, but we surmounted our divisive ideas, although not every issue has been dealt with. I don't believe the South will forgive the North and their invading military forces bent on changing our ways. Not in our lifetimes, that is for certain, but I believe that our fears and mistrust of one another will be lessened and assuaged. Class is also a factor in the South not solely amongst white and the freedmen, but against our Southern aristocracy, if you will. My point is that the world is not perfect. We are all humans trying our best to achieve and lead happy and fruitful lives. Some individuals like you do have a larger responsibility than others. You were given more by reason of your birth and intellect, and more is expected of you. At the very least, strength of character and stature. But I feel that it is your guilt for everything given to you, more than all your gifts, which drives you to take on these challenges. You could be as happy being with me, experiencing natural challenges like you and me discovering the great trail that Lewis and Clark have traveled!"

He looked down at her and laughed heartily. "What a presumptuous Southern Belle I've married! Continue Gaby, it sounds better and better by the minute."

"I know that you are doing the right thing, that we are doing right by the people of our world, darling. Questioning our lives and our motives is good, Jean-Louis, but too much of it will paralyze us. Your compatriots admire you. They see in you a source of hope and truth and loyalty. Through you they see a man who can help them achieve their dreams—a man who firmly believes in the advancement of all people through good peaceful leadership and negotiations with other nations. Although you fought against the South, your motives were admirable." A half smile eased her sexy pout. "You are a man of great integrity and vision. You can't vacillate now!"

"Amen, my Chérie." He laughed, clasped her shoulders and drew her close to him. "My wife, my best advocate, another smart decision on my part. I chose the right woman."

She wriggled in the arms that now encircled her waist, disbelief in her expressive eyes.

"I'm no advocate of anyone, Monsieur," she retorted, "I'm the person that you adore, the only one who has the power and the will to manipulate you and assuage your many needs. Do not forget it, partner! In effect, I was looking for an uplifting compliment Captain. Instead, I hear the same old serenade again." She started to sing. "It's all about Jean-Louis-Pierre de Pleyssis. Another great achievement . . . la la la la la."

He kissed her mouth shut.

"I can't envision my life without you, Gaby. You are my better half, Madame. Is that sufficient?"

Before she could answer him, a pleasant voice made them turn toward the nearby bridge.

"Jean Louis, Gabriella, what a formidable surprise. Hello dear friends!" Momentarily an expensive carriage stopped in front of them. Two elegantly clad women stood, one of them started talking to Jean-Louis.

"Chéri, I heard you were in Rome. Bonjour, Gabriella. What a pleasure!" she exclaimed looking coyly at Jean-Louis.

Gaby knew one of them well. She wished she didn't. Fernande Morat had been one of Jean-Louis' liaisons just before his departure for the United States. The gossips had been amazed. *Soi-disant*, they had been desperately in love. Nevertheless, Jean-Louis had left her two weeks before his departure. England had been her immediate destination to avoid the shame. She'd told friends that Paris was too painful. Every corner of every street reminded her of her forever love!

Gaby had met Fernande, at a *soirée* in Paris, and had not been impressed. Here again, her jealousy toward all of her husband's past lovers blinded her to graces any woman might possess. Although very much aware that her husband had been a despicable rake before their encounter, these constant meetings in the French capital always evoked anxiety. Italy had been wonderful on that account.

Usually a flute of champagne would help to lessen her jealousy. Jean-Louis was very gallant. He avoided most encounters that would place her in such a situation. None of these relations meant anything to him now—and not much then either. At times of insecurity, in the face of gossip, Gaby would remind herself that he had chosen her. He'd even offered to share his townhouse prior to their wedding. Had he not been disappointed when she had told him that she would not move in with him in Paris? Sometimes all the reassuring was not enough. She would ask him about the relationships, which he passed off with the comment: "All were passing fancies, Chérie."

"But could one of those past fancies return to tantalize you, Jean-Louis?" she would ask.

"No, Gaby, you are my world. Furthermore, stop wasting your time. Get a hold of your fantasies." That was usually sufficient to satisfy her, but Fernande caused a pinch in the pit of her stomach every time she saw her or heard her name. Now the lovely lady was in Rome. She knew that Jean-Louis and Fernande had visited Venice together years ago. Like herself Fernande had dabbled in opera, but she was nothing exceptional—chorus material. Nothing to compare with the gift that she had been blessed with. Nevertheless Gaby felt innerved by her presence in the Eternal City.

Jean-Louis stopped and placed his foot on the step of the carriage, Fernande came closer and spoke to him intimately.

"What are Your Graces doing in this enchanting and mysterious city?" he asked.

"Paris is boring and atrociously hot this time of the year. I needed change." Fernande promptly turned to Gaby. "*Le tout Paris* know about the unfortunate misfortune you were dealt, I can now see it in your face, ma chère. You are pale and much too thin. Need to *renflouer*, my chère. It is so hard to keep a husband these days—especially a man like Jean-Louis-Pierre, so demanding in all of the feminine graces." She looked coyly at him and winked. Jean-Louis didn't seem to notice. Fernande continued, "as for myself, it has been a very sad life. Le Baron died four weeks ago. What an awful time he had with his sick heart. He was paralyzed. You can imagine my grief and my dedication to his last needs. It was simply terrible, Jean-Louis-Pierre, I just need to be gay now." She turned to her friend. "You remember Catherine, love, she will help to lighten my sorrowful burden."

Jean-Louis nodded; it was impossible to place a word in edgewise with this woman. She looked as sorrowful as a freshly released prisoner *du Bagne*. Her whole demeanor spelled, I'm free and available!

She climbed down from the carriage, tall and shapely. Jean-Louis smiled at her. Gaby questioned if it was an ironic smile, or was he truly pleased to see her? Although not to be trusted, she had heard that Fernande was witty and charming in company. After the beauty's demeaning tirade, Gaby, who stood next to her, felt unattractive, her usual aplomb gone.

"Jean-Louis-Pierre, are you going to the club?" Fernande questioned, completely ignoring Gaby while she passed her arm in his.

"Please, please, take us there, Chéri. You need to be a member, you know, and we have not met anyone yet to vouch for us. Please vouch for me!" She looked at him with adoring and supplicating eyes as she flashed a magnificent smile. "For old times sake, Chéri."

Ready to kill them both, Gaby's green expressive eyes fired bullets at the attractive blond. Jean-Louis did not notice the anger building in his wife's spirit. Nonetheless, he carefully disentangled himself from his former mistress and reached for Gaby's hand. He noticed the coldness of his wife's skin. She was livid. He pressed her close to him and kissed her hair.

"*Mais oui, certainement* with pleasure, Fernande. We were going there ourselves; we'd love for you to join us. I know a few people who would absolutely adore making your acquaintance." Then he remembered the death of his father's card partner.

"I'm sorry about Henry. Please accept our condolences," he said politely. Certain that Gaby had been reassured, he asked Fernande and Catherine about common friends, the mood in Paris. The conversation continued to be lively as they were taken to a private club within the Cercle. The club was filled with foreigners. The French delegation and Gaby had to suffer all the admirers that a sudden French newcomer elicited. Of course with Jean-Louis around, no one would have dared to flirt with her. She was private property—very private property. No one dare to engage her for any extended period of time. The word was out—polite conversation was allowed. Anything more than that and anyone dared to counteract the Duke's order would suffer great consequences—their position essentially.

Gaby quietly observed the *va et vient*. Clearly, Jean-Louis enjoyed himself immensely. He looked relaxed. Earlier in the afternoon, he'd killed two men, maimed another and now he sat calm and behaved as if nothing had happened. She moved across from him to accommodate one of his aides. Lost in her thoughts, she inadvertently, must have been staring at her husband. He winked at her. She smiled back and then decided to use the powder room. Was she really pale and sickly looking as Fernande had said?

Walking towards the glass doors, she saw Jean-Louis' reflection as he gazed longingly at her. Other men starred approvingly as she passed by. Good, she needed a little reassurance. She walked inside. The Maitre D'hôtel offered champagne and canapés and she accepted both.

The Cercle was situated on a magnificent hill overlooking the city and its many monumental churches with their rich histories. Villas close by also displayed glorious private chapels. The Dukes, rich merchants and the Curia, commissioned some of the greatest artists of their time to decorate the walls of their private sanctuaries.

She paused by the ornate classical architecture balcony and then walked on the small terrace. The view was breathtaking. She wished their time in Venice and Rome had been more romantic. She wondered if Jean-Louis and Fernande had had a real romantic episode while in this historic city? All her plans—her surging career, studying with the maestro in the Teatro Fenice in Venice, here in Rome—now just a memory. Philippe had often offered to introduce her to famous maestros who would have given their right arms to work with her; essentially, she was not quite ready. Her plans had been altered. Jean-Louis had stayed with her on a few occasions when the Maestro had returned to the Palazzo, but she hadn't felt confident enough to stay behind in the residence, no matter how many guards were present. In many ways, it had been a wonderful opportunity to enter his world. She probably was one of the few women who had extracted such power. She loved him so, she thought. He did not care about breaking any rules as long as it served his purpose. She was his most pressing purpose. She felt certain of that. Lost in her dreams of the perfect life, she heard a familiar voice.

"*Ah Bella Stella*! What are you dreaming about, Gabriella, me, I hope?" Jacopo asked in a deep, enticing voice. "I saw your husband down below a while ago, I knew you couldn't be too far away."

"Did he see you?"

"I made sure that he didn't. I wanted to say my goodbyes to you, Gabriella. I am honored to have worked with such an extraordinary lady. I truly understand why your husband keeps you on a pedestal, far away from all these seductive Italian men. I am being amusing, Gabriella, I know that you could easily handle yourself without any supervision. It was my dismay. Nevertheless, I will never forget you. Now that I have met the perfect model for a woman and know that she exists, I will not stop looking until I find one with all of your spectacular charms and intellectual capacities."

"Thank you, Jacopo." A rosy blush flushed her cheeks.

"I presume you will be leaving very soon," he continued, cajoling her.

"I do not know. We are enjoying your beautiful city. Do you know something that I don't?" she astutely questioned.

Smiling back he pressed her to continue.

"I wish you could stay here much longer but I could not help but notice that the Tempête has sailed back in the bay of Civitavecchia. I felt your departure was imminent."

Because of the episode she'd suffered soon after her arrival in Italy, she'd developed a suspicious sense. Consequently, a bit uncomfortable about the questions asked, she retorted happily but assertively.

"I have not heard of any plans about our sudden departure."

He grinned maliciously as she proceeded to turn her back to him. A white veined marble parapet overlooked the Seven Hills. She leaned on it and admired the scenic view.

"Thus, Jacopo," she glanced sideways, flirtatious, "since our return is not on the horizon, I recall your promise long ago, the one about showing me the art works in these exact Gallerias. Will you make good on that offer?"

"Do I need permission from the Captain? I'm afraid that the Cercle is packed with his friends," he retorted.

She smiled at him. God, he was gorgeous. The Count ambled closer. She felt his sensual presence—tall, slim, dark golden skin with green panther-like eyes—a magnificent man. She loved his cologne. It was enchanting.

Unsure of her treacherous body, she quickly pulled away from the enchanting Count and strode to the gallery. Splendid Da Vinci paintings, sculptures from David, every one of these fine art works authentic, and Jacopo was an incredible guide. His knowledge of the paintings, of their masters and of the stories behind each painting was awe-inspiring. She now understood Renoir's passion when he'd traveled to Rome to copy the Great Masters. Oblivious of the time, she listened intently and enjoyed the Count's artistic details immensely. Apparently, the feeling was mutual.

As Jacopo commented on Michelangelo's tumultuous personae, he related to her that while he worked endlessly on the ceiling of the Sistine Chapel, Pope Julius II, who had commissioned the work, had disobeyed the arrogant artist. He'd entered the chapel without his permission. Minutes later a plank had fallen on his head, which had required the pontiff to spend several days in the infirmary of his palazzo. Michelangelo had fled under the cover of night from the Pope's wrath, only to be begged to return to finish his brilliant masterpiece. Gaby giggled as she reached for Jacopo's arm to guide him to the next galleria.

Flirtatious behavior, yes, guilty as charged, but she delighted in the moment. Why not? After all her husband was not paying much attention to her while he conversed gaily with his friends Fernande and Catherine. Lately, all was too serious. She felt like a tiger in a cage, looking for amusing things to see and to hear and to laugh. Oh, yes, to laugh. It felt wonderful. Unfortunately, she had chosen the wrong moment to be so cheerful!

A cavernous voice resonated high and bigger than life in the small galleria. Both jumped. Gaby almost lost her footing.

What she had not noticed beforehand came to light. The room was empty, except for the two of them-now the three of them with Jean-Louis.

"Gabriella, you have been gone for over an hour. I had Fernande check the powder room to make sure you hadn't drown, but now I see that you're enjoying yourself quite nicely with the Count. Good times always come to an end. We are returning to the villa," Jean-Louis said casually containing the fury in his smooth voice.

She flashed a delightful grin.

"Jean-Louis, it's been delightful! Jacopo has shared with me a wealth of information that you may not know. We placed these Grand Masters high up on the podium because of their creative talent, but their earthly lives were fascinating as well. We should spend more time studying the Impressionists when we return to Paris. Now is the time to learn about these great luminaries. I discovered so many amusing anecdotes, today, about many of these *tableaux*. We'll have to return so that I can share all the tidbits with you." She did not want to stop talking until his glance softened. It was not forthcoming. In order to avert another conflict, she walked toward her husband. Politely, she turned back to Jacopo.

"Good bye, Jacopo, and thank you for keeping your promise," she said with a smile not lost on her husband. "Good luck as well in all your endeavors." She waved at him, and hastened to the column her husband leaned against.

She had committed a grave error. A lump swelled in her throat. His eyes cast a glacial stare. She'd averted a huge scene this past afternoon. Could she do it again now? After all, it had been a friendly meeting. The emptiness of the galleries was dismal.

Jean-Louis had been engaged with his former paramour. Why should she feel guilty?

She stood in front of him, smiling. He did not return her smile. She felt vulnerable as she waited for the master to deign to take a decision. She would not give him the time of day. She reached for his hand.

"Shall we go, Jean-Louis?"

He straightened fully and pulled his hand from hers. He took her elbow without a word and directed her towards the club's main entrance. A few people acknowledged the couple, and Fernande hurried towards them.

"Where have you been, Gabriella? I looked for you. You were nowhere around. Did you meet un *petit ami*, ma chère?" she alleged ironically.

Gaby did not let the mean-spirited response pass.

"Unlike you, ma chère Fernande, I believe in the sanctity of marriage," she snapped back with blazing eyes.

"Thank heavens some of us still do," Fernande retorted shameless, as she winked at Jean-Louis. "However, please forgive me for noticing that I'm not the one who pulled *une petite escapade*, Gabriella."

Jean-Louis did not seem to notice or hear the women. He kept walking, clearing the path with his determined stride. He marched on outside. He did not flag his own carriage. He needed time to blow off some steam from his incensed spirit.

Gaby wished that she were not the focus of that anger! For the second time that day, she had to face his fury. This time there was no sensual smile or a warm embrace encircling her body. Instead, he let her pass in front to step into the carriage and then he sat down next to her. She did not dare move nor glance in his direction. She quietly settled in.

Furtive glances in his direction revealed that he was not unwinding. If anything, he appeared angrier. She tried to touch the hand that rested on the squabs behind her.

"Don't," came the curt reply.

Oh well, maybe she could distract him once they reached the villa. Small chance!

As they almost reach their final destination, Jean-Louis called to the coachmen to halt the carriage. He practically jumped out of the carriage without waiting for the footman. He held out his hand, pulled her forth, and lifted her out onto the graveled path. To reach the grand entrance doors, they'd have to walk through long covered paths decorated by graceful, highly ornate arches and a magnificent circa 1600's carved fountain remindful of the mythological roman gods. As they climbed, splendidly manicured gardens faced the last golden gilded gates of the palace. The keepers at the gate looked on, surprised to see the couple strolling. Actually they had been in Rome for a couple months and many had never seen them up close.

They walked briskly through the garden.

"We should come down here more often. I wish I wasn't so frightened all the time. I feel that I have missed the beauty of these beautiful grounds we were so graciously granted."

"You do not seem to have missed an opportunity to flirt and to conduct yourself like a loose woman, even in the most closed circles."

Flabbergasted, she stopped, faced him and raised her hand to strike him. He averted the slap and grabbed her wrist. He kept right on walking, not letting go of her hand.

"How dare you?" She gesticulated to free herself. "Stop, it's painful, I can't keep up with you." He released her hand and entered the palace.

The servants and the butlers waited. Some looked outside—no carriage.

"Upstairs, Gaby," he said in a non-negotiating tone.

"No, later. I'm famished. I need a little something to eat. I'm sure what you have to tell me can wait."

Very much aware that he was intent to force her upstairs and talk endlessly, she bolted the other way toward the dining room, placing herself out of his reach on the other side of the table.

"Gaby, do not push me, it really is not wise to aggravate this situation."

"What is there to aggravate? Your spiteful insults are going to hurt my feelings. I have no doubt. I do not deserve it. At the minimum, let me have a full stomach to regain some strength before I am forced to face my executioner."

She had touched a special chord.

"Sit down," she continued, "have a brandy and a full cigar." She tried humor. "Visualize all the mean things you intend to say and think of how sad . . ."

"Shut up! Eat and be done with it!" Actually, he did just as she had ordered. He walked to the side bar, fixed himself a brandy and walked back to the fireplace. In his great chair he sat and turned to the side table with the golden cigar case. He spent a few minutes choosing his favorite Romeo y Julieta. Finally he lit it.

While she proceeded to gorge herself, he glared at her. She swallowed as slowly as she could possibly could.

"Well, Madame, are you ready to talk now?" he questioned without meanness in his voice. His anger dissipated.

"Yes, certainly, I'll talk all you want . . . down here," she responded as sweetly as she could. "A bit of champagne and a tart, and I'll be fresh and sound," she smiled coyly.

"Gaby that's enough." He stood. "There are important issues that I want you to be aware of." He rounded the table.

Unwilling to listen to his tirade, she made a dash for the balcony and down the wide marble steps to the gardens. She ran aimlessly amongst the man-made lakes and intricately pruned trees.

He didn't follow her into the garden. Damn, instead of assuaging the situation, she had just aggravated it a thousand fold by this absurd impulse! Sometimes, a small lack of judgment could throw a game!

Here was the prowess of great leaders. Regardless of the exactitude of a well thought strategy, knowing when to hold back and when to act, when to bank on one's intuitions and when to rely on logic, was key to a successful strategy. She had multiplied her troubles when he could have been negotiated with and enticed to listen to her. Her only chance—he would keep on drinking. He had drunk quite a bit at the club already. Perhaps he'd continued to imbibe while waiting for her.

Dusk set in and she knew that her fear of the dark would bring her back to the house. He knew it too. She waited. An hour and a half, she wandered in the gardens, as she discovered a large cage filled with beautiful, brilliantly colored birds. At crepuscule, they were silent and lethargic. Their wings had stopped flapping but she recalled vividly their euphonious melody every morning.

Unfortunately, these beautiful songbirds were not free. Rather, they were imprisoned creatures placed in the cage and consigned solely to give pleasure to another species—humans. It saddened her. Had she had a key, she would have given these beautiful and joyless beasts their freedom! Let them fly away to the four corners of the world. That could have been her last act in Rome—an honorable gesture! At least they could sing and pleasure the world! An overwhelming feeling of sadness swathed her. She wished she could sing at times like that. She was trapped like these pretty songbirds in the cages.

Morose, she slowly walked back to the house. She opened the French encased windows and peeked in on both sides of the living room. Good riddance! Jean-Louis was nowhere in sight, his brandy glass was still on the table near the fireplace, half empty. She quickly filed in and gulped the last of the soothing brandy. Courageously, she strolled in the foyer.

The small smoking room faced the dining room; he often used the room as an office. Perhaps, someone had told him she'd re-entered the palace. There was security everywhere.

With heavy steps he marched to her. To make certain that she would not escape, he picked her up in his arms.

She should have known better. Jean-Louis never walked away from a confrontation. He let himself be gentled, yes, but although he advocated the position of never placing a person against a wall, in his personal life he would not give an inch when confronted in a dispute. She always lost those battles. Why waste her time and try to outsmart him or outplay him? Tenacious, he never gave up until he won. For her, it was a matter of pride.

"You can let me down," she proclaimed, dejected. I will not run anymore. It's dark, I'm scared."

Jean-Louis reflected that she should be more frightened of him. He certainly could do more damage than the lizards and rabbits she would encounter in the park! He felt her body relax in his arms. Gaby had an innately disarming demeanor. When she'd played all her cards and lost, she understood the futility of a beggar's lot. Had she been French and an imprisoned aristocrat during the revolution of 1789, she would have walked to the guillotine bravely, with her head high, unrepentant. Her eyes fixed pretentiously on the paupers who had sentenced her to the guillotine; she would have accepted her punishment.

He felt like one of these paupers now. Less than three hours ago, he could have battled with her. He kicked open their bedroom door, walked in, kicked it shut, and deposited his wife in the overstuffed day chair—the very chair where he'd made love to her that morning. She had come out of her bath-dripping wet, smelling sweet and enticing. He had wanted her so violently that, although fully dressed, he had pounced on her like a starved caged lion waiting for his daily ration of meat! He wanted her now, too. To hell with this afternoon! He had nothing to fear from the half-man Jacopo except that he suspected him of playing a deadly game for his own benefit. Jacopo was narcissistic and no one would stand in his way. He had heard some unsavory things about the fellow. From day one, he had been less than happy to have him involved in the negotiations. Furthermore, his wife's friendliness towards the Count had complicated the negotiations.

Looking up to him, Gaby understood that his anger had dissipated.

"Stop looking at me like that! Say what you have to say and be done with it! You have tortured me enough this evening. What are you waiting for? You like to see me grovel, while I beg you to spare your cruel comments? Well, no, it won't happen," she said gravely.

"I no longer feel like persecuting you, although I would have derived great satisfaction from it three hours ago." He bent down and kissed her lips, a hard sensuous kiss. He tried to open her mouth and feel her response. He kneeled down in front of her and proceeded to open her shirt and uncover her breasts. He pressed his lips to her soft nipples, which quickly responded to his moist mouth by becoming hard and full. Pulling her close to him he pulled off her shirt and slid his hands to the back of her skirt, tearing everything that resisted him! Content, he clasped her naked body to him, letting his madness unravel. He tasted every part of her and then turned her over on her stomach, resting his lips on her shapely, arrogant bottom. "I should have beaten it, instead of kissing it," he chuckled.

She lifted her eyes to the heavens. "In your dreams, mon Cher Duc!" she mocked back.

Instead he took his revenge by driving the little witch wild with sensations where her great control was no longer possible.

"Please Jean-Louis, I want you," she begged.

Good, he'd accomplished his goal. He pretended to hold back a while longer to hear her implore a little louder when a demanding knock at the door stopped him suddenly. Painfully, he pulled away and stood, he reached for his pants and belts, heaved a great sigh, and marched to the door. Someone called him and asked him to step in the hallway. He closed the doors behind him.

One of the so-called butlers flushed and embarrassed appeared to have difficulty to disclose the information he was privy to.

Jean-Louis felt his discomfort and brought him forth to his upstairs office.

"Yes. Speak," he ordered.

"*Eh bien*, Captain, a man . . . a so-called Jacopo di Castriodrianni was at the door, asking to see Madame." The butler began to sweat. "When we told him that she was not available, he replied that he wanted to see her for a last time. He brought her these chocolates . . . a shawl and a headscarf, which she'd supposedly left behind in the Galleria D'Arte. It's quite funny, Captain, for I do not recall seeing Madame wear any scarf since the kidnapping. We did not let him in. No one is accepted in this palace, except you and Madame. Security had seen Madame with the said man today in the Galleria del Arte. The guards found him once more, about an hour ago, wandering in the gardens—not far from your room. It's amazing he got that far. I beefed up security. He said that Madame left one of the garden gates opened, just in case the guards might not let him in. Anyway, we called the local police. We wanted him incarcerated. The Chief of Police, however, was having a difficult time. This man appears to be quiet influential. He was treated like a Lord by the local authorities—with great deference, indeed." The man stopped as he encountered the Duke deadly glance.

"Go on," he ordered

"He represents, we have been informed, one of the members of the opposition involved in the negotiations. The Chief also shared with us that he worked closely with Madame and knew you both quite well. He went further as to insinuate that we owe the Count an apology. We have not gone that far. We wanted to check with you first. We are not accusing Madame. Certainly, Madame had nothing to do with this sordid affair. But we are now combing the garden just in case he might have left some unsavory explosive device. Count di Castriodrianni most certainly displayed a great infatuation with Madame." The security chief finished, watching his leader's facial expression harden. He was not too certain how to read this latest development—but good it wasn't. The chief was glad that he had taken the initiative.

Jean-Louis' fury and jealousy resurfaced. When it came to his wife, the great Jean-Louis-Pierre de Pleyssis was not rational. He let his jealousy dampened his analytical mind. Only Gabriella could elicit such response, and he pursued his futile deductions.

Once again, everything made sense to him. He concocted his own play in less than sixty seconds, not unlike the drama that had taken place years ago in front of Notre Dame with her cousin the Cardinal.

Unfortunately for Gaby, a drama that she could not fathom took form in her husband's resentful spirit.

He dismissed the chief of security and ordered him to present the situation to Cunnan.

"I'll be down shortly." He strode away to his office to calm his spirit. He returned toward his massive desk, and poured himself another shot of brandy. Slowly he backed in his large chair to evaluate the new development. Now there was the reason why Gaby had pretended to escape from him in the gardens—to meet the traitor one last time. After all, meandering through the gardens had never been a point of interest—especially after the incident—she must have divulged to Jacopo the imminent departure. The little witch with great deftness, had played her game well, he fumed. Had he not placed the extra security, secretly, to insure her safety, her charade could have gone unnoticed.

Could they have been lovers? But when and where could they have met? She never left his side. In the delegation room . . . no, that scenario was unlikely. There were too many of his supporters and aides in these areas. She had had access to the private suites. No one had ever questioned them when they needed privacy. The Count, after all, had used these private apartments quite often for himself and his delegation. This was plausible. With rage mounting, the scheming scenario forged in his psyche. At this moment, Jean-Louis wrote and directed his own play! The laughs that the two of them had shared, he seethed, the desire to go out to coffee, to *déjeuner*, the meeting this afternoon at the club after he had banned Jacopo from the negotiations and barred him from the Club—from the French quarter anyhow. Of course, Jacopo was an influential man in his own right, a powerful member of the King's delegation but most probably as well a covert member of the opposition intent on keeping full control of his rich lands and estates. He invoked falsely the rights of the King's sovereignty. Jean-Louis was certain that the Count and his men were working to hasten the departure of the French troops from Civitavecchia after the Pope had been relieved of his temporal power over Rome.

Furthermore, their final goal was to oust the Monarchy as well and to retain full control of his assets and of his influence over the political process. This very afternoon, he'd caught Gaby as she fondly touched the Count's arm. Unaware that the crowd surrounding them in the Galleria had left, oblivious of the hours spent away from the bar, they'd been caught in a fit of laughter. How long could they have been in the Galleria alone? They were lovers. The Count was not bold enough to actually come to the palace without an invitation. He must have been madly in love with his wife . . . and maybe she with him, to even attempt such craziness. The gardens had been the perfect place tonight. All fell into place.

A blazing stare toward the upstairs apartment reminded him of Gaby, nude, waiting for him. How could she have been so amorous with him, if she had just met her lover less than an hour before? Gaby was sensual. He should not find that so difficult to understand. Not only was she deceitful, but also she may have affected the lives of thousand of people if she had revealed some of the secrets she was privy to. Everything he had been working for these past months gone in moments of lust! What else could she have divulged? How could she be untrue to him? Could she be in love with another man? That last thought overwhelmed him with anguish . . . and then blinding rage. He stood, stomped through the corridor until he reached their bedroom. He heaved a long sigh, his fingers rested on the gold handle for a long while, and then decidedly he turned it. The servant was dismissed immediately. He let himself into the foyer and crossed it. His muscular torso filled half of the small corridor that led to their apartment.

* * *

Jean-Louis had left Gaby so terribly involved in her sensuality, that the immensity of her poor judgment could not be fathomed. Frustrated from unfinished lovemaking, she pulled herself into the soft cushioning part of the chair and waited for her husband to return.

Naked on deep-seated goose down pillows of a white satin bergère, basking in a sea of emotions, the knowledge that their departure for France was imminent filled her with immense joy. His madness and jealousy had vanished or at least dissipated, she thought happily. She hoped that the culture and Jean-Louis' friends would bring back his joie de vivre.

Jean-Louis was a young man after all, almost thirty-four and yet the responsibilities that had been entrusted to him had aged him twenty years. He looked young and virile amongst the men he negotiated with, but his demeanor had become more like a man twice his age! He needed to slow down! A pretty smile lit her communicative green eyes. In gay Paris, he would retrieve his old joyous self. Tomorrow, he would be back in the palace for some parting words and signatures; another few days to tie up all loose ends; a going away masked ball in their honor would follow protocol. Perhaps in a fortnight they would be sailing back home on the Tempête.

Good heavens, the reunification of Rome to the Kingdom of Italy was at hand.

Philippe, her cousin had just been appointed Archbishop of Notre Dame in Paris. Who knows, God willing, the men in her life would cement strong relationships as they got to know each other better. Miracles did happen.

What a life she lived!

She prayed that these months abroad would not tarnish their romantic relationship. After all, it was normal for a couple to go through periods of turmoil. He was an influential man, and she had fallen in love with the man. All goes with the territory, the Mother Superior of the Convent in New Orleans incessantly repeated. Jean-Louis had not hidden anything from her. Furthermore, he'd encouraged her to take an active part in his professional life. She was his best friend and sole confidante.

The pretensions and the ambitions of many political leaders were so grandiose at times, that they would sometimes solve fractions of large issues. Meanwhile, the global crises were swept aside. Balance, along with a three hundred sixty degree vision, was needed to comprehend the full scope of a political stalemate. Minutiae always had the propensity to expand into larger global conflicts.

Jean-Louis possessed both of these energies. He never let anything deter him from his main goal—the progress of modernization on the continent. There lay his strength! He'd known when to compromise, when to cajole, and when to stay inflexible when confronted with the divisive factions.

He had achieved his goal. The Church would have its power consolidated in one enclave—the Vatican, but also in all of its churches throughout the world. The Catholics in France would be pleased with that development. Naturally, the Pontiff's recalcitrant demeanor showed by his unwillingness to leave 'his prison', but the brilliant man knew that the French would not stay in Rome's port forever. Victor Emmanuel II would eventually appropriate Rome as the new Italian capital.

This development was favorable to France. Not to discount the power of the lucrative trade market with the rest of Europe—and also with America. The United States were beginning to import Europeans goods—mostly French and Italian luxury items. The French called North America a continent 'in construction'.

The connections that Jean-Louis had made in the United States would become quite lucrative if he ever decided to return to live permanently in Boston! Naturally, all this was in the future. There was much too much instability in France and throughout Europe right now to dream of a distant future. He had won major concessions. Namely to hold back the forces of the Italian king into taking Rome by force, and secondly, he'd cajoled the Pontiff into accepting the unacceptable. Although there had been setbacks, the new treaties decided the fate of the future of European modernization.

Gaby was still lost in her thoughts, when she turned her head back and noticed her husband standing in between two large pillars. Jean-Louis stood straight, immense, somber, a conqueror's stare on his haughty features. What had happened in what seem to have been an eternity? What other disaster loomed? Would it ever end? An ominous chill trickled through her. What had he fabricated this time?

He came closer and froze. He placed his hand over his right forearm and stared down at her. Loud knocks at the door and the voice of Cunnan caught their attention. Jean-Louis turned back to her and shouted his scenario with venom.

"You would have manipulated the whole situation quite well, my chère, had you not been pre-empted by a simple security guard! Wonderful work, Gaby. It is terribly unfortunate for you that your deceitful interlude was revealed to me. Your friend was not as fearless as you would have liked him to be!"

Quickly she retrieved her aplomb. Calmness before the storm, she recalled the incident in Paris over Philippe's affectionate greeting. She jumped out of the seat and ran toward the safety of the salon where Cunnan's angry knocks hammered at the door. She became entwined in the discarded clothing on the carpet and fell head first against a glass corner of a small tea table.

Concerned Jean-Louis stepped to her, ready to take hold of the situation, but Gaby stood and darted towards the door. This last move did not appease him; instead, he followed with longer strides and blocked her exit. Separated by a very wide sofa, she intended to circle it many times as was needed until he came to his senses and explained his erratic behavior.

Jean-Louis did not relent. He matched her every step and caught up with her once more.

"Are you mad, totally crazy? What are you talking about?" she shouted. "It's a farce. How can you even accept as true these lies? There is a vast conspiracy against me."

He caught her upper arms and pulled her to him.

"Cease! You're hurting me, you coward. What do you want to do, kill me?" she screamed.

Mindful of her comments, he stared at her bloody lips. Quickly he let go of her. He paused and continued calmly.

"Eh bien, Gaby, you meet your lover and let him enter clandestinely in the garden? And not solely that, it appears that you have filtered some information. Unconsciously, I hope, I don't believe you could be so undeserving. Nevertheless, you talked openly about our whereabouts tonight. I should have asked myself earlier why of all nights, you strolled in the garden?"

In a glance of pure revulsion, she spoke resolutely as he closed in on her again. "Stop, stay where you are! You are doing the same thing you did this afternoon. You are jealous for no reason. What in the world are you talking about? My lover in the garden? Giving information? Jean-Louis, you know me better than that, you are mad! I just wanted a bit of fresh air, I was tired of arguing with you," she shouted.

Cunnan ran up the back stairs and kicked in the door. He bled when others hurt Gaby's feelings or if he found her morose. Gaby mistreated, that he could not fathom or tolerate!

"Jean-Louis," he roared, "Gaby is not at fault, the poor little angel. You were given false information."

Jean-Louis quickly reached for the coverlet that was lying on the spine of the sofa and wrapped it around his wife.

"We have just found hiding in the bushes a member of the opposition. He talked," Cunnan continued. "Members of the opposition had placed these acts of terrorism in action long ago—if perchance the treaties were approved. It was planned, Jean-Louis. Gaby is aware of nothing, poor child!"

The old sailor looked at Gaby. "How can you, you bastard?" he strode behind the sofa to her, and dabbed her cut lips with his handkerchief. Bright red blood smeared her chin and throat. "She is but a child!" The old man spoke with fury and distaste. Then he gathered her in his arms, tapping the back of her head.

"I fell, Cunnan," she whispered.

"My poor child, the pain we are putting you through, although no fault of your own!" He pressed her to him tenderly. "Wait here, my sweet, Jean-Louis needs to follow me downstairs. I'll be back shortly. Everything will be fine, my child."

Cunnan took the lead out the door. He turned to the Duke.

"Your attention is needed in the conference room. The men are awaiting your commands. Follow me," Cunnan ordered.

Jean-Louis massaged the back of his head, stared at his wife, and paused to assess the situation at hand.

Gaby walked quickly to him and forced him to look down at her. She gripped his upper arm. "I hate you! I despise you! How can you accuse me?" she demanded in a grave voice that overflowed with loathing.

Jean-Louis pulled away. He followed Cunnan out the doors.

She opened the doors slightly to overhear the dialogue downstairs.

"All was planned against Gaby," Cunnan continued, "since our very first association with Jacopo and his group. Gaby was a pigeon. I do not quite know yet whether her kidnapping was a direct result of these negotiations. There are so many factions in the opposition. It is hard to know who's for what. The guards that the locals sent over must have been cohorts of the ones who provoked the incident. I don't even know if our men spoke to the real Chief of Police. However, this fellow, the one we caught, must have seen her in the garden. He realized that she was the perfect alibi after you asked for the removal of Jacopo," the old man finished.

"As you can see, Cunnan, my intuition was correct," the Duke retorted. "May I point out that Jacopo is a traitor, and that I knew it from day one? He would not have conceded to anything the other members settled on. To think that my own wife played a role in that scenario is infuriating."

"Cease, Jean-Louis-Pierre, I will not allow another word against the little Princess. Gaby in the garden was a lucky hazard for Jacopo. After all, he worked hard at being seen with her in the museum. They were in plain view at all times. All was connected from then on. When she returned from the powder room, you were engaged in conversation with someone other than your wife, may I remind you." Cunnan's furious tone re-surfaced.

Jean-Louis remembered he had been thirsty for Parisian gossips.

"Jacopo was not willing to go in the *salle de jour*, knowing that you would ask him to leave. Yet he stayed, visible enough to concoct all these stories about the supposed relationship with Gabriella. The coward below confessed more than we wanted to hear. He further told us that Jacopo was enraged at her when she refused to follow him into the salon Dore. Still, he'd established visibility, and she could be accused of being his secret lover."

The Duke's expression hardened.

"Consequently, his presence in the garden would have been perfectly logical. It was a tour de force. Thank God, Gaby was not harmed. She came awfully close—from all sides." Cunnan's glare converged on the Duke.

Jean-Louis placed his hand to his forehead and then massaged the back of his head as Cunnan continued.

"He must have scaled the wall. Security did not see anyone. In my opinion, his men must have been casing the villa, or perhaps he might have known firsthand the location, you know of his reputation . . . we found him under your windows. We think we averted a catastrophe. I feel that we should keep this incident secret and release the leader to the national police with assurances that they also should keep their mouth shut."

The Duke nodded.

"This crazy ordeal is driving us all mad. Gaby had nothing to do with the intrigue," Cunnan pressed in his defense of the young woman he so tenderly loved. "She is being accused unfairly. She thought of Jacopo as an agreeable social contact with whom she shared an important role—for your sake Jean-Louis. She never in a million years would have chosen this path. Jacopo amused her; it was a distraction from her serious life. You know that she adores you," Cunnan proclaimed reproachfully. "She should never have been allowed in these negotiations. She would have been much happier, taking her singing lessons at the Académie de Musique and singing to her heart's content in gay Paris!" The old man turned his back to him and started to walk away.

Jean-Louis held him back and walked Cunnan to the privacy of his office on the second floor. He opened up as if he was a father.

"These past months were a real hardship on our relationship. We no longer joked or laughed. We were too absorbed in the negotiations," he remarked in a flat voice.

"We?" Cunnan retorted, "us, Jean-Louis-Pierre, us. Not the little angel!"

Gaby opened the doors and burst out on the scene. She could not bear to hear any more.

Shocked by her sudden appearance, but not willing to have others hear their conversation, the men returned to the couple's private apartment.

She trailed behind them.

"You see, you outrageous beast, I was the victim in this sordid affair. YOU, oh Almighty, accepted Jacopo's presence a year ago! I had nothing to do with it. I was still very much involved in my music. I hate your manipulative self," she shouted with venom. "You are never willing to accept guilt!"

"Cease, Gaby," he said in a hard voice, "don't try to convince me that you are proud of the fact that you were seen as vulnerable enough, malleable enough, stupid enough to be manipulated by an evil-minded, good looking, sweet talking traitor? It's incomprehensible that you would take pride in having been taken for an idiot, knowing that the world analyzes our relationship."

Gaby gasped. She looked at him in dismay. Dejected, she fell back down in the bergère. He was right, she thought. How gullible she had been—just for a few lighthearted moments in this smoke-filled atmosphere. She had been played like a fine-tuned piano!

She did not reply nor look at him with contempt. Instead, she gazed absently at the closed door.

He knew that she now realized the immensity of it all. There was nothing she or he could do. His anger subsided quickly.

Cunnan spoke first. "What should we do?" he asked.

"Take them to the local authority," the Duke said. "Hopefully, they will be incarcerated—for a while anyhow.

Keep everything under cover. Let's wait a while longer. As you said, no one should know what transpired in the villa. Tell the men not to utter one word."

Cunnan left, not before shooting a concerned glance at Gaby. Jean-Louis went to the side bar to fix a drink. And then he headed to the fireplace.

Lost in her own thoughts, Gaby was sick of all the intrigues. She had played the game well, as well as she could. What had happened to her husband? The man who loved to contradict society? The man who loved the social challenges? The man who never really played by the rules unless he wanted to? What had happened to them?

She had been his everything, his wife, his lover, his confidante, and his best friend. He would tell her everything and ask her advice, depending on her logic at every momentous step in the negotiations. In the heat of so much conflict, their little nest had become sad. Yes, sad she had to admit. Sexually, their desire for one another had not changed or so she thought. He was still as amorous as ever, as ardent, sometimes even more so, as if they lived in a world that could end any minute. However, their laughter had slowly but surely disappeared. Their lives consisted of work, balls and soirées, negotiations and sex.

The door had closed, and she knew that his conversation with Cunnan had ceased. Jean-Louis must have been in the living area. She would not force the issue. Oblivious to the searing pain on her swollen lip and chin, she dressed in a long and flowing nightgown and went to bed.

Where had he been all these months? Jean-Louis pondered. He gripped the mantle of the fireplace and held himself slightly back. Everything he'd heard a few minutes ago infuriated him. He'd had an uncanny feeling about the members of the opposition all along. The population that resided within the walls of the Papal city had been a source of concern—yes. But why had he not paid more attention to the opposition posed by the Counts and Princes, who in effect had lost fortunes and much influence. Jacopo was an influential and powerful member of the King's circle. It was a given that they engaged in reducing the temporal power of the Pope . . . but a Sardinian Monarch?

He should have been more careful. In retrospect, he should not have allowed his jealousy to blind him. He would have had more insights and control over the group. The following days would be critical and a lot harder than he'd predicted. He needed to rethink it all—quickly.

Gaby had rolled into bed. For some unknown reason, the lights had gone out in her room. As expected, her uncontrolled fears, her demons, as she commonly referred to her anxieties, had returned. Eyes wide open, immobilized, she lay in bed. Her endurance spent, she compulsively abandoned the bed. After all, she theorized, given that Jean-Louis behaved like her lord and master, consequently, he should accept that she would require his protection—like a lowly serf!

He heard footsteps.

Gaby enveloped in a white linen nightgown, looking like an adorable ghost, sprinted into the salon. She stood at the entrance of the room. A gentler Jean-Louis contemplated her beauty.

"Yes?" he asked with unmasked emotions.

She felt foolish, subservient, and weak, but at this particular moment, to assuage her anxieties alone, she could not fathom being with anyone else. It was too much. She would crack.

"The lights went out. I'm scared," she whispered.

The reason behind her appearance was apparent. She'd been humbled sufficiently this evening.

"Very well, I need to get some sleep anyway." He walked past her, then quickly returned to her and took her hand. She followed closely in the dark and stayed close by while he undressed. Before he climbed in, he picked her up and placed her gently in their bed. He possessively gathered her into his arms and positioned his body against hers. Her hips and legs pinned under his heavy thighs did not allow any personal movement. Oddly enough, her body relaxed. She felt protected and secure but unable to fall asleep.

"Jean-Louis," she started. "Will we . . ." she stopped.

An eerie sense of being watched overwhelmed her. Simultaneously, a haunting, birdlike whistle that would not end resonated through the open windows into the halls. It appeared to come from the tree facing the verandah. She lifted her head to the window when a deafening explosion blasted them out of bed and onto the floor. A heavy weight bore down on Gaby's back. Terrified that her husband was lying dead atop her, she glanced around.

"Crawl with me, Chérie," Jean-Louis ordered. Like snakes, they slithered their way toward the hallway. At that precise moment the salon illuminated. Another ear-piercing explosion struck, causing the walls to crumble, the foundation to unravel and to collapse to the ground floor. Projectiles of splintered concrete sprayed every corner of their private apartment. The windows exploded, shards of glass rained down from above. Numerous explosions of tremendous magnitude detonated, obliterating the northern section of the villa. They stumbled out of their smoke and flame engulfed apartment into the now uncovered alcove. A shattering bomb landed within fifteen meters. Gaby coughed, straining for breath.

Without delay, Jean-Louis picked up his wife in his arms and ran for the double doors that led out to the garden—their only chance at safety. He touched the panels. Warm, he noted. Immediately, he shook her out of her shock.

"Hold on tight, Gaby, we will be out of here quickly. Stay tight, Gaby," he repeated. He kissed her with all the love he could place in a kiss. She did not respond, but held on to him for dear life.

"I love you, Chérie," he murmured in her ears. "All is in your name in Paris, call Luke for help. *Je t'adore*, Gaby," he concluded, intense, as if speaking his last earthly words.

In one swift motion he kicked open the door, praying that fire had not engulfed the villa. His prayers were answered. He ran in between the two marble staircases that had been reinforced for just this very unlikely event. Fire razed countless magnificent palaces. The bombs ignited small fires throughout the city, and yet the local police was nowhere in sight! These damn bastards, the Duke fumed, they were not even able to protect their guests. Heads were going down, if he survived, he seethed.

Minutes later, guards ran up the stairs, the fire in the main house extinguished. Gaby held tightly to her husband, terrified. He gently put her down but kept her close to him.

"Where are the men who were caught in the garden earlier this evening?" he questioned, incensed. He turned to Cunnan, who stomped in right behind the guards. "Bring them into the conference room, Cunnan, I will question them."

Hours later, Jean-Louis and the officers were still interviewing the men they had caught earlier that day in the gardens. He finally came back for Gaby, who sat alongside the servants in the kitchen. The Northern section of the villa was completely destroyed. The security and servants were already fast at work, making accommodations in the smaller properties located on the ground of the large estate.

Incapable to stop the trembling, Gaby caught sight of her husband. She ran to him.

"Chérie, all will be fine." He looked down at her frightened expression and caressed her hair. Gently, he led her to the library.

"I wondered if it is an isolated incident, or if it is a plot to do away with us before the signatures tomorrow morning?"

She did not respond. Traumatized she stayed close by.

"Gaby, tell me, Chérie. What did you tell Jacopo?" he whispered calmly to her, no reproach in his voice.

"Nothing, Jean-Louis, I told you, I never, never met with him in the garden. I swear to you, I have been faithful always. He did press me yesterday afternoon. He seemed to think that our departure was imminent; he said he had noticed the Tempête behind the French Navy ships in the harbor. I felt a bit pressed. I quickly changed the subject and walked to the *Galleria Della Arte.*"

Without noticing it, the Duke took a deep breath.

"But why do you think Jacopo was behind tonight's horrors?" she questioned. "He may have been a bit smitten with me. Is it so ludicrous to consider? Perhaps it might have been just a coincidence. He brought chocolates, Jean-Louis, these are a far cry from bombs!"

"He was surprised by our guards in the garden, Gaby, which is where you were."

Stunned, she drifted into silence. "I do not know, Jean-Louis." She stepped closer to him and gripped the sides of his waist.

"He was taken at just about the same time you were in the garden this afternoon, Gaby. They took him to the local jail. The local police released him once they realized that he had ties to the King and to his delegation. He probably told them that he had fallen for you. It's a romantic nation. All Italians love great love stories. Anyway they let him out almost immediately, and now this. No one can find him. They have searched the surroundings. They will get the insurgents, Gaby."

A knock at the door interrupted the dialogue. One of the security men entered.

"Everything seems to be in order, Captain"

"Very well, unless they've found sympathizers close by, I want the incident to be kept secret. The local police will not expand on the story. From now on, we will use our own security solely. There is too much at stake."

"Yes, Sir. Everything seems to be in order. Your room, Captain, you can return to pick out a few things, but I would not stay in there, the windows are shattered and glass is everywhere."

"We will not," he interrupted. "Come with me and help me take out a few pieces of clothing. I don't want any servants in there either until we know more about the explosion. Prevent the servants from talking and let no one in the house and surrounding property—under no excuses," the Duke emphasized. "We will get to the bottom of this one, although I have a pretty good idea who's behind it."

He felt Gaby hold him tighter.

"Have the servants prepare a room for us. I want everyone in my study in ten minutes." The man was dismissed.

Gaby pulled away from Jean-Louis now.

"Oh, my God, he wanted to kill us, Jean-Louis?"

"I think so, Gaby." He was now looking down at her face and although not completely sure that she had not had a loving interlude with the bastard, he felt more secure in the thought that Gaby had been an innocent bystander. The story no longer made any sense. He left the room to return with a few pieces of clothing.

"Get dressed, Gaby." He pulled a grey day dress from her closet, and shoved a white mink stained with grey spots from the fire and a pair of grey satin boots at her. "The police might interrogate you. Do not say anything to them unless I'm there with you. I am no longer sure about anything or anyone in this damn country."

She nodded.

They both changed in what appeared to be a safe room. He pulled her into his arms. She was safe. For now, that's all that mattered.

Had she brought on this misery, Gaby pondered, with pleasantries and yes perhaps a bit of a flirtatious demeanor toward Jacopo? Had he really tried to kill them, because he had fallen in love with her, or had she been a stupid pigeon in a much larger scheme? With guilt in her heart, she now tended to believe the latter. She would listen to the comments their intelligence would divulge. How difficult it was to live in a land where no one could be trusted. What a horrible situation it had proved to be. She wanted to leave. She could not take much more. Jean-Louis would just have to deal with his challenges himself.

She looked up in the mirror and saw her swollen and cut lower lip. It was Jean-Louis' fault. How could she face all these people downstairs? How degrading! Well they'd heard the screams and shouts, she was sure of it. She was the victim in this sordid affair, but all these men probably would view this ordeal quite differently. Well she had to go, not showing up would actually prove the point of the morons down below, make their case that she was the traitor or, at the very least, a deceitful person!

She placed a little powder on her cheeks and rouge on her lips, and she rejoined Jean-Louis in the bathroom. Blood covered his feet. Glass, mirrors, and countless pieces of gnarled wood were scattered everywhere. Good, she rejoiced, he deserved to suffer as well, even if she had not inflicted it herself. Somehow, there was justice in this world!

He looked down at her, bent down, kissed her cut lips, "I'm sorry," he whispered.

"It's not enough, Jean-Louis. I hate you! Don't touch me!" She shouted back.

He washed his feet in the large marble tub, put on his socks and boots, picked her up and walked downstairs.

Everyone waited in the room. They walked in, hand in hand. Gaby was well aware that all eyes were upon her. She glimpsed at Cunnan's stressed face; deep frown lines crossed his forehead. He came forth, pulled her into his arms, and kept her there. Jean-Louis walked to his desk.

"Thank God, you're alive." he murmured as he heaved a sigh of relief.

She did not know what he referred to. The fall or the explosion? She did not care. She stayed close to him, comforted by his warm embrace.

The old sailor waited a long time before he gently pushed her back and walked her to the chair that had been placed for her, next to her husband.

Jean-Louis called the meeting to order, and she obediently sat by his side.

She sensed that it must have pleased many facing her to witness her obviously torn up lip and the bright red aureole that had begun to form alongside her chin. Back in a woman's place, she imagined their thoughts . . . she held way too much power over the Duke . . . he'd finally reined her in. There were some looks in the room that could have killed!

"Tonight we have suffered a setback," Jean-Louis began. "We could have been blown away from Italy." He paused. "If the terrorists had had their way, we would be dead in our posts. Months of hard earned work in limbo, and years of despair for the poor and desperate of the world. Modernization lost." He glanced around the room. Many shook their heads and stroked their guns.

"I have heard unfounded rumors about my wife. I repeat, unfounded," he declared louder than necessary. "Madame de Pleyssis had absolutely nothing to do with this act of terror. Once again, she was inadvertently the victim in more ways than one in this sordid affair."

Gaby knew that he was still angry with her. She hated him. Nonetheless, she appreciated being the first order of business as he quelled all gossips.

He went on with his orders. Everyone needed to stay in, on guard, until all negotiations ended and were sealed with his signature. The chain of command was now fully enforced. Anyone caught disobeying an order would die. Too much was at stake now.

An hour later, after delineating every detail that needed to be followed until further notice, he asked if anyone had any questions. "Now is the time to ask questions," Jean-Louis clipped, "before all enforcements are to take place."

One officer raised his hand, sheepish as he fleetingly looked to his sides for support and emotional assistance, which was awkwardly given.

"Captain, I heard what you said, but with all due respect, your wife . . . Madame de Pleyssis," he quickly caught his faux pas, "is a foreigner. There are thousands of lives that will be affected by this treaty and a hundred of those of us present, could lose their existence if the negotiations fall through. Treason from only one of us will have us all killed and will defeat our nation and long term goals." He took a long deep breath, and turned around once more, looking for support that was absent now. The Captain's eyes were fixed on him, as if any minute now, the sailor would be struck dead. The man continued. His voice trembled.

"We love and admire Madame. As you know we have dedicated ourselves to her security . . . but she is a foreigner, Sir, an American with Italian origins at that, and we were wondering, *eh bien* . . . treason is a great offense, you understand . . ."

The Duke did not budge.

"Make your point!" Jean-Louis ordered.

"*Eh bien*," the officer was encouraged by the question and foolishly went on. "Madame, Captain, knows it all. She has attended the most secret of all sessions at your side, Captain, and now the allegations that she might have divulged some of these secrets to the Count are still alive. Should we still allow her to be involved? Some of us are wondering if some sanctions should be taken." Seemingly proud of himself for having had the courage to make his point, he once more turned to his fellow officers self-importantly. That was strong leadership, he mistakenly assumed.

Gaby was shocked. Jean-Louis looked at his wife and then at the young officer. Calm and still as a marble statue, his forefinger on his cheek and the rest of his fist over his mouth, the Captain glared down at the officer. The young man's courage waned; he looked around, searching for emotional support from the others security officers in his unit. None was forthcoming.

"Come here," came the ominous voice.

The man hesitantly walked alone to the Duke.

"Are you saying that my wife is a traitor and that she should not be trusted? Is that what that speech inferred, Lieutenant?"

"Well, no, but the evidence is here, Captain, the garden, the gallery, the bomb."

"What facts, officer? These are absurd babbles."

Towering over the now visibly shaken young man, "Madame de Pleyssis has the full trust and support of the Emperor and myself." the Duke countered.

The man trembled.

"How dare you doubt the confidence of the Emperor and of your superior officers?" As the last word was uttered, the poor man flew across the room. Fast as lightning, Jean-Louis followed the roll; he lifted the man by his torn shirt and forced him to look up at him. "You will be court-martial upon our return." He released the limp body.

The man fell back once more on the marble floor where he continued to bleed profusely.

"Please, Jean-Louis, stop!" Gaby stood and tried to walk towards her husband. She could not fathom to watch the developing carnage on her behalf. Two strong hands pulled her back. Cunnan gathered her to him firmly. He first held her face next to his chest and then gently turned her around. He whispered in her ear.

"Chut, Chut, my lovely, Jean-Louis is right, say no more. Let him do what needs to be done."

She saw her husband roll the moribund man with his boot towards the approaching guards.

"You are lucky, you are still alive," he told the failing officer.

He now turned to the rest of the assembly.

"I do not want to see him until we reach Toulon." He proclaimed haughtily to the rest of the assembly. The Duke's last gesture was to bend down and to tear off the man's épaulettes.

"Anymore questions?" he asked giving the room of assembled men a three hundred sixty degrees glare.

The room was silent, the marble floor bloodied. A pin could have been heard falling.

"Very well, the plan is set, no changes, just a few adjustments. Dismissed and carry on." The officer was taken away. Jean-Louis walked to his petrified wife.

What had happened? In less than twelve hours, her husband had killed two men on his ship, insulted and mistrusted her and now this carnage! Was he ever going to return to the man she had fallen in love with. Had he been that ruthless during his other campaigns? Was she on the verge of falling out of love with this somber man? Confusion overwhelmed her. She could no longer be sure of anything.

The Duke approached her, reached for her shoulders and led her toward the second floor where new accommodations awaited them.

Gaby understood all too well what had just transpired. They thought of her as a traitor. She hated herself for having gone into the garden, and she wondered about Jacopo's dark plans? Young, handsome, vivacious, and brilliant—a dashing man who could make any woman forget herself. She had been duped. Now her anger for the Italian shifted to mental anguish. The idea that she had been used to have her husband killed was too much for her to bear.

She looked up at Jean-Louis' face. He was stoic. His face displayed no emotions. She pushed her body closer to his, and placed her hand over his low back. She held his side forcefully to reassure herself that he was still hers.

Madness set in, she concluded. Less than two seconds ago, she'd questioned her love for Jean-Louis. Now the thought of losing him was too horrific to consider. She hoped that it was all a bad dream.

A bit surprised at her gesture, Jean-Louis looked down at her, no emotions in his eyes.

She placed her hand on top of his and squeezed it once more.

"I love you, Jean-Louis, I have been faithful, and I always will be," she whispered.

He did not acknowledge her comments.

They reached the room that had been prepared for them. Quietly they undressed.

Jean-Louis lay in bed flat on his back, his hands behind his head. Mentally he reviewed the scenario that had changed their plans these last few days. He still had some doubts about his wife, but more and more it seemed unlikely, unconceivable as he struggled with the scheme.

Gaby rolled onto her side. She held her torso upright on her elbow. She needed a response from him.

"Jean-Louis," she whispered, "look at me, I swear to you, to everything that I hold dear in my life, you and our relationship, I never had any relations with Jacopo, nor ever wished to have any relations—never, ever, with anyone other than you. I did not, I repeat, did not divulge any information to him!" She insisted. "I'm smart, Jean-Louis."

He looked away.

"Look at me, damn it!"

He finally stared at her.

"It just felt good to be flirted with, that's all. A huge mistake, in retrospect, but I would never have jeopardized what we had, what we have, nor what we both believe in."

He did not respond.

"Answer me!" She knelt on the bed, placing her hands on his chest. "Look at me, not through me, damn you! I did not do anything wrong. I spoke with someone and shared a few laughs. You did the same thing yesterday with Fernande. You laughed, you remembered old times."

"No, Gaby, I make sure that you always come first," he retorted candidly.

This last statement could not be denied. It was true. He had walked away from Fernande's side to come to hers. Dejected, she pressed away from his body and rolled to her side of the bed, her head fell wearily on her pillows. How could he even entertain such absurdities?

They both lay awake for a long time. Then he rolled onto her and took her solely to pleasure himself—or to relieve his stress. She did not know.

Lying awake, she recalled how her trustful soul had thought their relationship to be unique—one locked in divine love. They also shared a partnership, an exchange of ideas, unusual for this era. Now, it came down to jealousy, distrust, gossip, and treason. Submerged in resentful discontent, tears flooded her eyes. Had she not proven her love and dedication a few months ago? Did Jean-Louis think that she could be manipulated that simply on Affairs of State? Did he think of her a non-entity, an imbecile? Tears rolled down her cheeks freely now, and she turned onto her side. No need to let him bask in glory.

Her muffled sobs stirred Jean-Louis. He gazed at her shapely body. Gaby's hair had not been brushed and her long curly mane covered part of her shoulders as it sank in the tiny fold of her waist. He pushed aside her hair away from her body and kissed the back of her neck.

"Gaby," he said, "you are my world." He held her tightly.

"Your world?" she asked, incredulous.

"I believe your words, but be aware, if I ever, ever catch you with another man," he paused, "I'll kill you both!"

"You're mad!" she snapped.

To seal his words with a formal action, he pulled himself up, ripped her gown down to her bottom, took her body out of it, and pressed her to him for a short moment before he entered her powerfully like an ancient conqueror scaling a coveted castle!

She did not expect much more from him tonight. After the act ended, he covered her body possessively with his own.

She attempted to push him away.

"You're hurting me, Jean-Louis, you've hurt me, please leave me a bit more space."

To no avail, as if he had not heard her protest, he pressed her even more tightly to his body. A short while later, she felt his slow rhythmic warm breath on her shoulder.

They had lived through many difficult times together. Where would the scale tip? Happiness versus sadness and confusion? She questioned if she would trade her heavenly moments for a less passionate, but more even-keeled relationship or no relationship at all? No, her whole being screamed—her life did make sense. She relaxed in his arms.

He must have felt the subtle movement as he tightened himself to her once more.

She hated him again. She knew exactly what he was doing, grasping at all her controls. He was just impossible. She tried to move to disturb his sleep. She couldn't sleep. Why should he?

"Stop, Gaby." He placed his hands on her waist and stomach to immobilized her with the weight of his larger body.

She swallowed hard. She felt him stir.

"What's wrong with this story?" she shouted, "I should be the one who's enraged."

His hands radiated over her lips.

"Hush," he said, "go to sleep." He kissed the top of her head. She relaxed her body once more, vanquished. To release his grip, she nipped at the fingers still lingering on her lips.

Another kiss landed on top of her ear and his hand slid sensuously over and down her breasts enveloping her tender skin in his large hand.

She sighed. He chuckled.

The episode was over—at least, as far as he was concerned.

Chapter 24

The treaties with the Pope's ambassadors and with the envoys of the Monarch had loosely been agreed upon. Victor Emmanuel II and his generals would walk into the Vatican and meet the Pontiff—a first political meeting between the two great political entities in Rome. Rumors persisted, however, that the population within the Walls would attempt to thwart the secret gathering, the new Italian Ambassador communicated to his French counterpart. Jean-Louis had contacted Cardinal Thornsen, and other arrangements had been made so that the first talk between the two key players, King Emmanuel II and the Pope, would occur in Rome under the stealth supervision of the French troops still in the city—and himself.

The last ball that they would attend in the Eternal City was given in their honor. Gaby, still enraged about the garden incident and at the inconceivable reproaches aimed directly at her, unleashed her anger on all who surrounded her. Even Cunnan was on the receiving end of her sarcastic remarks. On this very evening, she'd informed the Duke, she would do as she wished and she would have a wonderful time. They would depart from Italy soon. In the residence where the ball was held, her safety was assured. The host had requested a few arias from the 'extraordinary soprano'. Amiably, she'd acquiesced. The look of distaste on her husband's face as she was ushered into the ballroom was apparent. She glanced back pretentiously and boldly sauntered on.

With ill-concealed annoyance, the Duke scoffed. His wife was not aware of the events that would unfurl hours from now.

Everything was on track like a well-honed Swiss carillon.

He descended the steps leading into the ballroom and accidentally, encountered the wife of the French Ambassador, who by all accounts was the new furor. In effect, she was splendid, elegant with flamboyant red hair and expressive brown eyes. Her past . . . no one really knew. Had she been, perhaps, a courtesan? Her claim to fame had been in the salons of the philosopher Jean Courtier, a pillar of Paris society. The French Ambassador to Italy had taken her as his mistress and her ascendancy in the Grand Monde had climbed at a vertiginous pace, Fernande had shared last week. She appeared at all galas, symphony gatherings at the Jardin, at plays, at operas, at the Emperor's fashionable masked balls. She was charming, while the Ambassador was pretentious and hideous. No love between the two. She was his trophy and he was her pedestal. All theater!

When faced with the mores of his world, Jean-Louis considered himself extremely lucky. There was his portrait, he reflected. He would have wed an aristocratic woman and carried on tradition in a loveless marriage, had he not found Gaby to adore. Love in a marriage was a rarity. He smiled as he observed the impudent little brat across the dance floor. She sang divinely to her heart's content. Her magnificent voice echoed in all the salons. Soon, they would reclaim their lives in Paris—if he survived.

He continued down the staircase, inadvertently, finding himself face to face with the very enticing Marie-Hélène Noveaut. She shot him an audacious glance. Very much like a schoolboy who sees an opportune occasion to shine in the eyes of his beloved, Jean-Louis decided to take pleasure in the niceties. Making his wife aware that he was still very much in demand would not be that unpleasant a task with the beautiful and very loose Marie-Hélène Noveaut.

He stopped in front of the beauty and sensuously smiled at her. Women adored that smirk.

Two stairs below his, she sensually smiled back and bent slightly forward to display her opulent breasts.

"*Monsieur le Duc*, what a pleasure," she intoned deviously as she extended her gloved hand to him. "Ever since our arrival, your name is on everyone's lips."

"Lovely to see you, Marie-Hélène. What brings you to Rome? Rumors had you staying in Florence," he retorted as he gallantly lowered his lips to her hand. Jean-Louis pretended great interest. Allegedly, Marie-Hélène had been away from Paris living with her husband, a wealthy English man, who'd owned large plantations in the West Indies. The man had died of malaria. She'd returned quickly to Paris and had met the Ambassador in one of Courtier's salons.

"Love at first sight, *Monsieur le Duc*! We have not been apart since that fateful day." She smiled a devastating smile.

She knew of him by his less than enchanting reputation— before the Gaby era. Very much accustomed to adoring conduct from most men she met, the gorgeous woman was quite taken by her easy conquest of the celebrated Duke. His purportedly adored wife was no match to her charms and good looks, she concluded—a bit disappointed that it had been effortless.

The couple lingered on the marble staircase, apparently enjoying the moment. Not willing to let her go, the Duke stepped down in clear view of the dance floor. Many heads turned and mouths wagged.

Later that evening, having lost sight of her husband, the pretty Duchess began to search the smoking salons, where men usually congregated, for her spouse. To her horror, she found

Jean-Louis entranced in conversation with someone she did not know—but who looked splendid. He appeared to be charmed. She knew that look quite well. However, she had never seen it focused on anyone but her. Jealous, she could not take her eyes off of the couple standing entranced partly hidden behind a large marble pillar facing the dance floor. The shock stopped the conversation she was engaged in. Soon, many in her entourage followed her gaze.

No, the couple was not talking to one another. Rather, they engaged in a flirtatious banter, as Marie-Hélène granted the Duke a full view of all her charms.

Gaby burned with jealousy!

Grins flashed on many guests' faces as they observed the charming couple. She heard the amused remarks as she left her acquaintances and began to hasten toward the staircase. Her pride in shambles, Gaby walked with purpose toward her husband who seemed involved in an enjoyable conversation with the beauty.

The Italian high society was intrigued. Everyone understood by now the strong bond between the Duke and the lovely Gabriella. No one had been able to divide that unusual couple. Now, a French woman appeared to be doing the unthinkable!

French women possessed that *je ne sais quoi*. A smart and pretty French woman could always get her way with men. But it also gave hope to the young Italian beauties that now saw a chance to enchant the attractive Duke de Bourbonne. He was handsome, powerful, and highly desired by many females, not to mention a few males, as well!

Marie-Hélène Noveaut had taken the first step toward unraveling the romance. By the looks of it, the Duchess did not like it one bit.

Gaby was irate. Was he mentally challenged? Was he trying to enrage her? To make her repent for her insolent behavior? For God's sake, she had been faking her *joie de vivre*! Even tonight she would have loved to have been happy with him. To laugh, to dance and to forget all of the catastrophes that had happened in this difficult country. She longed for nothing more than to return to Paris. She continued her determined walk across the ballroom. The Duchess was quite a sight as well. Her determined demeanor caught the attention of the dancers.

Inflamed, she reached the place where her husband stood. Two other men that she had met before, and several women not in her connaissance, circled the two lovebirds!

She faced her husband, who did not acknowledge her arrival. Annoyed, she called to him none too sweetly. Instead, seemingly fully engaged in the conversation, Jean-Louis ignored her—once, twice, the third time her heart broke. Marie-Hélène enchanted him, she thought, tears swelled in her beautiful green eyes. Neither mortified nor angered, she sauntered next to him, dejected, in a trance. Her misery revealed.

Immediately, Jean-Louis sensed the devastation. When it came to her impertinent behavior, he did not regret bringing her down a notch or two. However, he could not fathom to see her sad. At that precise moment, Gaby appeared distraught.

Disgusted with himself for placing her in such a distressed state—essentially just to assess her sentiments—he immediately changed course. Proprieties, no longer *du jour*, he broke away from the group. Questions that he had been so intent to respond to while he schemed his painful game were now left unanswered. He kissed Gaby on her cheek and took her hand, tears were ready to spill down her lovely face. Her expressive eyes always betrayed her—she adored him. He now recognized that nothing had ever happened between her and Jacopo, except for the truth she had shared with him.

Poor Gaby, life had changed so drastically since their first arrival in Italy. From the happy go lucky life they had led in Paris to these most serious, constantly anxious and dangerous moments they had lived through these past months.

Unfortunately, as he envisioned the next few days, her trust would be shaken once more—he was certain of it!

He promptly took her elbow and escorted her downstairs.

"Why, Jean-Louis? Why were you so cruel?" she asked reproachfully. She looked up to him, allowing herself to be led to the terrace.

He did not let her continue to fill him with shame. His lips pressed to hers and his arms encircled her waist so tightly, that she had to push him away to prevent a misstep.

"What were you doing? She mesmerized you? How could you treat me so heartlessly last evening and handle yourself in such a cavalier fashion with this woman this evening? How?"

He did not respond. Once again he kissed her with a daring that was quite difficult to renounce.

She let him direct her and followed silently.

At the beginning of the soirée, she'd decided that nothing would deter her gaiety and carefree demeanor. It worked for a while and it was fantastic! Now, however, sadness resurfaced. All of the mariners, whom she respected, now despised and distrusted her. And all that mistrust for a few laughs, everything had been so light. She needed some lightness for goodness sake. *Mon Dieu*, she was only twenty-five years old!

The mean and cruel emotions she had felt yesterday toward her world returned. She did not know how to disengage. Jean-Louis, her only strength and support at difficult times, had been the precursor to all this chaos! And now, she'd caught him flirting with another woman! What had happened?

"Why are you deserting me? What is happening to us?" she inquired. She glanced down at the ballroom and noted the hundred of eyes upon them.

The crowd seemed curious, as they sensed the tensions between Gaby and Jean-Louis.

"I presume that theatrics has come to an end," the old dowager Signora de Paoli sliced. "After all that is said and done, our own sordid relationships are just normal. Let's now wait for act two to begin." A round of sympathetic laughter broke out.

Jean-Louis preempted the critics and directed the whimpering Gaby down to the gardens. Her tears rolled down her pretty visage forever, or so it seemed to Jean-Louis. He sat next to her on the cold concrete bench and took her into his arms as he rocked her like an infant. Thank goodness, she could not talk, he thought, that would give him time to explain his erratic behavior.

"Gaby, it is my fault, my darling. Last evening you said that you wanted to once again feel the butterflies that a flirtatious relationship brings about. Tonight, I wanted to see jealousy in your eyes. You know that none of these women excite me and never will. You are the only one in my life and always will be, Gaby. I adore you, Gaby."

The tears stopped. He continued.

"These past months, we have played a political game of cat and mouse. It has caught up with us this week. It will not happen again, darling, I assure you. We will laugh and have a fun life once more when we return to Paris. This is a dangerous place, Gaby. It has been demanding to all involved. The passions are great on both sides. It is difficult to keep a clear perspective."

He stopped, pensive. He was unwilling to share with her the danger that lurked for him, just a few hours from now.

Gaby would want to join him. Instead, he gathered her into his arms and just held her.

Gaby would not understand, he thought. She would manage to extricate from him a compromise. She would demand to be included. That could not be done. She would be placed under considerable danger. God knows what sordid, crafty arrangement they would have to devise. No, Gaby would be a burden. Her safety was paramount. He would return to her. They still had much to accomplish together. They stayed on that bench for a long time, silent as if their hearts translated their passion. She slowly moved in his arms.

"We should return to the ballroom," she whispered.

Once more the lovers dealt a blow to their differences. Conciliatory glances showed the crowd that the altercation had been settled.

Marie-Hélène, confident of her devastating charms, strolled toward Jean-Louis and Gaby. Her conversation quickly became one-sided. Madame Noveaut was making a complete fool of herself!

Jean-Louis-Pierre and Gaby only had eyes for one another.

Knowing smiles re-appeared on the faces of many in attendance. "The Duchess is the only one who counts in his life," it was murmured. "The Duke's polite demeanor is still very much in evidence," others stated, "after all, he ambled in the world's greatest capitals, but his heart belongs to his wife." Rumors persisted. But most acquiesced that the couple was truly endearing—the giant and the dwarf, hand in hand, their trademark.

"I tremble at the Duke's sensual bearing when he wraps his arms around the Duchess' shoulders. Although engaged in conversation, he gathers her to him to reassure her that he never forgets her presence. How romantic," the Countessa di Padaluva exclaimed.

Their love had been the talk of many a ball that they did not attend. In a strange fashion that love had given a window of hope to many young women and some men that passionate relationships were not necessarily an unreachable dream with a spouse. Although, most still believe that marriage should seal family fortunes and names. Love could still be fulfilled with lovers and mistresses.

Chapter 25

The soirée continued to be a joyous affair. In the early morning hours, the revelers took leave of their hosts. Gaby and Jean-Louis followed hand in hand. They climbed into the carriage that would return the couple to their villa.

The horses thundered down the wide arteries. Suddenly the coach slowed. Gaby leaned toward the window and parted its curtains. Jean-Louis pulled her back and drew the curtains across the window, but not before she realized that they'd entered a strange part of town. An unusual number of men with black cloaks walked so close to the carriage that one of them touched its door.

"Where are we, Jean-Louis? Look!" She squeezed his hand and moved forward, wanting to see more. Jean-Louis stopped her a second time. Social gatherings were not that unusual in Rome, the local residents loved their late night festivities. The carriage, however, drew to a stop.

Gaby pressed close to Jean-Louis. She looked up to him, and his kiss on her forehead did not reassure her. "Everything is fine, Gaby, I love you," he murmured. "One of the horses might have been injured. I'll go and see."

He stepped out of the carriage. She waited a few moments, and then she trailed after him.

One of the cloaked men moved so close to Gaby, she gasped. Where was Jean-Louis? Many of these faces were familiar—too familiar—her butler, Jean-Louis' manservant, the cook, and many other men whom she'd seen walking the halls of the villa. Why were they here? Two carriages suddenly crossed paths at a diagonal. More men emerged from carriages . . . some walked toward . . . a boat. As she began to register her surrounding, Gaby realized they'd been driven to the port. She noticed more human shapes meandering in and out of carriages. They were far from the villa.

Jean-Louis returned to her.

"Jean-Louis, this is our help. What are they . . .?" Her question left unanswered, Jean-Louis clasped Gaby's arm and in one smooth motion, he covered her long mahogany mane with the black mink hood attached to the collar of her coat. He motioned to her to be quiet. Totally confused but very much aware that life in Italy was anything but serene, she kept quiet.

Cunnan reappeared on the scene. The butler gave Jean-Louis a large stack of documents. All moved silently as in a well-rehearsed ballet. All knew their roles. Gaby followed the drama through shifting eyes. Finally, Jean-Louis walked to her once more. In one quick, sweeping motion, he kissed her tenderly and passionately.

"I adore you, Gaby, more than my life," he whispered in English, "I'll see you soon. Follow all instructions given to you quietly and quickly."

Her silence broke. "No . . . Where are you going? Jean-Louis, tell me!"

She saw her husband nod to Cunnan. A strap of rough clothing passed hands. Jean-Louis grabbed the cloth and gagged her while tenderly sweeping her up into his arms and handing her over to Cunnan. "I love you, Gaby, for as long as I'll live and beyond." He brushed her forehead with his lips, and then quickly he slipped the hood over her face.

Her moaning silenced, in Cunnan's arms, she was swept away in the dark. The salty scent of the Méditerranée reminded her of their nearness to the pier. She was lowered in a boat. The cloak's hood slid down to rest on her shoulders. Suddenly, she noticed a form, which appeared to be a heap of rags or old fishermen's nets, rise in the dark. Men emerged from the nets and slid onto the seats in the boat.

Cunnan lowered his human package in the barge. Three waiting boats now silently sped towards the Tempête.

Gaby felt paralyzed. Was Jean-Louis taking another route? Why had she been silenced? Perhaps, he sailed aboard the large barge positioned behind them? Her thoughts scrambled and tumbled over the dark precipice of despair. Her husband was not part of the group that now rejoined the ship; her intuition told her that much.

As soon as they embarked, the boat left the dock and sailed away. The rest of the men, as well as Gaby, were shoved inside and brusquely pushed under the heap of rugs.

What was happening to her? Why? Where was her husband? Why had they split up? Was he staying behind? No, Cunnan surely would have gone with him? Be calm and composed, she ordered her indomitable spirit. If she'd learned anything from all the complexities she had experienced in Italy, calm and clear thinking were essential qualities to maintain. She parted the rugs and lifted her head just to scan the horizon above the outer edges of the barge. She waited to adjust to night vision. Additional boats appeared near the Tempête. As they reached the fully equipped war vessel, men she recognized as her former servants, filed off the boats and onto the ship.

Cunnan appeared. He did not remove the gag. She shot a supplicating gaze to him. He smiled back a reassuring grin, but he still did not remove it. Instead, he lifted her out and onto the ladder. He placed his forefinger straight and perpendicular to his mouth—the international signal that implies that a disturbance of any kind could pose a grave danger. She complied while she looked around her in search of Jean-Louis. Everyone settled in the proper station. She heard the murmurs of the rowers down below. The Tempête set sail, silent and lightless as it departed the harbor. The horrific truth dawned on Gaby. Jean-Louis was not aboard the craft.

The first officer stood at the wheel, the small fishing boats were left to float away at sea.

Still muzzled, Gaby watched as Cunnan prepared the crew on the upper deck. He took the decisions that her husband usually took. Jean-Louis was not on board. She felt absolutely certain of that fact now.

Cunnan approached her next and removed her gag. "I'm sorry, Gaby. Jean-Louis will meet us soon, probably within the next three days. He will tell you all about it. Don't fright, and please try to get some sleep."

"Sleep? Cunnan, please tell me what has happened? Where is Jean-Louis? Where did he go? Please, I beg of you! Why . . . why such secrecy?"

"There was unrest, Gaby. We accomplished part of our goal. The parties are at the table, talking. That is good. What it will be worth next year? I would not bet much gold on the Pontiff keeping Rome. It will be Emmanuel's capital sooner rather than later."

Your cousin, Cardinal Thornsen, will meet Jean-Louis in Rome. I think the Monarch and the Pope will honor our hard work. Everything is in place for his safe return. Please do not fear," he answered reassuringly, not revealing the dangers of the mission. A larger crisis looms, Gaby. The Emperor has declared war on Prussia. It was no longer safe for us to remain. The French Navy is still in Civitavecchia, but I don't know for how long?"

"Where is Jean-Louis, Cunnan?" she asked desperately.

Cunnan started to walk away. She stalked him, asking countless questions, until the first officer blocked her.

"I am sorry, Madame, orders!" he exclaimed clearly uncomfortable at having to challenge her.

Cunnan continued on to the bow of the vessel.

"Why wasn't I told?" she questioned. Then, she realized the futility of her question. Not even her adoring cousin Philippe had confided in her. First resentment, then sadness overwhelmed her. Tears welled in her eyes and rolled down her cheeks. Defeated, she sobbed.

Cunnan glanced back one last time. The devastating gaze in his little angel's eyes made him spun on his heel. He drew her into his arms.

"Gaby, my dear child, this was one of the many complications that we predicted, and prepared for. Everything will go smoothly, Gaby. Jean-Louis did not want to place you in danger again . . ."

"So you knew all along . . . Jean-Louis is in grave danger. If the Vatican does not agree to all of the terms, Jean-Louis is a sitting duck. I doubt that Victor Emmanuel II will come to his rescue. He will push forward to Rome with his army," she interrupted.

"Jean-Louis wanted the copy of the translated treaty given to the French emissaries in Rome.

"Does Louis Napoléon know about this latest development? Is there enough security to assure Jean-Louis' safe return?" She pressed vehemently.

Unwilling to give her false hope, Cunnan left her questions unanswered. "Please, Gabriella, get some rest. I need to act on Jean-Louis' behalf now."

She marched over to Jean-Louis' study. She tossed the mink on his chair but kept her cloak, although it was a balmy July night. His scent was everywhere. Why had he not confided in her? She'd known that their departure was imminent, but she'd expected a few extra days.

In fact, Jean-Louis had not trusted her. How quickly these months had gone by. Only last night, she'd retrieved the man that she adored. Presumably, the negotiations had taken all of his living hours so as not to leave any leaf unturned.

Now, France was at war! Oh, dear God? While her friends, *les artistes* in Paris forged a more natural, less preoccupied existence, Jean-Louis pursued his duties on behalf of his country, conduct instilled in him by his aristocratic roots. Gaby pondered on the futility of risking his life for any cause, even this lofty and admirable foundation. He had more than served his time. He loved and needed her. She loved and needed him. Wasn't that enough? Why would he want to sacrifice their relationship for name and country? There were so many others who enjoyed their lucky birth. Why did Jean-Louis feel this overwhelming guilt? she brooded selfishly.

Chapter 26

Jean-Louis rode east, back to Rome in the company of four of his officers. Louis Napoléon had set the wheels in motion with his strong push toward a modern world. The magnificence of the new Paris, a center of culture and commerce, connected the great cities of Europe with its new railroads. Trade between nations and a new world order where education of the masses, the financial elevation of the bourgeoisie, and perhaps in the next century, the cessation of wars on the continent would facilitate great advances toward modernization.

"If Bismarck had not embarked on his conqueror's path, and would have agreed to stop its war machine and abide by the philosophy of the French Emperor, Prussia and the Germanic States would have shared in the fruits of the newly formed Italian union." Jean-Louis stated.

"Bismarck was sent to Russia, England and France as Ambassador to test us," Gerard nodded. "I will admit that historians will study this age for a long time. The sly fox, to embarrass the Emperor in such a way—sending the Bad Ems Dispatch to all ambassadors throughout the Continent!"

Jean-Louis had been convinced prior to the Italian assignment, while still in Paris, that the Prussian minister would force Louis Napoléon into a war. And he had!

Spain had been without a ruler for two years since the demise of Isabella. Placing a Hohenzollern on the Spanish throne would have encased France on its northeastern and southwestern borders. The perfect ploy for the wily Bismarck.

The Emperor and his Ambassador to Prussia Vincent Benedetti and certainly the Duke de Gramont, the French foreign minister had misjudged the whole affair. War was the only path acceptable to Louis Napoléon and his army advisors, to bend the enemy to his will. France was poised to embark on a path destined to devastate its citizens for years to come. The Empire would come to an end, and France would be forced to pay considerable reparations.

Although an aristocrat, Jean-Louis-Pierre de Pleyssis, did not behave pompously, nor did he showed disdain for anything that was not aristocratic. He had seen middle class in action in the United States and although the sacrifice that France's proletariat would have to endure at this time was viewed as inevitable, he believed fervently that he pursued an honorable path—essentially what was expected of him.

The French populace displayed great ambiguity toward the aristocracy and the non-titled class, appearing to envy the polished demeanor of their former autocratic rulers. They copied the learned comportment of the royals and their descendents—the craving for that luck of birth devoured a whole population! And then there was the rising bourgeoisie, which pursued everything noble. They pursued their endeavor to the utmost. The difference—the aristocracy performed it without pretense. They had been raised with the coveted facility of life.

He closed his eyes and reposed his head back against the tufted squabs. The next few hours would be decisive. The plans had been delineated. His concern was no longer Italy but war with Prussia. He would be called and he would serve.

Chapter 27

Gaby fell asleep as she pondered life with Jean-Louis and his philosophy. She glanced at the clock. It was past two in the afternoon. Through the port, she noticed the sun positioned high in the blue sky. The surging swells rolled her toward Jean-Louis' pillow. The Champagne and the excitement from the night before must have lulled her into a deep slumber. Calmly she rolled out of bed, walked past his desk, caressed its black leather-writing table and came to burrow into Jean-Louis' wide and scuffed leather chair. His scent reminded her of wild flowers in the Tuscan hills, its fragrance suffused every corner of the cabin. Her hand settled on the engraved silver cigar case. She lifted its corners and pulled on the golden ribbon that kept the cigars in a perfect line up. She pulled out his favorite and caressed the rough brown leaf. Perhaps he would recognize her scent when he'd placed the tip of the cigar to his lips. A loud bang coming from the upper deck jarred Gaby out of her *rêveries*. A thud against the hull made her run to the hatch leading to the outside lower deck. She couldn't see; but she heard the mariners hauling a load on deck. A *frisson* of disquiet shook her. Jean-Louis was back. She bolted out onto the deck.

Cunnan stood nearby, scanning the horizon for signs of Jean-Louis. He looked haggard from fatigue, but with a determination in his eyes that contradicted his physical appearance.

"What was that, Cunnan?" she demanded anxious.

"Nothing of great importance, Gaby. One of the lifeboats fell overboard."

"I must have taken your advice and fallen asleep, Cunnan." Gaby spoke calmly, but disappointment was written all over her face.

"Good for you, Gaby. We should see signs of Jean-Louis in the next ten hours or so."

"Can I stay near you this evening and sleep on the cot. I loathe being alone; all types of horrific plots torture my soul. I'm so worried. Why isn't he here? Do you think something has happened?"

"Well . . . Gabriella, something must have happened." He responded calmly. "The Roman campagna is filled with insurgents. Jean-Louis knew it, and he was prepared."

Cunnan never minimized the immensity of a problem. She loved him for his straightforward nature and the obvious respect he showed by not lying to her. At this moment, she wished with all her heart that he would treat her like a mere young woman of her time. She wanted comfort and expressions of hope and faith. Instead, she was treated like a responsible partner, one who could face hardship and yet be sensible and calm. In all other occasions, she certainly could hold her own, but when it came to Jean-Louis she believed in miracles.

She automatically began to hum an aria from La Bohème. She stopped herself. Damn all these operas, there was never a happy ending! The women always died. She did not want to die. She did not want Jean-Louis to die. They still had lots of passionate moments, lots of good times together, lots of laughter and passion ahead of them. She closed her eyes and prayed fervently. *Please God, don't let him die, bring him back to me, I beg you, do not take him away, bring him back to me*, she repeated softly just for her ears. Her faith resurfaced. For a while her spirits lifted. Deep in her soul she knew that it was too early for their life mission to end so darkly.

She returned to the captain's bridge to stand beside the ship's wide, dark wooden helm. She observed the fingerlike projections of the Italian mainland. Squinting, she scanned the horizon for the scantest movement on the serene Mediterranean Sea. As day turned into night, there was still no sight of her husband. Cunnan slept on the other side of the wheel. He had requested a cot so as to return to his job promptly if need be. The commanding officer remained silent. The crew prepared for the worst, and a sense of doom settled over the Tempête.

By mid-morning, the sea became agitated. Gabriella sobbed uncontrollably as she approached her husband's great chair. She sat in it and leaned her head on the fur that trimmed the collar of his leather jacket. His scent remained powerful. Something had happened to Jean-Louis. She knew it.

Cunnan was grim; the optimism that had kept a ray of brightness alive, all but vanished. Relentless, turbulent waves hit the sides of the ship and spilled onto the deck. Everyone was vigilant. Cunnan kept her close by. She was thankful. He looped his arm around her for a short while. Neither spoke as they hoped against all odds for a miracle.

The rest of the day and into the night the sea was relentless. By early morning, the storm passed. An island pierced the horizon. "Sardinia," she heard someone shout, but the two days vigil overpowered her will. Her small body wrapped in blankets lay exhausted on the bench, racked by sporadic spasms of uncontrollable tears. She had not been willing to return to the stateroom for fear that her morbid thoughts would overwhelm her fighting spirit.

Slumber had overtaken her however. When she woke, later that morning, a single glance at Cunnan brought her closer to desperation. The dreadful expression on his face confirmed her darkest suspicions. Everyone feared the worst. The mission had failed or it had been botched. What had happened in the Roman campagna, no one knew yet?

Poor little Gabriella, Cunnan thought, still filled with hope. She had been so vehement about it that, for one entire day, everyone on the ship had predicted the return of Jean-Louis and his four men. The Captain would show up miraculously and break the horizon in a barge or maybe a French naval vessel, all surmised. Alas, after the fourth day all had lost hope once more. Gaby roamed the deck with the spyglass raised high on her face. She must have literally fallen from fatigue, Cunnan thought, for he had found her lying down on one of the mess's wooden benches in a fetal position. Not prepared to awaken her, he'd covered her small fatigued body with the driest blanket he'd found. He had pushed the bench against the wooden bulkhead of the lower cabin, just in case she should become restless in her sleep, and he'd further positioned several thick ropes left on the deck, to break a fall.

What would his little angel do without Jean-Louis-Pierre? Cunnan wondered. He hated to see the gloom and sadness that now permeated her entire persona. And yet, there was not a damn thing he could do about it. He loved the little angel like a daughter or as close as what he could perceive a father's love could be. He looked down at her for a few more minutes and then returned to the helm. He lifted the bronze spyglass to his eye, and he checked the compass and its circular metal balls that simulated the magnetic field of the earth.

Silence reigned. It was over. He felt it in his old sailor's bones. Jean-Louis-Pierre had been clairvoyant, he concluded with great sadness. He'd forced the negotiators to copy more than one reproduction of the original signed document. Furthermore, he had insisted on taking the original inside the Aurelian walls himself. Copies had been sent to the Vatican and to the King earlier in the week. Before their stealth departure from the Eternal City, he'd waited just long enough for the copies of the documents to reach the Pontiff and the King. The beginning of his last mission. Whether or not the mission failed, he would terminate the work that the young and brilliant statesman had envisaged and, in fact, achieved. The Empire could not be fully trusted. He would return. The hard steps had been taken. He would need to tie up the loose ends and give credit where credit was due. He would make sure of that. Great odds had been surmounted. He hoped that peace throughout this very dynamic and volatile region would prevail. Modernization would stabilize France's economy and avoid conflicts between the great powers as delineated by the Vienna Conference in 1815. Trade would bring a new dawn of economic stability and prosperity to France, to the nascent kingdom of Italy, and to the surrounding nations.

The first officer had taken over the watch. A weary Cunnan held on loosely to the helm, absently scanning the horizon. He recalled the years he and Jean-Louis-Pierre had spent together at sea. Their first adult meeting, he had known Jean-Louis Pierre as a young child, was on a French vessel. It had revealed his young friend as a brash, young, arrogant aristocrat with a valor and temerity that mesmerized. From the very start, they had bonded. He had known his father, a smart and brave warrior, but dull and serious, compared to his son's sharp wit, gregariousness and bad boy reputation. Although, strongly disliked by all mariners who sailed with him, Jean-Louis-Pierre was admired and respected for his bravura. He had no patience for the weak at heart, and he led his life accordingly. He had followed the whims of the moment, accomplished the goals he had set for himself, and embarked on another challenge. There had been no rest for the young Duke. The harder the battle, the harder he fought . . . always bigger than life.

What had happened? Cunnan wondered. A betrayal? Could Gaby have leaked plans inadvertently? Had she said something that might have tweaked the plan? No, she knew nothing that could endanger anyone. Jean-Louis-Pierre was too concerned for her safety.

A few officers had asked him to let her spread valuable but downright false information. He had not been willing. The plan had been abrogated. Translating was one thing, he had full control of what Gaby would review but involving her in such a stealthy conflict was something he had refused to entertain. Jean-Louis-Pierre must have fought to the end.

Had he been ambushed, or was he a prisoner alive in some medieval dungeon? No, no one in his right mind would take the chance to imprison him. Jean-Louis-Pierre and the four were dead. Why had he led the expedition? Total control was often the perdition of powerful men. Jean-Louis-Pierre demanded absolute control. He never trusted anyone but himself. This time he had lost the game. They'd passed the meeting place three days ago. Tomorrow they would have to leave these waters.

The old seaman wiped the salty tears running down his nose. Although his vision was blurred, he discerned movement to the right of the small island he'd focused on for the preceding seventy hours. Pirates' attacks in these treacherous waters remained viable. He passed the long spyglass to the first officer. He noted the intense gaze, the taut set of his jaws. Damn, a small barge was sailing their way. A signal? A blinking light coming from an *éclaireur* from a pirate's ship? Cunnan was fully alert now. He took the lead. No. A slow moving barge heaved through the rolling waves. A half smile hung down on the officer's lips

Chapter 28

Far on the horizon the shifting peck bobbed on the waves. Then the boat emerged. It popped up and then rapidly became engulfed below the swells. Behind it was a lighthouse on the coast of a small isolated island.

"*C'est eux!*" the éclaireur shouted at the very top of the mast. "*C'est eux!*" he repeated.

The spyglass focused on the sight. Cunnan recognized Jean-Louis-Pierre, escorted by three of the four men who'd accompanied him on his venture. The rough seas made it difficult to distinguish it, but clearly, the Captain's head was recognizable. Cunnan steered the vessel toward the grey wooden fishing boat. It finally reached the barge. The ladder was tossed down at sea and the four men climbed on-board. The Captain reached the deck last. Cunnan hugged him while the rest of the crew saluted with respect. The three other men, wet and covered with dark seaweed, were taken to the ship's infirmary. Jean-Louis refused.

Gaby was fast asleep on the bench as her husband walked onto the Captain's bridge. He stood above her curled up body, staring lovingly at her. They still had a future together. She had been his only focus these past twenty-four hours, seeing her again had been his only consideration.

"She hasn't slept in almost three days," Cunnan murmured to his friend. "I don't think the sound of a cannon would wake her now. We found her there about an hour ago.

"Watching her gave all of us, grown men, a feeling of melancholy," Cunnan confessed. He tapped gently, the rough fabric that covered her body.

With Cunnan in tow, the Duke lifted his wife and began to walk slowly down to his cabin. He placed her tiny body on the wide and extra long bed and pulled the blankets up to her shoulders. He kissed her damp, curly hair before he ambled back to his chair. Cunnan waited.

"We were ambushed by Jacopo and his men, just before we reached the French Embassy in Rome. Did the Vatican change its mind at the last minute? Did some Counts decide that they had given up too much, too quickly? I am not sure." The Duke looked away, melancholy in his usual composed demeanor.

"What happened to Gérard?" Cunnan questioned.

"We lost him as we stormed the Porta Pia's entrance," he replied seriously. "Fierce fighting erupted at the Leonine Wall. General de Barilla was ordered to stop at the wall. The Italian artillery feared insurgents. Because of it, we received their protection, although we understood later that many habitants of the Leonine City wish to become Italian citizens, rather than to stay under the temporal power of the Pope. Lots of confusion, Cunnan, and we were, of course, the key figures to capture in order to blackmail the King of Sardinia and the Empire. Luckily, Count Edward of Sardinia met the radicals, a fierce battle between the parties ensued, and it gave us a cover to reach the port. The King gave us asylum under the strict conditions of total silence. He wants Rome and its port as his capital. We essentially gave it to him. Our troops will leave for the front soon. A day later, he gave us an escort to Pisa. Unfortunately, the strong currents, courtesy of the Mistral, veered the barge westward, our fresh water barrels rolled out to sea. We took a chance and landed on a miniature, uncharted island—the cause for the delay. Voila!"

"You know our mission is over. Now, more than ever, I wonder about the part the court of Otto von Bismarck played in this sordid and delicate affair. What games is he playing now that he has defeated Austria? Is he intent on unifying the German states if and when he defeats the Empire? I heard in Rome that Louis Napoléon has abdicated. He is being held in the Hohenzollern's castle of William I. I will leave Gaby in Loire, and I think that we should return to Paris. I believe that Bismarck will set siege to Paris. He wants it, Cunnan. It's what I told Louis Napoléon before my departure. Unfortunately, he listened to his generals. I was right then, and I'd bet my fortune that I am right again!" the Duke concluded. "I will move my Grandmother and family out of Paris upon our return. I think we will need to stay and fight."

"I think that you should spend some time with your wife when you reach Loire," the old man retorted. "What's driving you, Jean-Louis-Pierre? You let guilt rob you of what you should justifiable enjoy."

Cunnan sipped a bit more of the strong cognac they had been drinking, and he tapped Jean-Louis on the shoulders once more. "We have our work cut out, again, when we arrive in France, Jean-Louis-Pierre. Will we stop in Toulon?"

"Yes," he replied with authority, "I would like to change ships and arrive in Brest on a French military vessel rather than the Tempête."

He was going to watch all sides carefully now that Bismarck was on the warpath. The Prussian man of State would not stop anytime soon.

They sat a while longer while Gaby slept. In the wee hours of the morning, Cunnan took his leave.

Chapter 29

Quickly, Jean-Louis removed his wet clothes and walked toward the bed where his wife lay asleep. He rolled in and gathered her, blankets and furs into his arms. He buried his head in her hair, "I love you," he whispered. He stayed with Gaby in his arms, as he savored holding on to the most precious gift in his life, his legs tangled with hers as he imprisoned her small body.

The sky was still dark when Gaby woke up. She must be hallucinating, she thought at the sight of her husband. She turned back fully and touched his arm. She caressed his lips . . . perhaps these past days had been a horrific nightmare. He'd always been near her.

"Jean-Louis!" she shouted as she pushed him onto his back. "Jean-Louis," she called out again to assure herself that her dream theory was erroneous. She bolted out of bed and ran to the bridge.

The first officer and Cunnan stood there, both rested and happy. Grins on their faces suggested that Jean-Louis had returned.

"They are back, Gabriella, they are back!" The men looked at her, happy.

Wild emotions took over her usual analytical state of mind—indescribable happiness at the realization that her husband had survived against all odds. Unfortunately, certainly because of sleep deprivation, lunacy set in. An overwhelming anger stirred within her, something she had never felt toward him, even in their worst moments. After all she had gone through for her husband, he had not trusted her, had not even hinted at his last mission. Everyone she knew was aware of the mission but her!

"Damn him! I'll kill him!" she shouted in English. "I swear, Cunnan, he'll pay for this deception." She raced out of the deck area.

So contrary to what they had come to expect from the young Duchess, both men followed her down in the Captain' s cabin. Gaby was an excellent shot. She'd lost her fortitude. Perhaps, a sense of loss, the lack of sleep tormented her. It often had a bizarre effect on a person's character. She stormed into the cabin, the two mariners on her heels.

"Jean-Louis, wake up! Wake up . . . now, damn it!" she screamed.

"I'm back, *Chérie*, hush. Come to bed, Gaby, I'm too tired to explain now," he said his voice filled with the irritation of disturbed slumber.

"Hush? Come to bed, Gaby?" she fired back incensed. She noticed the belt he'd flung on the rug, she reached down for it and struck his shoulder. Then losing all rational common sense, she strapped every part of his body as hard as she could.

"Gaby, stop it. Cease, *Mon Dieu!*" Suddenly awake, Jean-Louis rolled over onto the other side of the bed to stop the assault on his body. She ran to the other side, where he had taken refuge and once again she used the belt on him to her heart's content.

Flabbergasted by this crazy turn of event, the two men stood motionless by the door.

The beating took its toll. Jean-Louis was now fully awake. He clasped the belt in the air, spun toward Gaby, reached for her waist, and pulled her none too gently to him. He held her hands behind her back and rolled his tired body atop hers. "You're impossible, Gaby," he murmured with ill-concealed annoyance. He gestured to dismiss the two startled mariners. The door slammed shut.

"I thought that I would be greeted with warmth and unsurpassed emotions. Instead, I have received the beating of my life," Jean-Louis whispered with an ironic smile.

She was going to respond in no uncertain terms that he did not deserve her, when he kissed the words out of her mouth. "We will talk later, Gaby. I love you, darling." He fell once again on her.

"I hate you, Jean-Louis, I loathe you!" she raged, conquered. She lay quietly in his arms and encircled his body in her arms.

She had not been dreaming she reassured her weary spirit. He would suffer her wrath soon, but now God had granted her wish. All was well. She took his advice and relaxed in his arms. Sleep eluded her. She lay quietly. They would soon be back in France.

Chapter 30

He woke her up early. He wanted her. The rapture was intense. Everything they'd previously shared and everything that was to come, was wrapped up in this one moment. They held onto one another as if they were the only two beings left on earth. The world became inconsequential. Death had not taken him away from her. They had each other, and it sufficed. Nevertheless, he would pay for the lack of trust he had displayed. Of course, she would have fought him tooth and nail had he told her about the dispatch. Why had he gone? The challenge was not warranted. He had her, for God's sake. She should have been sufficient, she opined.

The following two days, she spoke to no one. She refused to discuss anything. She walked away after their shared meals. She practiced shooting, wrote and slept. Even Cunnan could not assuage her anger. Sometimes she would cast a furtive glance at her husband while he sailed the vessel. He would catch her every time. The man must have had eyes on the back of his head! He would smile. She, in turn, would change position and look away. Her attitude toward the crew and the officers turned downright rude. They had not trusted her in the darkest of hours. Although Jean-Louis had given the order, they should have divulged a bit more information. She had been kept in total oblivion. She now hated all of them, even Cunnan.

The evening of the third night after Jean-Louis re-appearance, however, she crossed the line of impertinence. They were having their common meals. The strategy on how to re-enter French national waters was the topic. She stopped all conversation.

"Please, gentleman, your comments bore me. They are unfit for my feminine, foreign ears!" she declared loudly. "How can you trust me with such important information such as the communication signals. Aren't you frightened that I could perhaps divulge all the information presented to a passing vessel? *Oh non*, please *l'étrangère* is amongst your ranks. Beware!" she exclaimed with her fabulous theatrics.

Her green eyes shot darts at the attending officers at the table. "After all I suffered myriad humiliations and panic in the name of France," she continued, now only bitterness surfaced from her perfectly rounded lips, "but surprisingly enough it is not sufficient for French Nationals such as you. Non, non, non, non," she mimicked the Gallic accent, "I'm *une étrangère*, have a care gentlemen. I may be a risk, a liability . . . personally, I feel that you are arrogant, self-impressed, and haughty idiots who could not feel lightning if it struck you!" She looked down at her plate and picked up a piece of meat. Slowly she masticated the hardened dry and salty morsel.

An uncomfortable silence fell throughout the room. All appeared astounded. Even Jean-Louis had no reaction to this attack.

"Mon Dieu, you do not trust me. I wonder why?" she pursued, irate. "Do you know anyone else more trustworthy than I? Now, I no longer care. I despise you all!" Her voice was distinct in her accented French, and her green eyes, which she disdainfully posed on everyone sitting at the table, snapped with utter fury. The pretty Duchess clearly meant each and every word she spoke.

The Captain stood, walked to her chair, and pulled it out. He bent his head and nodded toward the lower deck as an ironic smile tugged at his lips. Not quite sure what to make of it, she picked up her tray, stared at him arrogantly and made her way to the cabin.

He closed the hatch behind him.

Once they reached their cabin, cleverly, she placed her tray on the other side of his desk. In turn, he stared at his pretty wife. "Come here, Gaby!"

"No," she answered. "No, not in a thousand years. I meant everything I said. I did not deserve the treatment that you and your men showed me. Not even Cunnan said anything to me!"

"Very well." He stood up, walked around the desk, lifted her up, and sat her on his lap.

She loathed his controlling demeanor when he didn't even attempt to be subtle. With Jean-Louis it was his high road or the high way! She secretly feared loud men's voices. Out of nowhere, Jean-Louis' tall stature revived some awful childhood memories. Angry he was not, annoyed or perhaps even amused, and that was good news. They almost had been separated eternally.

He sat deeper in his chair and he gently pressed her cheek close to his heart.

"We need to talk, Gaby."

She knew by the tone of his voice that a choice of conversation was not in the cards.

"Gaby tell me, how would you have handled the situation if you had been in my place. Tell me, *Chérie*?"

She paused for a moment. She'd prepared many retorts to his questioning—which she knew was bound to arise, but not this one.

"Differently," she replied at a loss for a pertinent response to his question.

"How Gaby?" he repeated.

"Well, first you should have told me."

"And you would have listened?" he questioned, his eyebrows lifting.

She moved her head from side to side.

"That would have placed you and me in grave danger. We had no time for altercations, Gaby. You saw how quickly everything turned sour. We lost Gérard. Everything happened very quickly."

He looked away. Gaby knew how much Gérard meant to him. He had been the head of his security for many years in France. His wife and two children had died while on a crossing to England. Distraught, he had chosen a more challenging life and had served Jean-Louis with honor.

She lifted her hands around his neck and kissed him tenderly. It could, just as easily, have been Jean-Louis who had perished. Weapons did not pick and choose their targets.

"I am so sorry about Gérard. I knew how much you admired him, Jean-Louis."

She did not have time to finish her sentence. He placed his hand behind her neck and just held her head tight against his heart.

"You saved my life Gaby, your vision was a perpetual cord around my neck, pulling me out of the chaos. I love you, *Chérie*," he ended simply, gathering her closer.

"What an insulting way to profess your love to me. I heard the subtle reference to ball and chain?" She smiled, forced herself nearer, and kissed him passionately. "I adore you too, Jean-Louis," she whispered against his lips.

The couple emerged from their cabin an hour and one half later, as if the quarrel had never existed. The sound of their laughter echoed across the ship's deck.

She would save his life again, but, in much more perilous times.

www.ingramcontent.com/pod-product-compliance
Lightning Source LLC
Chambersburg PA
CBHW020827260626
47169CB00003B/860